Tonight You Are Mine . . .

"Perhaps if the Khan does not take you for his own, I could come close to the stature of a tarkhan, and claim you. Together we could follow the sinking sun toward Frankistan and find wonders more royal than those in Cathay. Dreams can be formed and made real if courage is the clay, little princess."

"Why would you do that for me, James the Frank? We have known each other just a few hours, out of all the centuries that have passed."

"We have known each other since birth, and beyond," he said hoarsely. "Except that it has taken this night to clear the scales from our eyes and make us see the truth. I have drunk wine tonight, but my head is clear of fumes. Another kind of potion has seized me —one I've never tasted before. It makes me swear my soul into your keeping, whether you wish the gift or not. You can't refuse. Tonight I defy the gods. I claim that your life is my life, and one day I will claim you in truth. And if it can't be done by James the Frank, then it will be done by James the Mongol, a soldier of the Kha Khan, with grease on my face and blood on my hands."

JOHN JAKES
I, BARBARIAN

(a new, revised and enlarged edition of the
original work written under the pseudonym
Jay Scotland)

PINNACLE BOOKS • NEW YORK CITY

This is a work of fiction. All the characters and events portrayed in this book are fictional, and any resemblance to real people or incidents is purely coincidental.

I, BARBARIAN

Copyright © 1959 by Jay Scotland
Copyright © 1976 by John Jakes

A Pinnacle Books edition, published for the first time.

Produced by Lyle Kenyon Engel

ISBN: 0-523-00971-2

First printing, August 1976

Cover illustration by Dean Cate

Printed in the United States of America

PINNACLE BOOKS, INC.
275 Madison Avenue
New York, N.Y. 10016

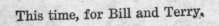

This time, for Bill and Terry.

CONTENTS

Special Introduction
to
The Pinnacle Edition

I, Barbarian was the first historical novel I wrote, and the book with which "Jay Scotland" finally resolved his identity crisis. The poor pseudonymous wretch had "written" a couple of earlier mystery novels, but began to specialize in historical fiction when this book was finished.

The editor of the original edition was dead set against using the name John Jakes on the cover. "Sounds like a piece of machinery, unfit for big-scale stuff with a lot of action and romance." So much for Jakes as Historical Novel Writer; he had to wait around for another fifteen or sixteen years until Lyle Kenyon Engel geared up to produce the American Bicentennial Series. (During those intervening years, "Jakes" wrote a good deal of science fiction; evidently a clanking, clattering name is all right for science fiction.) It was Lyle, bless him, who rejected the idea of using Jay Scotland as the name on the Bicentennial Series and insisted I use my own.

Old Jay (the pseudonym) was originally conjured in less than five minutes by expanding my initials to a first name, and using the atlas as a springboard to an acceptable last name, just as Cornell Woolrich did when he put William together with Irish. "Jay" wrote five more historical novels before he retired.

Speaking as "Jay," I must say I had always been interested in history and was startled to find it so much livelier than its presentation in high school and college classrooms. I don't recall precisely what prodded me to pick Genghis Khan as a central figure for the book; perhaps it was a desire to try to do a proper job on him. (Purists will note I chose to use the "second" spelling of the great warrior's name. "Genghis" is more familiar to general readers, I believe, than is "Jenghiz.") I do remember seeing a film, produced, I believe, by Howard Hughes, in which John Wayne was forced to play young Temujin. John Wayne is the world's greatest Rooster Cogburn, but he looked strange and uncomfortable with Mongol eyes. The picture was a flop, albeit an interesting one, and it may be that it got me digging into the history of the amazing general whose mounted hordes terrified Europe in the early thirteenth century.

In the time period covered by *I, Barbarian*, the Third Crusade was still relatively recent history. There were castles—and civilization—at the other end of the world (an area which the Mongols described with the catch-all term "Frankistan"). The father of the protagonist of this novel had gone on the Third Crusade; had seen, if not served under, Richard Lion-Heart; and had wandered into High Asia with his small son. (Writers as well as readers sometimes puzzle over the past histories of characters. I don't know to this day whether James' father ever married the yellow-haired woman mentioned in the text, or whether he sired his son out of wedlock. I suspect the latter.) After writing about Genghis, I became sufficiently interested in events at the other end of the known world to do a Jay Scotland about them as well. That book is *Sir Scoundrel*. King Richard is a prominent character.

Considerable research went into the preparation of *I, Barbarian*. I wanted to make the world of Genghis Khan a real world. I dislike historical novels in which a character takes "a drink" and wears "clothes." I want to know *what* he drank and *what* he wore; not to the point of boredom, but I want to get something of the feel and flavor of a period. I think readers do too.

A lot of purple prose went into the early version as well. The current edition has been re-edited from start to finish, and a few tons of adjectives and adverbs have disappeared in the process—though for better or worse, I have kept most of the flavor of the original. I was enthralled by Edison Marshall when *I, Barbarian* was first in the typewriter; perceptive readers will see, I think, an attempt to duplicate the style of a master storyteller.

A reissued novel is much like a child who walks out the door at age 21 and doesn't come back for another decade or so. The bemused parents wonder if they really spawned that unfamiliar adult; they privately admit that, with the benefit of hindsight, they might have done many things differently. But they still love their offspring.

Thus I enjoy seeing *I, Barbarian* back in the

world after so many years. I thoroughly enjoyed working my way through it again. And I certainly thank Andy Ettinger and Pinnacle for the opportunity to share the book with you.

JOHN JAKES

I, BARBARIAN

BOOK ONE

THE ROAD TO
KARAKORUM

Chapter 1

To Dare the Gods

I, James Frankistan, began the strange and gore-streaked unraveling of my destiny on the high Gobi in the late summer of the Christian year 1217.

At my feet lay a magnificent roebuck. I had slain him from horseback with my horn bow and bone-tipped arrows. Nearby, my pony wandered among the reeds at the fringe of a small slate-colored lake. The sky and the wind-tortured barrens of the Gobi plateau matched the color of the water; it was an ominous afternoon, with clouds flying away to the north and a few bleak tamarisks dancing on the far horizon.

The sound of my own breathing roared in my ears. I was proud, but I was afraid, too, and the explanation of that is not simple. I was not one man, except in body. I was a Frank by birth, a Mongol by upbringing. Sometimes I thought as one, sometimes as the other, and sometimes in a tangle of both.

The wind and sun of the high Gobi had burned my skin brown, but it was still lighter than that of most Mongols, and no weathering could hide the yellow of my hair or the light color of my eyes.

I had been raised a barbarian, and taught about the barbaric gods who ruled creation. Sometimes—thinking as a Mongol—I believed in them and called upon them. At other times, my Frankish blood asserted itself—as it had when I slew the roebuck. Game had been scant that year, and I was hunter enough not to be content with wretched marmots in the cook-pot. But in slaying the animal, I had violated The Yassa, that code of laws created by the Kha Khan for the protection of his vast empire. Specifically, I had broken that statute which forbade the killing of certain animals during the spring and summer months so that game might be more abundant in the wild white winters of the plateau-land. When I killed the animal, I knew in the Mongol part of my mind that the gods had marked my presumption.

I was young, and the young often risk more than their elders. So I had not considered the consequences until after the buck was dead. The moment he was, I began to think as a Mongol again, and wondered whether my impatience and my hunger had led me beyond safe boundaries. If so, the gods would have some special penalty for me.

True, I carried the horsehair-tufted lance. I wore the felt footsocks, the sheepskins, and the leather coat sewn with animal gut. I rode my pony as well or better than the best Mongol horseman. But I was still an outlander, an adopted child of this terrible, barren land. So I was

4

doubly punishable. I had violated the law of the Khan, and not as one born to it, but as a man of alien blood.

Crouching over the dead animal, I felt a shivering on my backbone. I glanced at the sky, convinced suddenly that I had indeed defied the Gobi gods in unacceptable fashion.

Taking care then to offer slight appeasement, I followed the rule of The Yassa and refrained from cutting the throat of the killed roebuck with my short sword. Instead, according to custom, I carved open the chest, thrust my hand up through the wet guts, closed my fingers around the beast's slimy heart, and gave it a sharp tug.

The gods would not be appeased.

A clap of thunder racketed in the north. Black clouds came hurtling across the sky. I had lived most of my one-and-twenty years on the Gobi and was well acquainted with the storms that could be born suddenly on a summer's day, yet the peal of thunder struck me as more than a coincidence of weather: I had been marked for my solitary deed. The gods in whom I half-believed had not been pleased by my audacity. They had already responded, setting in motion events which could not be stopped. . . .

I laughed a little, nervously. Then I tugged the heart farther out and stared at it glistening in the gray stormy light. Cutting it free, I held it up to the sky to show whoever or whatever might watch. At that instant, I beheld a horseman riding toward me through the barrens, coming from the direction of the small yam station where I had been raised.

I replaced the heart in the carcass, took my lariat, and hitched the bleeding animal so that I might drag him behind my pony. By that time, the figure of the rider revealed itself to be my friend and companion Tadda, the huge, childlike, and soft-witted Mongol.

Tadda and I were as close to being brothers as was possible for creatures of different bloods. Together, we made up the only family which the kindly old bearded Mongol, Kojin, had ever called his own.

Tadda waved and hailed me in an excited manner. "Leave the beast, brother! Ride swiftly with me back to the yurts. Our father Kojin is much alarmed."

"Alarmed that there will be no food in the pot and that his spindly old shanks will wither, I don't doubt," I replied. The remark caused Tadda to scowl and fret one of his fingers by chewing at it. His speech became thick and clumsy as it always did when he was agitated. I perceived that he was genuinely frightened and put my hand on his arm to calm him. He blinked several times, then smiled shyly. More thunder shook the sky.

"I'm sorry I made light of your message, brother. I will ride with you at once. But first tell me what troubles our father."

"The—the coming of a fine caravan from Cathay," Tadda stammered, his leather cloak flapping in the rising gale. "A courier arrived from the daroga only an hour ago. The road governor bids us give the caravan shelter for the night, since the tengri have loosed the whirlwind." *The tengri?* I thought. *Yes, but they have a reason.*

Whatever the reason, the fact of a coming spell of violent weather could not be denied. The tengri, the mythical creatures of the upper air, did indeed seem to be preparing to unleash a mighty storm. As I mounted my pony, Tadda went on:

6

"Kojin is worried because he doesn't think we can entertain the lords of the caravan in style, and its leader is one of the mightiest of the Raging Torrents."

"What is his name?"

"Hargoutai."

"Hargoutai the Falcon?"

"Aye, James—returned from Cathay with spoils of war."

"Truly he is known to be one of the most savage of the Khan's great warriors."

"Is he not a tar-khan?" Tadda asked, blinking like an infant in the whipping dust.

"He is. No time to lose, brother. Ride ahead and I'll drag the animal as quickly as I can. We can't afford to leave it behind. There must indeed be food of quality for the tar-khan, or else he may be truly displeased."

I signaled to Tadda to be off, and he wheeled his pony. On my own mount, I followed at a slower pace, but still pressing for all possible speed.

The noise of thunder grew louder, and dust and sand stung my face as I rode. Ominous thoughts boiled in my head. There was no accounting for the whims of the tar-khans. They reigned supreme among the Khan's warriors. They had the right to enter the royal pavilion at any time without ceremony. They were exempt from all taxes and immune from the death penalty nine times. They passed their noble privileges to their descendants through nine generations.

Hargoutai the Falcon, fresh from victory in Cathay ... another bad omen! I only prayed the storm would abate after a single night, so the caravan would press on to Karakorum, one hundred leagues to the north and west, where the

7

Khan sat in splendor. Should we displease the great warrior, we might all be strangled or suffocated in cloaks. The cruel humor of those favored by the Khan was sometimes without bounds, and the name Hargoutai was whispered along the caravan road from Cathay in tones of terror. Through the mounting gale, dragging the roebuck I had slain in defiance of the law and the gods, with poor frightened Tadda a speck in the murk ahead, I truly felt that for my insolence, the gods had tossed me into the maelstrom of a perilous, unforeseeable future. . . .

Our yam station was a poor place at best: half a dozen felt yurts in the midst of gray wilderness; lonely lime-coated and picture-painted tents whose dome shapes withstood well the fierce winds of the Gobi. The yurts, plus the rude sheds containing barley and hay for the two hundred ponies we tended, had comprised the center of my existence during all my years of growing up. I had never been more than a few leagues from the way station since I could remember. In the shadow of the yurts, I had hunted wild dogs and rats with a club when a child, and ridden wild sheep with my fists deep in their wool. It was my world. Kojin was its lord, a father not of my blood whom I yet loved beyond all bounds.

Kojin, my adopted father, performed his official duties well. In the vast loneliness of the Gobi, he always had ponies ready for the couriers who traveled back and forth from Karakorum to Cathay in twenty- and thirty-league relays. When I had reached my fourteenth year, Kojin had made me his clerk, for poor Tadda had not the brains for the task. Thus it had become my duty to note down, in the Ugur writing which Kojin had taught me laboriously over the dung fire, the

8

name of persons passing, at what hour they passed, what merchandise they carried, and also at what hours the Khan's couriers arrived and left. These records were submitted regularly to the road governor, the daroga, forty leagues distant. My world . . .

Of late, however, its horizons had been pushed back by Genghis Kha Khan. Some travelers said he would go to the world's end before he was done.

In the year 1211 the hordes had ridden across the Gobi into fabled Cathay—into Shan-si and Chih-li—investing walled Taitong-fu and forging alliances with the Men of Iron, the Liao princes of far northern Cathay. When the Cathayan emperor Wai Wang, more at home painting on silks than wielding the weapons of war, fled in terror below the Yellow River, the mighty Khan pursued, undeterred even by snow-choked gorges across which his warriors had worked their way on spear shafts and logs bound with chains.

The great General Muhuli, early in this same year 1217, brought the campaign to a decisive close by storming and burning Yen-king, where the emperor, the Son of Heaven, had once sat at a splendid court. The fierce Cathayan general Wang Yen prayed one final time to Kwan-ti, the god of war, then wrote his confession of failure upon the lapel of his robe. He drank a cup of poison as Yen-king flamed; Genghis Kha Khan was ruler of Cathay.

And where once our yam station had seen only a few solitary travelers and couriers, now hardly a day passed without the appearance of a treasure caravan bearing back to Karakorum the riches of the conquered land. Long processions of two-wheeled curtained carts drawn by bullocks rolled by, each cart heaped with precious floss-silk garments, rich leathers, fabulous jade, grain wine, and ivory. Long-whiskered Cathayans in padded coats, strange holy lamas with yellow hats and prayer wheels, professors of the Buddhist faith, mystics and near-naked fakirs, Nestorian priests, and countless others streamed through our tiny outpost, setting up a restlessness in me such as I had never known before.

I began to wonder what lay across the barrens, at Karakorum and beyond. Wealth beyond dream? Heroes beyond imagining? Beauty and adventure to dazzle the eye and excite the mind? Of course I could not say. But the chore of labori-ously noting the day-to-day commerce of our post grew all the more tedious as a result. Perhaps this same restlessness had prompted me to turn my back on the laws of The Yassa and kill the forbidden game. If I had dared the gods and lost, I would soon know.

Arriving at the yam station, I was met by old Kojin in his sheepskin robes. When he saw what I dragged behind my pony, his sharply angled eyes widened in horror.

"Will you bring down the curse of the Khan upon me, oh willful son?" he wailed. "I cannot doubt that the caravan of Hargoutai the Falcon is scarcely two leagues distant. There is much to be done. What poor provisions can we offer? What soft lodging place? None, none! And now you add to my difficulties! You bring that ac-cursed animal strung to your lariat. You will be my undoing!" He wagged a hand at me. "You are a foolish creature, James the Frank. Woeful was the day when your barbarian father wandered out of the sandstorms to seek refuge here and die."

10

"Enough talk, old man," I laughed in an attempt to reassure him. I swung off the pony. "If the caravan is still two leagues away, it will take some time to negotiate that distance in this blow. By then, the roebuck will be cleverly disguised with other oddments in our common pot." I struck bewildered Tadda on the shoulder. "Come, brother. We'll do the women's work since there are no women to aid us. My father, make the yurts ready. Tadda and I will prepare the food. No guest will ever guess he's eating forbidden meat."

"The gods know," Kojin replied with a piercing stare. I felt an unaccountable shiver on my spine. "The gods always know, James." He gathered his sheepskins around him, bent into the wind, and hurried toward the yurts.

The sky had turned black. The air was thick with dust and sand. Thunder crashed almost continuously. Tadda and I struggled through the gale to the storage sheds and set about furiously butchering and dressing animals, I the roebuck, Tadda a pony which he cut from the screaming, frightened herd. Lightning blazed blue-white on the raw flesh of the roebuck as I carried armloads of it into the largest yurt.

Kojin had lighted fires of horse dung in the center of all the yurts to warm them. Beneath the smoke hole over the fire in the yurt the three of us normally used for ourselves, Tadda and I dumped flesh into the pot. Then we dragged forth leather sacks of kumiss, hoping that Hargoutai the Falcon would be content with a homemade stew and fermented mare's milk. It was all we had to offer, apart from a cheerful fire and a warm interior whose walls were hung with a few spears, round lacquered shields, one precious bamboo bow case, and a single ancient Bokhara carpet.

"Perhaps the weapons will make the noble tarkhan feel welcome," I said as I dropped hunks of marten flesh into the simmering pot.

"They will make it easy for him to dispatch us to heaven" was Kojin's dolorous reply.

Tadda reappeared at the entrance flap of the yurt. His excited face was streaked with rain. "The caravan approaches, old father! Two warriors have already ridden—"

Without warning, Tadda was thrust from the entrance by a pair of swaggering, booted Mongols in garishly lacquered leather breastplates and felt caps.

A commotion could be heard in the yard above the rising rainstorm. As the remainder of the procession milled into the yam station, the two warriors stalked this way and that about the yurt, scowling critically. Their faces, greased heavily against the bite of the wind, gleamed like wild masks. One stuck a finger in the pot, licked it, then asked, "Who is master here?"

"I am, Lord," Kojin replied, stepping forward with all the politeness and quiet pride of a true Mongol noyon. I was immensely proud of him. He hid every trace of his earlier misgivings. "Word of your coming was sent to us," he said to the savage soldiers. "We have done our best to prepare a warm refuge away from the perils of the storm. Our dwelling place is humble, its appointments far less rich than the silken pavilions of Cathay. Yet if hospitality is the measure, then you lords may find this a more satisfying place of rest than the palace of the Son of Heaven himself. Bid your men enter and warm themselves."

"Well said," replied the Mongol who had tasted

the pot. But I disliked his looks, especially since he cast curious, and even unfriendly, glances in my direction. His companion nudged him, then pointed. A new dread seized me as the two stared at poor half-witted Tadda. Unless Kojin and I could divert them, the notorious Mongol bent for vicious humor might expend itself in entertainment in which Tadda would be the hapless victim.

The warrior who had spoken pulled aside the yurt flap and bawled something into the storm. The clatter outside was ferocious, with much screaming of animals and rattling of cart wheels. The Mongol stepped smartly aside again, holding up the flap and announcing, "Bid welcome to Hargoutai the Falcon, tar-khan of the Anger of God, Genghis Kha Khan."

Even he, a member of the tar-khan's own retinue, sounded fearful.

Chapter 2

The Coming of the Falcon

Lightning-lit rain gusted into the yurt, making the dung fire dance. Then Hargoutai stalked in.

He planted his hands on his hips and swept the company with his gaze. Dressed in a long quilted coat and white felt cap with upturned circular brim, he was of commanding height, with a brutal countenance. The crudeness of his features was relieved only by an almost feminine mouth and by alert dark eyes which clearly showed him to be a man of mental as well as physical prowess. He stank of the rancid grease with which all exposed areas of his face and neck had been swabbed. For an instant he stood scrutinizing us. Rain and wind howled through the flap, and firelight put mountains and plains of shadow over his features. I was struck by a notion that here was one of the tengri brought to life, an evil spirit sent from the gods to deal punishment to me. I cast a glance at the bubbling pot. Hargoutai appeared not to notice.

He loosed the collar of his greatcoat and commenced a tour around the circular yurt, sniffing and studying. With his collar down, a hideous red crescent scar on his neck became visible; doubtless it was an old wound badly healed. It made him appear all the more cruel if that were possible. He sniffed the common pot, spat loudly, and nodded. "Not the sweetmeats of Yen-king nor the tender reindeer of Karakorum, but I suppose it will do." He waved at Kojin. "If you are master here, send your louts to make my party comfortable. I wish to delay as little as possible, though it appears I'll be forced to spend at least one night in this sink of desolation." With his knife he ripped open one of the sacks of kumiss, then snorted disgustedly as the fermented milk spilled out upon the floor. "Pfaugh. Suck for children. Bring me rice wine."

One of his flunkies scuttled outside as he undid his coat and seated himself on a bench near the fire to warm his hands. Kojin signaled to me and Tadda that we should go outside to attend to the remainder of his company.

I counted at least fifty carts of Cathay and nearly as many inhabitants of that land, oppressed slaves who might once have been nobles in their own country. In addition, Hargoutai traveled with a personal guard of fifty Mongols, a boisterous, quarrelsome crew we quartered in three of the yurts. A fourth, small and poor, was given over to the Cathayans, who jabbered in their own tongue while snapping off bits of tea bricks to prepare over the fire. Apparently that was all the food their captors provided.

We were forbidden to enter the last yurt since

15

its residents had already quartered themselves inside. With wondering eyes, Tadda listened close to the flap. We both heard girls talking in bright, chirping syllables. Then a Mongol soldier cuffed Tadda away.

As we worked feverishly in the hay sheds, soaked clean through but forced to provide fodder for fifty ponies, Tadda whispered, "That last yurt—"

"What about it?"

"Women, James. Maidens of Cathay for the couch of the Kha Khan." He gave a shy giggle.

At the moment I cared little for all the beauties of creation. The insufferable airs of the soldiers of Hargoutai filled me with anger. I felt myself fully as good and as capable as they, and while I worked in the storm, I imagined all sorts of plots and schemes for proving my worth. Each plot, unfortunately, seemed to lead to instant execution once my reason subjected it to analysis.

With the Cathayans quartered and the Mongol soldiers soundly started on a drinking bout—several had already lurched from their yurts, vomited noisily in the storm, and returned, a sign of full-scale revelry—Tadda and I crept miserably back to the yurt where my adopted father sat listening to Hargoutai's accounts of his many achievements in Cathay.

Disgusted, I noted the cook-pot was well-nigh empty. Tadda and I would go hungry. Besides, we could not get close to the pot without causing a scene. Hargoutai still dipped an occasional hand into it, licking his fingers between pulls from a sack of powerful rice wine.

Tadda and I sank down on the benches farthest from the fire—the place normally reserved for children in a Mongol family. Hargoutai and his

16

two lieutenants left the yurt to vomit. Kojin threw me a glance, indicating that the evening was progressing tolerably well. I was about to make comment when I spied a figure in the shadows, on a bench to the left of where Hargoutai had been seated.

My breath caught in my throat. It was a girl.

I saw her eyes first. I shivered, for I felt the wheel of destiny turning again while I gazed at her.

She was Cathayan, no more than sixteen years old. Her exquisite oval face had a sad, bemused quality that stirred me strangely. After turning away from my glance, she bowed her head, hands clasped over her knees.

I kept staring. She grew conscious of it. When she raised her head again, I thought I saw a smile in her slightly tilted eyes, though there was none on her lips. Mingled fear and a plea for kindness shone in those eyes for a moment.

I could tell that her body had already reached the first bloom of womanhood. Her breasts were small, high, well-formed. The sight of them stirred me in a way I had known only once before, during my first experience with a wench. That had been three years past and had involved a caravan slut. It had been a crude, unsatisfying affair, yet wondrous, too, as a man's first union with a woman always is.

Now, gazing at the virgin of Cathay—for she could be nothing except a virgin if she were being borne back to Karakorum as a prize—it was as though a chord of sweet music rang through my head, making me dissatisfied again with my dull, narrow world. Never had I seen a creature so lovely and so desirable.

Hargoutai had clothed her in the Mongol fashion, in a long gown of purest white felt. Yellow girdles bound her dress at waist and breast; a gleaming cloak of sable fell back from her shoulder. Her headdress was shaped of birch bark, decorated with colored silk; tiny coins and ivory statues gleamed in the lustrous folds of her dark hair. A curl fell deliciously over each tiny porcelain ear.

I must have been gaping outrageously, for Hargoutai and his compatriots chose that moment to return, belching and grunting, and all three noticed my attentions. Hargoutai scowled, sat down, and helped himself to another pull from the leather wine sack. Then he patted the maiden's leg. "We have given these rustics a feast for the eye, have we not, Cho Soo? In return for the miserable fare of their pot, we give them a banquet of beauty. I'll vow they've gotten the best of the bargain." He chuckled, pinching one of her breasts. "A hundred leagues to Karakorum, and then you may no longer deny me. Doesn't the prospect please you? Concubine of a tar-khan of the Kha Khan?"

The eyes of the maiden Cho Soo flashed with defiance for a moment, but she forced herself to answer politely. "Of course, Lord." I was surprised that I understood her so well; she had evidently studied the language of her captors.

Pleased with himself, Hargoutai turned to Kojin. The little demonstration of his sway over the Cathayan girl made me dislike him all the more. But before Hargoutai could speak, one of his lieutenants swaggered to his feet and pointed a finger at Tadda.

"Lord Hargoutai, that one strikes me as addle-witted. Do you think we might find amusement in making him perform a trick or two?"

Tadda blinked and clutched my arm. I felt my belly tighten. Fortunately, however, Hargoutai cast his gaze in my direction.

"Perhaps later. I am more interested in finding a pale-fleshed, yellow-haired youth with sky-colored eyes in the middle of the Gobi. What is your name?"

"I am called James the Frank," I replied.

Hargoutai could not control cynical mirth. "You are noted for your frank nature, eh? Famed far and wide for your outspoken manner? How odd. You've sat like a wet lump of wool since first you entered. I find your name exceedingly unfitting."

With a burst of anger, I answered him. "My name comes not from my character, Lord, but from my origins. My father, whose name I don't know, was a soldier of Frankistan."

"Then there really is such a place as Frankistan? I've heard tales, but I never quite believed them."

"There is indeed, Lord. One day I hope to return there and seek my true origins."

"Very ambitious," Hargoutai muttered after another swig of wine. He meant presumptuous. "But how did you come to the Gobi?"

"The exact way is unclear, Lord," Kojin interrupted tactfully. "Many years ago, a dying Frank stumbled into my yurt leading a babe but five or six years of age. The Frank was almost delirious. He babbled about having wandered far, and truly that must have been the case, since he knew enough of the Mongol tongue to converse with me. He lived just a few days, but in that time he told me a tale of being a poor man of Frankistan who had gone off to fight a holy war against someone named Saladin. He spoke of great pos-

19

ters showing barbarians defiling a religious tomb. Of fighting where the sun shines hot all year. Of a place called Acre, of which I have never heard since. And of a man called Richard, with a lion's heart, of whom I also know nothing. The Frank never spoke of the lad's mother, except to say her hair was gold in color and she was not a Frank. I adopted the boy and raised him for my own, because I was wifeless and childless. The other, Tadda, is a distant orphan relative of my family. He too I took in at an early age. Both have been good sons."

"A half-wit, a yellow-headed savage, and an old man," Hargoutai chuckled. "Gods, what a fine group to entertain a warrior of the Khan!" Again he fixed me with his gaze. "But come, James the Frank, exercise your vaunted tongue. What is your true ambition? Certainly not to be a prince of the yam for the remainder of your days. Since returning to Frankistan is clearly a dream beyond your reach, you must have another."

For an instant I didn't know how to reply. Then, across the firelight, I caught a glance from the eyes of the Cathayan maiden. Unless my brains lied, I again detected warmth and a hunger for kindness in a land where there was none.

Her glance gave me courage. So did something else: I had not drunk of the rice wine, but of a headier draught—the thunder of the Gobi; the promise of great turns in the road of my destiny, if I could but survive the snares of the gods along the way. Thus I dared to speak out in a bold way, deliberately meaning to stun the insolent Hargoutai.

"Lord, my ambition is to be a warrior of the Khan."

The thought had popped into my head unexpectedly, but I was not entirely surprised by it, nor displeased by it, either. Perhaps the idea had been slumbering in my mind for months, while I fretted against the narrow confines of my world.

Hargoutai and his companions were convulsed.

"A warrior as mighty as Hargoutai the Falcon, I suppose?" one of the lieutenants jeered.

Then anger and the wild fury of the whirlwind took possession of me. "No. Mightier."

The laughter stilled. I caught the intake of Cho Soo's breath, sharp and fearful. The lieutenants exchanged scowls. Hargoutai, however, appeared unmoved. He continued to subject me to close scrutiny, his eyes gleaming in the midst of his greasy face. I was suddenly aware that calm might signal greater peril than wrath.

Hargoutai said softly, "Ambition without a leavening of tact can be the ambition of a dead man."

"But as you yourself remarked, Lord, my name prompts me to speak out and say—"

Kojin would let it go no further. He leaped to his feet and boxed my ears. "To the shed with you! Still your insolent tongue!"

In his eyes I saw no anger, only a fear that Hargoutai's anger might explode in the pull of a blade, thus taking one or both of Kojin's adopted sons from the face of the earth. My fury was tempered with the understanding that Kojin's blows were given with love.

Kojin gestured. "Tadda, go with him!"

As the bewildered creature shuffled ahead, I went out without another backward look.

The storm howled across the dark Gobi, nearly blowing us from our feet. Finally, drenched, we staggered into the shed of barley sacks. There we settled ourselves uncomfortably for the night.

21

The world was possessed by shrieking wind-devils. But somehow they did not terrify me. In my mind burned the image of the virgin Cho Soo—especially her eyes. It is said that through the eye, love enters and escapes the body.

Never would I forget her glance of encouragement at the moment when I needed it most. If I had not cared for her before that moment, I thought I cared for her now, though I knew well the price I might be forced to pay if I dared to covet a tar-khan's concubine. I would be a prudent man—if I had truly become a man on this momentous day—to banish her image from my mind.

But I could not. I thought of her for an hour, then another. I cared for her with the hasty passion of the young; but that made the caring no less real. I cared for her too because I despised the man who kept her a prisoner. So instead of forgetting her, I said a prayer to gods, Christian and pagan, whose names I did not know. I prayed they would keep the tengri flying and the whirlwind abroad for one more day and one more night, though I suffer death at the hands of Hargoutai the Falcon because of it.

During the night Tadda whimpered and sobbed, caught in bad dreams. I felt he must be visioning the cruel face of the Mongol leader, even while I, fully awake, feasted on the dream-image of the Cathayan maid.

Tadda crawled against my chest. I held him in my arms until his whimpers stilled and only the storm cried on. Then I drifted off, still dreaming of her.

When I awoke early the next morning, I did not open my eyes. I listened. I heard the bitter cry of the wind; the savage pulse of the rainstorm; the thunder.

The caravan would be forced to stay. The gods had answered my prayers. Whether to destroy me soon, or lead me a few more steps along an enticing but ultimately fatal road, I did not know.

Nor did I care.

I only knew I would see her again.

Chapter 3

The Girl from the Clouds of Heaven

Wrapping my leather cloak about me, I stepped over Tadda's slumbering form and set out through the storm to explore conditions at the yam station.

Little could be seen of the surrounding landscape. It was hidden by the rain pouring from the sky. The dung fires had gone out in four of the yurts, the three belonging to Hargoutai's elite guard and the one occupied by the Falcon and my adopted father.

The aftermath of the Mongols' prodigious capacities for strong drink was apparent everywhere. Outside the yurts of the soldiers, several of them were sprawled on the soaked earth, lying in their own sourness, blissful and content that they had once more proven themselves men by being drunk, sick, drunk, sick, drunk once more, and sick still once more, wine sacks without end.

I made my way from yurt to yurt, stoking the

fires until healthy plumes rose to the smoke-holes. Inside the yurts, too, the soldiers lay about in postures of drunken slumber, most snorting heavily. One opened a bleary eye, raised a boot to kick me and was unable to summon strength, his leg falling back to earth with a thud. I held back a smile. The lethargy of the camp made my dangerous task a bit easier.

In the largest yurt, a similar scene presented itself. Hargoutai and his two officers slept beneath their leather cloaks. Old father Kojin huddled on a bench in his sheepskins, dozing fitfully. I stoked the fire, threw fresh meat in the cook-pot, and proceeded to the yurt housing the fifty Cathayan captives.

Most of them were asleep as well, although one or two bearded grandfathers, yellow-cheeked and sad-eyed, chattered to each other while I bustled about. One silk-robed servant sat by himself, gazing into a shiny brass globe. I wanted to ask him what the stars foretold for me in the next few hours, but I did not.

A delicate chatter greeted my ears as I waited outside the yurt which housed the Cathayan maidens. Since Cho Soo had not been sleeping near Hargoutai, I assumed she was with the others. Taking a last look around to make certain no warrior was stirring, I called softly, "Are there any within who speak the tongue of the Mongols?"

The chattering hardly abated. I was afraid no one had heard me. I opened my mouth to speak again, more loudly, even though it meant danger of discovery. Without warning the flap was drawn aside a few inches. I glimpsed eyes that I recognized with surging heart.

I could not clearly read the expression of those

eyes. They contained fear—of that I was certain—but I thought I detected another, bolder light, although this might have been only self-delusion. Bending close to the flap, I said, "I have brought chips to warm the fire. If you will step away, I will place them inside the entrance of the yurt and shield my gaze at the same time."

Cho Soo lifted the yurt flap slightly. I caught sight of the hem of her white felt robe with its yellow girdles. I knelt and began to pile the chips just within the entrance, watching my own hands tremble. Cho Soo remained at the edge of my field of vision, holding the flap for me. I dared not gaze at her for fear of losing my composure. A touch of some Cathayan scent radiated from the girl's body.

The last of the chips unloaded from the crook of my left arm, I whispered, "If the storm prevails one more night, will you come to the hay shed when the rest are sleeping?"

Though the rain dinned its fury around us, I heard her answer, "I will."

My being sang with joy and triumph. Still, I felt obliged to add, "Evil could follow you."

"I will come."

Rising quickly, I risked one glance. Written on her face I saw the light that had shone in my dreams only an hour earlier—a light of gentleness; of subtle passion; perhaps of defiance of her captor. The flap dropped into place. Her small ivory fingers disappeared.

I think I reeled away from the yurt with the same reckless step of a Mongol warrior displaying his capacity for wine. I threw back my head, flung wide my arms, and let the rain pelt my face. The wind whipped my hair, and I let out a low, wordless cry of victory. The gods had accepted my new challenge to their power.

Gaining some degree of control, I made my way to the fodder sheds. Tadda was stirring. I set him to tending the Mongol ponies, going myself to the hay hut, rooting around and shifting the stuff until I had created a warm, fragrantly dry nook. It was a rude bower indeed, but the best I could arrange. As I looked down at it, the sight seemed to suffuse me with a kind of holy warmth.

I placed my cloak in such a way that no rain could possibly reach the snug depression. Then I went to aid Tadda in his chores, my heart lifting. Tadda noticed my good mood; it brought a smile to his face.

Shortly old Kojin came forth to find us. The rain had slackened somewhat, but the wind had increased in intensity. The ponies, Mongol war horse and yam courier animal alike, huddled together for protection. Kojin shivered in his robes. "The tears of the gods stop, but their breath is still violent. I fear a buran."

"A black storm?" I asked.

"Yes, and one that may continue another night at least. The tar-khan may find it necessary to remain with us."

"Well, our hospitality was acceptable, wasn't it? Notwithstanding his unkind remarks?"

"I do not believe we displeased him," Kojin said. "Apart from your remarks about your ambitions as a warrior. They were hardly prudent. You were fortunate Hargoutai did no more than reprove you with his tongue. He might have done much more."

"I only said what I believed, old father."

"You acted like a fool!" Kojin exclaimed. "Hargoutai is our master. We must respect him.

27

He is one of only a handful elevated to tar-khan by Genghis himself."

"With all due respect, father," I said, "no man is my master."

Kojin's Mongol heritage recoiled at such words. "The Kha Khan and his lords are masters of *all* men!"

"Legally, perhaps. But there is a difference between loyalty and slavery. Hargoutai treats everyone as his slave. I am a Frank, not a Mongol. I owe him no such allegiance. I will not pay it, no matter what the price."

Aghast, Kojin seized my arm. "My son, what evil spirits possess you that you utter remarks of a kind I have never heard before?"

I could only shake my head. "I can't say. I know something's changed. Yesterday I felt like a child. But today I do not. A man can change quickly. Many things—the slaying of the roebuck, the rage I felt when Hargoutai looked on me as no better than a fox cub, good only for tossing in his cook-pot—many things have changed me, old father. I cannot begin to explain them. Perhaps I have talked to the gods."

"Madness!" Kojin seized my other arm and shook me. *"Madness!* James, you are my dearest treasure. You are my son. I do not want you taken from me!"

"That will not happen. At least not soon. I think there is a long road ahead."

A watery gleam, no part of any storm that ever rained from heaven, entered his eyes. "A road? Away from me? I am an old man, James. I want you to remain by my side the rest of my days."

Gently, with all the affection I had felt for him across the years, I touched his withered hand where it lay on the sleeve of my coat. "And very likely I will," I said. "You're right, my talk is foolishness. I drank kumiss when I left you last evening." I was lying for all I was worth. I could not bear to hurt him. "Do not alarm yourself. I'll be with you for many years to come."

Reassured, old Kojin dabbed his eyes. His manner became authoritative again. "Take care to stay out of the way of Hargoutai today. His mood is black after so much imbibing. Practicing discretion is no reflection upon courage. I hope you will promise to remember that maxim until the caravan departs."

"I intend to practice the utmost discretion, old father," I answered, straight-faced.

"Good. Excellent! My son has regained his sanity. Now to work. At least two horses must be slaughtered. A fresh stew prepared. . . ."

My duties did indeed keep me from the path of the tar-khan for the rest of the day. Thus it was possible for me to concentrate on the loveliness of Cho Soo, rather than on the ugliness of her master. I congratulated myself on my cleverness at the door of her yurt. Asking whether any inside spoke the Mongol tongue had worked better than I had hoped. Only the preceding evening, the maid had answered her lord in Mongol, leading me to surmise that he had been her teacher on the road from Cathay. I shuddered to think of the additional lessons he might teach her in Karakorum.

Occupied by thoughts of the coming night, I busied myself with the slaughter knife, with sheaves of hay, with a dozen menial tasks which the arrogant Mongol soldiers haughtily ordered me to do.

As Kojin had prophesied, the wind developed to

a buran, a terrible gale that would have upset the yurts had they not been dome-shaped and securely staked. Late in the day, the Mongols started drinking again. Several one-string fiddles appeared. The keen of the wind was multiplied by a dozen male voices pealing chorus after intoxicated chorus.

I noted soldiers laughing and boxing one another's ears. A mood of good feeling seemed to prevail, in spite of the delay in the journey to Karakorum. I was required to enter the large central yurt only once. Hargoutai the Falcon was away, for which I was thankful. A glimpse of his face would have ruined the picture I had formed of the coming meeting in the hay shed.

Tormented souls seemed to cry across the Gobi that night. The one-string fiddles planked endlessly, one loud voice dropping away, then another and another, until only a few remained. It seemed I had spent hours waiting in the warm depression under the cloak in the hay shed; waiting while doubts assailed me. . . .

Cho Soo had only answered yes to my proposal because she wished to torment me. She and Hargoutai the Falcon were doubtless laughing over my discomfiture this very moment. . . .

No, she meant to come but could not, because Hargoutai had thrown caution aside and was taking his pleasure with her rather than waiting to deliver her unsullied to the Khan at Karakorum. . . .

No, she meant to come, but it meant nothing more to her than a moment's respite on an otherwise gloomy pilgrimage from her homeland. A few cordial words, a touch of my hand, and she would return to the yurt, then journey on and forget me, and one day laugh about the blue-eyed creature she had met on the Gobi. I could mean nothing to her, even if she came . . .

And she would not come.

The hour was growing late. The yam station was silent. Voices had died. Could that be a faint smear of light eastward in the direction of the Great Wall? No! I leaped up. The patch of lightness was the white of her gown, blurring out of the windy wastes.

I clasped her hand. She uttered a little exclamation of fright.

"I didn't mean to alarm you," I said clumsily. "I—I thought you were not coming."

"Hargoutai bade me sit beside him until he fell asleep. It takes much wine to bring slumber to that one." Her voice was even more delicate and lovely than I remembered. She spoke the rough Mongol tongue with something less than perfection. Yet with a charming lilt which must have had its origins in her birth as a girl of Cathay.

"I promised I would come to you. I have kept the vow because I wished to do so."

"Here, sit with me." I showed her the place I had prepared. "It's warm under the cloak. I managed to steal a small sack of wine."

Modesty and courtly grace manifested themselves in the way Cho Soo took her place in the warm depression. She folded the lower ends of her yellow floss-silk girdles about the hem of her gown. I, in turn, lowered myself to a half-crouched posture. It was uncomfortable but necessary if I were to maintain a proper distance between us, and not seem the same sort of mannerless lout as her Lord Hargoutai.

Wordlessly I held out the sack. She took it in tiny hands. With bowed head and averted eyes she sipped, then returned the sack. The buran whined and cried outside the shed, but it could not disturb our warm haven.

Finally, after another swig from the sack, I summoned courage and said, "You took a great risk coming here, my lady."

"I told you I wanted to come."

"To see me? Or to defy the tar-khan?"

"If you must know the truth, a little of both."

"Well, I'm all at once doubtful about whether I have the courtly words to make your risk worthwhile."

"It's payment enough to spend an hour in the company of one with a kind voice and clean skin." She wrinkled her nose. "Your flesh does not stink of that dreadful grease."

"It's plain you're not fully accustomed to the ways of the Mongols."

"Definitely not! Nor will I ever be."

"I have seen a few Cathayan women pass this way on the journey to Karakorum since General Muhuli burned Yen-king. None has possessed your refinement." Though I felt I might hurt my cause by asking, I said, "Are you from a royal house of Cathay?"

Cho Soo gave a nod. "Among the Hat and Girdle People, as the Mongols call us, I was a princess of the royal house of Chin. The Golden Ones. I lived in the imperial palace. I attended T'ien tsi, the Son of Heaven Wai Wang, and subsequently his son when the emperor fled to his enemies, the Sung, rather than face the fury of your Khan."

A glint of anger for her emperor, a shine of courage from within herself lighted the delicate oval of her face.

"I remained at our court, the Clouds of Heaven, with a few other proud and foolish people. I knew I should have fled but I didn't. As a result, I was captured by the men of General Muhuli, who is now governor in Cathay. He presented me to Hargoutai, either as a concubine or a gift for the beast who sits on the throne at Karakorum. Either fate is unwelcome. I would gladly dare all the dangers of the earth to have a few moments in the company of a decent man."

I laughed. "You forget, princess. I have spent my life among the Bow and Arrow people, as Cathay calls the Mongol race. I am brother to them. I have the same faults. The same appetites—"

"No, that is not true. I saw differences when you spoke boldly to Hargoutai. Your form is just as manly as the strongest Mongol soldier. Your arms are as well muscled. Yet in your eyes I see none of the barbarism I have witnessed among the Mongols."

Bolstered by the rice wine, my head throbbing slightly, I answered, "I would be the most cruel and most barbarous of all, if the task were defending you from those who would hurt you. By rights you should look on me as a clod. A yellow-headed fool wrapped in sheep's wool and staining my hands in the cook-pot the same as the others. Your very coming pays me more honor than I have ever known. It warms my heart, Cho Soo, but—" The wine spoke for me then; the wine and the darkness and the sweet scent of her. "—in one respect I'm like all men." I reached out and touched her small, hard breast, the contour of which I could feel beneath the white felt of her robe.

I thought she would pull away. She did not. Instead, with a sudden intake of breath, she clasped her hand over mine and tilted her head back, eyes closed, while her fingers pressed against the backs of mine, and I felt the tip of her breast harden with her desire.

Chapter 4

The Vow.

We kissed then. Her mouth, not overly large—it matched the delicacy of the rest of her—still had a surprising mobility and passion. Her lips parted. She darted her tongue out, a sweet, spiced caress.

I held her breast more tightly. She swayed a little; I think she would have let me take her then, and in truth I wanted to; I was rigid. Yet something checked her.

She broke the embrace. Not angrily, but with a decisiveness that said she knew we were both on the verge of surrender to one another, and it must not be. In a way I was achingly disappointed. In another, I was elated. She was no casual creature; something more than sheer loneliness had drawn her to me tonight. If not love, then at least the possibility of love. That was some compensation for the torment I felt because she had roused me so.

She attended to a loose lock of hair, and then began speaking again, still with a courtliness inherent in her nature, yet in a more friendly and intimate way.

"James—that is your name, but do I say it properly?"

"You say it beautifully."

"James, you misjudge yourself. You are not like Hargoutai."

I smiled. "Why, didn't I prove that I was a minute ago?"

"No," she teased, "you only proved your own words. You are a man. That is still a far different thing from being a Mongol." The way she pronounced the last word told me how much she hated them. "I wouldn't have come here if it hadn't been for that touch of difference. You may dress like them, and speak in their tongue, and eat raw flesh, but you aren't of their blood. That is important, because in Cathay, we place great store in the perfect detail—the minute difference. A small and perfect moment shared with you may be the last one granted to me for the rest of my days."

Sensing the sadness in those words, I tried to reassure her. "Your life at Karakorum may not be too difficult. Especially if you should be chosen as concubine for the Khan." The thought hurt. "Though savage in battle, he is said to place great store in the workings of the mind. Besides, doesn't he have a learned Cathayan as counselor now?"

"Yes. The venerable Ye Liu Chutsai is with him. He is a great scholar, versed in the teachings of T'ang and Master K'ung. It was he who told your Khan that although he had conquered a mighty empire from the saddle, he could not govern in the same way." A gentle sigh escaped her lips. "He may be of some help. But I really don't believe it. I'll become the goods of Hargoutai the Falcon. In fact, I'll be lucky to reach Karakorum at all without being subject to his desires—especially if this drinking continues."

Her brief flirtation with the subject of virtue kindled fires in my belly again. I edged closer, driven by the intoxication of the wine. I was prepared to touch her hand when something made me stop.

The kiss had shown me a kind of bond already existed between us. It was born of mutual loneliness—we were both outcasts in an alien land. Yet I knew somehow that the bond was potentially much stronger. I wanted the locking of our bodies to seal the bond—and in the depths of her eyes I thought I saw the same desire.

Yet I held back. It would not be fair for me to destroy her one advantage, her one means to survival: the demonstration of her perfection. Virginity could deliver her from Hargoutai into the favor of the Kha Khan.

So I fought my own feelings and occupied myself with still another tilt of the wine sack. Time had stopped. The wind moaned, and I knew that the eastern light would never break; we would remain together forever.

I knew I was a cursed Frankish fool. I tried to speak of something that would divert both of us from the dangers of our passion. "Cho Soo, help me. If I am ever to seek a place in the world, I must know something of distant lands and other people. Tell me of Cathay, of your house and your pastimes."

She touched my arm. A smile of spontaneous thanks brightened her mouth. "Gladly," she said with a little sigh, as if she too knew she must deny her own desires. She began to describe Cathay, presenting a colorful and splendid picture to my limited imagination.

She conjured vivid pictures of a civilization over five thousand years old, more learned and ancient by far than the primitive Mongol tribes. Her words wove dream-patterns in the hay-sweet dark, painting as though on invisible silks delicate pastel scenes of great cities where barges floated on pleasure lakes, where women carried little silver bells in their hands, and noble mandarins took the sun beneath umbrellas.

Within the great palaces where screens of silk kept out devils, life was calm and measured, devoted, as she had told me, to the pursuit of perfection, the tiny detail in which the whole meaning of the universe might be revealed. I *saw* the colored tiles of pagoda roofs and the poets writing their verses with brushes of silk. I *heard* the temple gongs and the words of the Bamboo Books.

In those swift-flying moments, she carried me to battle with Cathay's mighty war lords, each of whom had his own temple in camp wherein he prayed to Kwan-ti before battle. I saw twenty-horse chariots, machines which threw heavy stones, crossbows that required ten men to wind them, war engines which could catapult fire and rock when two hundred artillery soldiers drew back the ropes. The wonders were nearly beyond my comprehending, and I was ashamed that I had ever been content with the narrow confines of my barren Gobi world.

I could hardly conceive of roads which crossed great rivers on arches of stone, or of the fabled Great Wall, all stone and brick and running miles and miles, a tower at each gate and topped by a parapet so broad that half a dozen Cathayan horsemen could gallop abreast . . .

I shook my head. "Truly I have lived as a child for too many years. I never dreamed such sights lay beyond the desert. If Cathay is so magnificent and mighty, there must be equal beauty to the west in Frankistan, whence came the father whose I remember."

Uncontrollable now, I seized the hand of the maiden of Chin. "All at once you have made me know that I, too, have been made a prisoner here in my own homeland. My captor is no less real than yours. It is the ambition I described to Hargoutai, the desire to be more than a herder of animals among the barrens."

"You at least have the chance to realize your ambition," Cho Soo replied sadly. "My own end is ordained. I'll live out my days in this ugly land, and bear Hargoutai's flat-nosed brats, and never again set eyes on my beloved country. If I have fired your mind, James the Frank, it is at the price of recalling my own woeful state."

"Perhaps—" Again I was possessed, as I had been when boasting to Hargoutai. "Perhaps if the Khan doesn't take you for his own, I could come close to the stature of a tar-khan. I could claim you! Together we could go to Frankistan and find wonders more royal than those in Cathay."

She smiled. "A pretty dream."

"Dreams can be made real if courage is the clay, princess."

"But why would you do that for me, James? We have known each other just a few hours."

"Long enough," I said. "Some spend years on this earth and never come as close to another as

39

we've come tonight. My old, childless father, for instance—"

Cho Soo closed her eyes. "A pretty dream. Pretty talk...."

"Don't jest with me!"

The storm of my emotions broke fully then. I fumbled with the clasp at the throat of her gown and opened it, reaching beneath and laying my hands on the cool, bare perfection of her breasts. The tips were sharp and hard against my palms. She moaned a little, leaning toward me to increase the pressure.

"Listen to me, Cho Soo. I have drunk wine tonight, but my head is clear of that. I've also tasted something else. Something far sweeter. A draught I've never tasted before. It makes me swear my existence into your keeping, whether you wish the gift or not."

"James, James! We must not. There is no hope, no possibility—"

"There is! I think the gods are favoring me at last. Yesterday I killed a roebuck—forbidden by the Khan's law. Doing that, I defied the gods, too, and they haven't struck me down. Tonight I defy them—and the Khan's power—a second time. I claim that your life is my life, and I vow to you that one day I'll claim you in truth, whether you will or not. And if it can't be done by James the Frank, then it will be done by James the Mongol, a soldier of the Kha Khan. Grease on his face. Blood on his hands—"

She uttered a cry, whether of pain or pleasure, I couldn't tell. But suddenly she was close against me, her arms around my neck and her mouth open and eager against mine.

When we drew apart, I stared at her and damned myself as a drunken oaf for spilling out such a profession of love. But I could not help it, because the works were true, and I would have spoken them even if I had known the tengri would seize me the next instant.

Breathlessly, I watched her shining face. I waited for the courtly, girlish laugh which would signify the acceptance of my words as nothing more than youthful ardor. I waited for her to say I was fully as peculiar and boastful as the scar-necked Hargoutai. Any moment she would deny me; would turn aside in derision or anger; would call out for assistance.

She touched my cheeks with her palms. Tears welled in her eyes. "I take the gift and the promise, James the Frank. I give in exchange the gift of my heart, for what reason I do not wholly know. As you say, we are both strangers in an alien land. Yet my feelings suddenly leap beyond such common explanation. It may be that we have been bound together since birth, and shall remain so till death, though I doubt whether we'll ever see each other again once Hargoutai the Falcon moves on to Karakorum."

"Don't say that! *Don't!* I swear I'll come to you."

"The promise is worth the deed," she answered softly. "If I could only give you a tangible gift in return—the one prize above all others woman-kind can bestow. My heart cries out to give it. My whole being cries out—"

Then her words grew muffled, because I could hold back no longer. My arms circled her shoulders and I tipped her backward into the fragrant hay, covering her mouth and eyes and lovely skin with kisses. She transformed me somehow. I was no longer a cloddish clerk but a true and full-

41

fleshed man who had at last opened the miracle-book of love.

It seemed only a moment until the yellow girdles were torn aside and the fastenings of the felt robe unbound. Her small ivory breasts were beneath my hands again. I caressed them while her fingers stole to the root of my wanting, and touched, and stirred new savagery in me. I bared her below the waist and saw the loveliness of ivory, dark-tufted and trembling. I was marginally conscious that the wind had died, to be replaced by a peculiar keening in my ears—the song of a blood-yearning older than time.

Our hands and mouths grew even bolder. In another moment, I would have lifted myself onto her and brought the joy to completion. But then I remembered where she was destined to go. The memory destroyed the moment.

No pain before or since was as anguishing as that which made me tear myself from her, retreating across the tiny bower in the hay. Tears glistened on her cheeks, and stung my own eyes as well.

"No!" I said hoarsely. "No, I cannot. You must find favor with the Khan."

"There is torment in me," Cho Soo exclaimed.

"And in me!" I poured all the truth of my love into my words. "Keep the memory, Cho Soo. The memory of what we almost had tonight. The memory of my promise that I'll come and claim you—somehow. I have sworn it."

"We have sworn it, beloved," she answered through her tears. "It must be so."

Gasping, I stumbled to my feet. She drew the folds of her felt gown close about her. For the first time I grew aware of a diminishing of the

42

wind and a definite radiance on the eastern horizon.

"You must return to the yurt. The hour of dawn is almost—"

I stopped, struck dumb. I looked both right and left and saw no succor. We were prisoners in the hay bower in the breaking light.

Out of the pearly gray came a Cathayan maid, dragged by a lieutenant of Hargoutai the Falcon. The Mongol's eyes lighted vengefully. I turned to Cho Soo who stood beside me. I still could not speak.

The hostile gods had gained revenge.

Chapter 5

Caught

Before I had a chance to gather my wits and struggle, the officer and his unwilling captive were upon us.

The officer's lance, horsehair tuft, keen point, cruel hooks and all, touched my breast. The Mongol said curtly, "If you attempt to flee, yellowhair, it will go hard with the Cathayan maid. I will slay her in spite of my master's instructions. Though it's doubtful whether she remains a maid," he added, making a great lewd show of inspecting the hay and Cho Soo's white robe for signs of telltale blood spots.

The terrified captive handmaiden made gestures of entreaty to her mistress, blurting sorrowful explanations in Cathayan to Cho Soo between bursts of tears. The Mongol officer shouted, summoning three of his fellows. We were marched rapidly in the direction of the largest yurt.

I felt a chill foreboding, chiefly on behalf of

Cho Soo. I was the one responsible for drawing her to the hay shed. My vow of a few minutes earlier now seemed like a ghastly jest. The officer pricked me frequently in the spine with his lance. I would have attacked him but for his threat to harm the princess. The handmaiden continued her wailing until one of the soldiers cuffed her and sent her sprawling.

"Do not blame Ti Po," Cho Soo whispered to me, referring to the fallen girl. "Hargoutai sent his officer to summon me. When I wasn't in my proper place, the officer threatened the poor child with death. She told him she thought I'd crept off in the direction of the sheds, though I didn't realize a single soul was awake when I came to you. Hold no anger in your heart for her. All the maidens have been harshly treated on the journey for Yen-king. Their spirits are crushed."

"I hold anger only against myself," I said softly. "For my rashness in involving you—"

"They're cooing!" the officer exclaimed, digging me again with the lance point. "No, that's wrong. I've got my animals mixed. They weren't cooing but bleating. Imagine the spectacle! The white deer mounted by the wild ass!"

All the soldiers bellowed with laughter. My cheeks burned with shame. But I had no more time to dwell on my folly, for we arrived at the yurt and were thrust inside without ceremony.

The officer dismissed the disappointed soldiers and prodded me to the fire. He kept his hands off Cho Soo. She followed me closely, her chin lifted, the fear she must have felt concealed behind a regal expression. Stillness descended over the yurt. I could have sworn I heard the wings of the doom-birds flapping. . . .

Huddled on a bench beneath his prized bamboo

45

bow case, old Kojin regarded the pair of us with dismay. Sad, soft-brained Tadda crouched at Kojin's feet, arms wrapped around the old man's spindly calves, head against his knees, great eyes luminous with dumb fear.

The dung fires crackled. The two lieutenants waited. My own gaze was drawn irresistibly to Hargoutai the Falcon.

The mighty tar-khan was half-dressed. Sheepskins were tied loosely about his waist with a sinew. Only his breastplates, garish lacquer shining in the fire-glow, covered his vast and grease-glistening torso. A kumiss sack was slung over one shoulder for convenient drinking.

For several moments Hargoutai marched back and forth on the opposite side of the fire. His big splayed feet struck down rhythmically like an angry heartbeat, the only sound in the yurt apart from an occasional pop of the fire. As on the night when I had dared to speak to him boldly, whatever plots and furies boiled in his brain were concealed behind his face. But his wound-scar looked particularly hideous and scarlet on his muscled neck. I wished suddenly that he would seize a blade from one of his lieutenants and rush at us; I could defend myself. I had no defense against his measured stalking and his unreadable expression.

Kojin broke the silence. "I beg you to heed me a moment."

"What do you want?" Hargoutai growled.

"To explain. The boy's brain was addled with wine! He did not realize the nature or magnitude of the offense he was committing."

No matter what the risk in any other course, something told me I dared not let Kojin paint me as a coward or I was lost. I said, "I would not lightly dispute the words of my good father, Lord Hargoutai. Yet he does not speak with precise correctness. Though I had been drinking, I knew full well what I did. I forced my attentions upon your prisoner. By means of threats, I persuaded her to accompany me to the hay shed."

But Cho Soo undid my lie. "And I also dispute the son of Frankistan, Lord," she said in a clear voice. "I went willingly to him. No threats or violent measures were employed. I was eager for an adventure. I led him on. He is blameless."

"Obviously both of you are making great efforts to convince me that the other partner is free of guilt," Hargoutai remarked in an ominously quiet way. He glanced at neither of us, studying the fire instead. "That leads me to suspect that each of you bears equal guilt." His eyes flashed up at me. Never before had I experienced such a stare of absolute cruelty. Tadda began to whimper.

"Silence that wretch!" Hargoutai ordered. One of the lieutenants stepped forward and clubbed my brother with the butt end of his lance.

Hargoutai laced his fingers together, a wild figure with a greased, gleaming breast, there beyond the fire.

"Well, it's a nice puzzle we have, isn't it?" he remarked. "I am a party to the discovery of your erring ways, princess. I wakened early and drank a certain amount. I also did considerable thinking. Would you care to know what I decided? Very simple. I decided to keep my choicest gift to myself. I decided to enjoy it this very morning, in fact, and face the anger of the Khan later. Thus you may blame my own weakness for your undoing. Now let us begin to attempt to solve the puzzle of guilt. I can only assume both of you were bemused and out of your senses. Certainly there is no other reason to make a princess of the Golden People seek a rendezvous with a yam clerk, nor any other reason why a loutish foreigner would dare to ask after the favors of a virgin nobly born."

The words came hot to my tongue. "I was not seeking dalliance. I *love* her!"

Kojin leaped to his feet. "My son, take heed of what you say!"

"Keep silent, old one!" Hargoutai snarled. I noted a new, harder edge to his voice, as though his calm was cracking. To Cho Soo and me, he said, "I can excuse the prating of a clod raised among sheep and mares. But I would find it exceedingly surprising to hear similar words from your lips, princess. On the other hand, a curious expression on your face leads me to believe that such a circumstance might come to pass." He smirked, baiting her. "Can that be the case?"

"I do indeed love the Frankish man," Cho Soo answered in a whisper. "But that does not prevent me from recognizing my duty to you, as well as the extent of my crime. I pray that you punish only me."

"*No!*" I shouted. "If guilt is placed, put the kang on my shoulders!"

"A wood yoke to prison the neck and wrists is hardly suitable for this crime," Hargoutai replied, his tone lowering still again. The smoke rising to the hole at the top of the yurt was stifling. Slowly, the tar-khan rose. "You both annoy me with your sentimental gush and your protests of guilt and innocence. I'll have no more! I must

48

deal fairly with the situation, choosing one of several alternatives which lie open."

He cast a sidelong glance in my direction, making me understand that the inevitable punishment would be anything but fair. I thought of seizing the lance of one of the officers, slaying Cho Soo and then myself. But I was not quite ready to surrender life so quickly.

Hargoutai raised one hand, spreading his fingers. He addressed himself to them in the manner of a scholar disputing a point of law. His calm was grisly. "First, of course, The Yassa explicitly provides that persons guilty of adultery may be slain at once by the person wronged. Further, if either of you had chosen to deny that you willingly participated in this meeting, you could be judged innocent, since under the law of our mighty Khan, no man is termed guilty unless he confesses. However, you show no willingness to deny guilt. You have, therefore, confessed to committing adultery in spirit if not in act." Abruptly his voice grew louder. "Thus I am free to slay you."

Hargoutai halted his pacing. A neck muscle wrenched. I judged that only by sheer exertion of will was he able to keep from turning on us both and killing us in a twinkling. His rage was balanced on a perilous precipice.

Fearing for my safety, my old father Kojin chose this moment to rush forward and fling himself at Hargoutai's feet, grasping the tar-khan's legs. "I beg mercy and generosity, Lord!" Kojin pleaded, trembling. "The tar-khans are famed far and wide for their magnanimity as well as for their valor. I supplicate in behalf of this foolish boy, who is dear to me beyond life itself."

"Father," I said, my head drumming, "do not abase yourself before such a creature."

Hargoutai's eyes flashed. He glared at me, then pointed at Kojin's trembling head.

"Kill the meddlesome wretch."

Chapter 6

The Slow Death

I plunged forward to leap through the fire and stop it. One of the officers swung his lance in a wide arc. The lance hit the side of my head, driving me to my knees. Hargoutai kicked free of Kojin's grip and stepped to the side. Another blow to my head. Through the intervening curtain of flames, I saw the beloved face of my old Mongol father raised in a final plea for mercy. Only a crude croaking escaped his throat. Rheum welled at the corners of his eyes. All at once he saw death coming. The second Mongol lieutenant thrust his lance into Kojin's chest. He gave a twist to engage the hooks. Then he twisted it until it came free, bloody barbs, bits of flesh and all. Blood poured from Kojin's wound. His hands stretched out in an appeal to tormentors his eyes could no longer see.

Hargoutai the Falcon waved. "Another stroke."

The lieutenant put all of his power behind the

thrust. The lance cleaved Kojin's breastbone and flung him down. The lance vibrated. The officer placed a boot on Kojin's bloody chest and wrenched his weapon loose. Tadda wailed, covering his eyes.

The officer dragged a fox pelt from behind a bench and covered the ruin of my old father's body. Then he began cleaning blood from his boots by scraping them on the floor.

I endured agony during those moments, unable to do more than scrabble about on hands and knees, still dizzy from the blows of my captor. Visions of blood and Kojin's glazing eyes floated in my head. At last I gained my feet. I bit my lips to keep from shouting curses.

"One day," I whispered to Hargoutai, "you will die by my hand for what you did."

This amused the tar-khan. He took another pull from the kumiss sack and sat down on a bench, appearing utterly relaxed. "I very much doubt that, clerk," he said. "You should certainly know that tradition forbids shedding the blood of a Mongol chieftain of high birth. So you would have to concoct some kind of clever scheme to disguise a murder. To judge from your behavior, I think you lack the brains." Annoyance turned him toward Tadda. "Unless that simpleton can cease making cat-sounds, I'll give him the same treatment the old meddler got."

"Tadda" I said. "Be still, if you value your life."

My brain had already absorbed so much horror that I was ill-prepared for more. But it took no special insight to see poor Tadda's mind was even more unbalanced as a result of the killing he had just witnessed.

Beside me, Cho Soo drew her sable cape tight

around her body. She treated Hargoutai to a glare of loathing. It bothered him. He was making himself less and less of a man in her eyes, yet because of my insults, I knew he would not let me off lightly. To compensate for Cho Soo's scorn, I suspected he would punish me with extra severity.

He struggled to control his voice. "To resume our discussion of the laws governing the crime of adultery, it is further written in The Yassa that if a man shall steal a horse, or goods of comparable value, the punishment shall be death with the body severed in two parts. Of course a deflowered virgin of Cathay foolish enough to take up with a Gobi-rat of doubtful origin would not be judged to have the same value as a prime pony . . ." Hargoutai directed his words to me, their poisoned meaning to Cho Soo. ". . . yet a case could be argued for punishing you, Frankish man, in this way. You have stolen something of considerable value. Still, I cannot bring myself to admit it is as valuable as a pony, in which case it falls under the classification of a lesser theft."

"Kill me and be done. Or can you only slay the old and helpless?"

"You will judge my talents for slaying soon enough. But your death will come when I desire it, and in the manner I desire—no sooner. Theft of an item of lesser value than a horse may be punished by blows of a stout staff—seven blows, seventeen, or as many as seven hundred. Even seventy blows laid on well by one of my warriors would see you dead, but again it doesn't strike me as fitting. Of course you might escape the penalty altogether by paying nine times the worth of the prize taken. But I confess I can't estimate the value of nine times a maidenhead. Can you?"

"He didn't touch me!" Cho Soo cried. "I am still a virgin!"

"The body can be virginal and the head that of a strumpet, princess." Hargoutai stared at her in a cold way. "You have betrayed and shamed me. Your worth is destroyed."

"He would never believe you in any case," I said to the Cathayan girl.

Hargoutai the Falcon stroked his chin, picked at a speck on his lacquered breastplate, studied his toes, prolonging the pronouncement of sentence still again. My gaze roved to the fox pelt, beneath which lay lifeless meat that had once been a man. Finally Hargoutai said, "There *is* one punishment permissible in this situation. I encountered it when our horde invested walled Taitong-fu five years ago. Carrying it out may delay our journey to Karakorum, however ... ah, well. The waiting is worth it. It is known as the slow death, the torture of Cathay, yellow-hair. Have you heard it?"

Before I could reply that I had not, Cho Soo screamed and had to be restrained by the two officers. "You will *not!*" she cried. "He is innocent! I swear it by the funeral raiment of my sacred ancestors!" Twisting in the grip of the officers, she raked them with her fingernails and used all manner of female tricks, even biting, to try to free herself. Hargoutai stepped forward and struck her. She tumbled to the floor of the yurt.

The officers dragged me around the fire, pushed me to my knees beside a bench, and held my left arm pinned atop it. Hargoutai the Falcon picked up his small sword from a divan and tested the sword's edge against the fat part of his finger.

"The outcries of the princess trouble me greatly," he said in pleasant tones. "After all,

54

didn't the soldiers of Cathay invent this clever practice? Simply explained, yellow-hair, your limbs will be cut from your body over a period of many hours."

Grinning, he lowered the sword blade over my left hand. The keen edge scored the flesh of my smallest finger, just behind the nail. "All your limbs," said Hargoutai. "One joint at a time." He leaned on the sword hilt, forcing the blade straight down through flesh and bone, cutting off the tip of the finger.

I cried out. I could not help it. My vision blurred. Distantly Cho Soo exclaimed and prayed to her gods in the Cathayan tongue.

"Hold up his head so he doesn't faint!" Hargoutai ordered, flinging away his sword and rummaging for the kumiss sack. "Gods, I'd give my soul to be back at The Black Sands and amply provided with wine. This mare's piss sickens me."

Nevertheless he made a great show of swigging, then examining the flesh of his belly to test its firmness, all the while the officers kept holding up my head.

The pain from my hacked finger was so fierce it kept me wide awake. Hideously fascinated, I stared at the discarded sword. Ages seemed to pass. At last Hargoutai picked up the weapon again. He examined it; spat on it; smiled at me as he tested its honing against hairs plucked from handy pelts.

Would he strike now?

No, he was turning away; reaching for the kumiss sack. I had been spared for a few more seconds. The mental torment was almost worse than the bite of the sword.

He raised the sack for a drink. I closed my eyes. The officers yanked my hair. I opened my eyes, thinking that I had still a moment of respite before the game began again.

Too late, I reckoned that Hargoutai had wished me to think exactly that; he had wanted to lull me; to tease me into believing the blow was to be delayed. While my eyes were closed, he had dropped the sack. The blade was a blur of gold light hacking down across my vision, then— *crack*—across the second joint.

I screamed.

Hargoutai turned his sword about, holding it by the blade and offering it to one of his officers. "The privilege of taking the next joint will be yours. I have to relieve myself." He turned away from the fire.

Pain became a beating all along my arm. It spilled through my chest, swept down my legs, numbing my senses at last.

The officer chosen to perform the next cut took the sword. He circled to the other side of the bench, kneeling in front of me. He applied the blade lightly, sawing back and forth but not slicing deeply at first.

Hargoutai's blurred form wavered at the edge of my vision. I had forgotten everything except my own pain, wondering how long the game would continue before I died of loss of blood. I bit my tongue as the officer kept sawing. He remarked to Hargoutai that the meat seemed lean and stringy, making the butchering hardly worth the bother. The Falcon replied with coarse laughter.

A flurry of white motion swept past the fire as the last joint severed. I swayed backward and toppled over.

As though borne on noisy winds, Cho Soo's imploring words drifted into my head: "Lord Hargoutai, heed my words. Stop the ghastly game or a prize truly will be taken from you!"

"What the devil do you mean?"

"This, Lord. I know your tongue speaks anger, but your heart is still filled with lust, I think. Stop the torture, now, and I will be yours not only in body but in mind and soul until my dying hour. This I promise in the name of my sacred ancestors, who will smite me down if I ever break the vow. If you don't heed me, then a blade will find my breast one night soon, for though you guard me with a hundred handmaidens and a thousand warriors, I'll find a way to deprive you of the treasure you coveted all the way from Yen-king."

Hargoutai tried to laugh. "You're threatening to kill yourself if I don't stop, is that it?"

"No threat, Lord. On my word as a princess of the house of Chin, I speak the truth. I promise faith if you do as I ask, and my certain death if you don't."

Through a reddening veil, I tried to cry out to her; tried to beg her to call back her words. The bond she promised in order to save me would separate us even more completely than death. My tongue worked but no sound came. Red lights danced in my skull. Pain pricked and stabbed all my body.

"I accept your vow," Hargoutai answered. "Tonight, when we leave this unspeakable place, you'll bind it with your flesh. Leave the Frankish dog where he lies. If he bleeds to death, it's no longer our concern."

"You must tend him before we go!" Cho Soo cried.

"No, I must not. That was not part of the bargain. Not another mark shall be made on him, nor shall he be touched in any way. Go quickly to your women. Gather your belongings. The fury is gone out of the buran and I want to take the road for Karakorum for more reasons than one."

"Lord, I beg you, implore you! Sear his finger with fire so he doesn't—"

"*No!*"

I thought I heard her weeping then. Her voice came to me faintly. "Then let me touch him once before I go away."

"*No, you may not!* One word of endearment from your lips breaks the vow. Touch him and I'll kill you both."

"He'll bleed to death if we don't—"

"Go!"

I heard soft footsteps, fading.

Cho Soo you are gone, and where shall I find you again? Sworn faithful to Hargoutai, how can you keep the vow we made?

Half out of my wits with pain and dizziness, I soon heard the jingle of caravan bells, the clatter of ponies on the road to Karakorum. Sprawled bleeding beside the dung fire, I heard the sounds fade to silence. I wanted to die. The slow death would have been preferable to the slower one waiting for me if I survived the night. All my life—if I had any left—I would perish slowly for the loss of her.

But it seemed I would find release much sooner. The red agony of my mind dimmed suddenly to utter darkness.

Chapter 7

Fate's Wheel Turning

The months following the departure of the treasure caravan were the saddest and bleakest I had ever known. I did not die but often I wished that I had. I considered myself less than a whole man because my left hand bore only four fingers. In place of the fifth, a blackened, slow-healing stump.

For many days after waking in the fireless cold of the empty yurt where I had been tortured, I wandered in a dizzy haze while the poisons worked themselves from my system. It turned out that after my plunge into unconsciousness, Tadda, in perhaps the final fully rational act of which his damaged mind was capable, had thrust and held my blood-gouting hand in the dung fire. This I remembered not at all.

The consequences of Tadda's act were twofold. The stench of my fire-seared flesh must have provided the final push which drove him into a shadow-land where he would dwell for the rest of his days, unable to even speak to me, making instead sad puling sounds while spittle ran from his lips. The other side of the coin was the cauterizing of my wound, which prevented my death. My own strength and vitality did the rest. After a time, the thought struck me that I might be fortunate to have but nine fingers left. Such signs were highly regarded by the Mongols, especially since nine was a mystic number among them, and the infirmity might somehow serve me well, one day.

I thought endlessly of Karakorum. My heart and my life lay there. I wanted desperately to go, not knowing what would befall me on arrival, but convinced that any peril would be more than repaid by nearness to my beloved. One thing prevented me from going—poor Tadda's sorry state.

Alone and almost mindless, he had no one to comfort and tend him. I could not bring myself to turn my back on him, and journeying with him to The Black Sands would have placed him in terrible danger, for he would have become an object of cruel scorn.

Sometimes I puzzled over the condition of Tadda's mind. Most often, he seemed lost in his private madness; yet on occasion, there were brief, eerie moments of lucidity. One such came of an evening, when I had apparently been pensive for quite a while, gazing into the dung fire. I felt him touch my arm and turned to find him staring at me with clear eyes.

"Brother?"

"What is it, Tadda?"

"Do you think of her?"

I started. Here was odd proof that something of my feelings for Cho Soo had registered on him that ghastly night when Hargoutai took the sword to my hand.

I lied to him. "Only a little."

"You—you want to see her."

"She's in Karakorum, Tadda."

He understood perfectly but repeated, "You want to see her."

Another lie: "No, I don't think about that, because I'll never see her again."

"I know why." His face grew sad. "I know. Because of me." He began to whimper, rocking back and forth until I comforted him. By that time, his eyes were lackluster again, and his mouth slack, and I wondered if the brief period of alertness had been imagined.

So I resigned myself to dwelling at the yam station with him, possibly for the remainder of my days. It seemed as good an end as any, I reflected on occasion. What was Karakorum but self-torture anyway? Cho Soo had vowed faith to the tar-khan. She would not break the vow. Nor would I have her do so.

At least there were no repercussions from my supposed crime against the tar-khan. Emissaries of the daroga who came regularly to collect the yam reports did not mention it. I began to suspect Hargoutai had said nothing of the incident to the road governor; Cho Soo's hand again became apparent.

By the time the first emissary journeyed to the station a month after the caravan left, Kojin had been safely buried near his yurt. My report of a hunting accident was accepted without question since I was his adopted son. I was appointed to take charge of duties at the station, and given promise of a Cathayan slave to help. The promise was never fulfilled.

Winter closed upon the high Gobi, attacking with fierce snows and winds. It was a life even lonelier than before. Tadda and I slept beneath many cloaks of leather in the central yurt. I could not guess what peculiar dreams filled my brother's head, but one dream alone occupied my nights, heartbreaking and empty of hope though it was.

Karakorum—The Black Sands—

And my promise that one day I would claim my maid of Cathay for my own . . .

What futility even to entertain such visions in slumber! I was convinced the gods sent them to torment me.

Most agonizing of all were the dreams which showed me taking part in a Mongol wedding, drinking myself sodden with joy at the ikhudur—the festival—then entering the yurts of the Cathayans to pursue my bride, engaging according to ritual in a sham fight with her handmaidens until at last I overcame them and carried my wife to my horse and rode off with her toward Frankistan, exactly as the Khan had carried off his empress Bourtai Fidjen from the tents of the Bourchikoun, the Gray-Eyed People. The Khan had been only seventeen years, and still called Temujin.

The gods, I think, sent me those wedding dreams, too—reminders of my foolishness in defying them. It seemed there would be no end to my punishment.

The cold time passed away. Great flocks of migratory birds began to wing north again toward the white tundras in the land of the Tungusi. The pale ghost-lights which shone in the black sky throughout the winter evenings slowly waned. The gray face of the barren land reappeared, and the dust storms began once more. Caravans and couriers arrived more frequently. I performed my duties but did not try to mingle with the travelers, who treated my yellow locks and my nine fingers with many an odd glance.

In the spring of the year 1218, a band of gray-robed Nestorian priests came by. I prevailed upon them to conduct a ceremony at the grave of old Kojin. This they did, using mysterious words I did not understand. I had buried my old father without religious ceremony, fearing reprisal from the daroga's official should they examine his corpse and question me. The Nestrian ritual put my conscience to rest on that score.

The days stretched on and on. Cho Soo ... Karakorum ... Hargoutai. Tormented dreams. Hopelessness. Only the pitiful sobbing of a mad child in a man's body gave company.

What happened to Tadda in the early summer should have been foreseen, I suppose, and would have been, except for the fact that I was too bemused by self-pity. I had noticed that when we went among the skittish pony herds to tend them, Tadda had to be guided with care. But I gave it no special thought, merely looked after him as best I could. Often Tadda stumbled and fell among the ponies, dropping to his knees and not having sense to rise while their playful but dangerous hoofs cut the air about him. On a particularly clear, fresh summer morning when the vast Gobi plateau could be seen stretching for miles on every hand, we went among the herd with barley, I from one direction, Tadda from the other. Much stamping and whinnying came from Tadda's side.

"Have a care, brother," I called out, emptying my barley sack. "That stallion has been in bad temper these last few days."

Tadda seemed not to hear. His eyes dull, he stumbled into the very horse I had warned him about. The stallion reared, whinnying wildly.

"Tadda, be careful!" I shouted—too late. He disappeared among the mares around the stamping stallion. A cry of pain carried across the herd.

I ran with all my strength, doubling a woven lariat in my hand and using it to lash the mare's back. The stallion swung his fine head at me, lowered it, then reared again. His hoofs came slashing at my head.

I whipped him once, then a second time, as hard as I could. His hoofs missed me. One more lash of his flank and he trotted off behind his fillies.

"Tadda, where are—?" The words caught in my throat. I saw him sprawled on the ground, where the stallion had hammered down. Bone showed through his broken temple. So much blood had spread across his face, it glistened like a scarlet mask. Vomit climbed in my throat.

I knelt and gathered him in my arms. "Tadda—brother—it's my accursed carelessness that's brought this to pass."

He started, trembling in my arms. His great, mooning eyes opened wide for an instant. In their depths I saw perfect sanity. His lips worked, frothed with red bubbles.

I put my ear close. One of his huge hands worked spasmodically on my arm, telling me as best it could that he had loved me through all our years of being brothers. Then he whispered, "Now—now you can go."

Abruptly, the flow of warm breath against my cheek ceased. I lowered Tadda's head in the crook of my arm. I felt a black guilt on my soul. Tadda had been seeking a means to die and set me free. Angering the stallion had been no accident.

For one inhuman moment, I gloated. I *was* free. Then, cursing my own weakness and folly, I bent my head in sorrow and shame, and wept.

The stallion trotted close, nickered, and dropped his head toward Tadda's body, as if curious about why Tadda lay so still. An hour later, I buried my brother alongside our father's grave. The wheel of destiny was revolving once again, like the prayer wheels of the Yellow Hats and Black Hats who traveled along the road. I must only wait for my chance; somehow, after Tadda freed me of the burden of tending him, I knew it would not be long in coming.

As spring waned and summer ripened, bringing again its sudden thunders and rains, courier activity in both directions on the road to Cathay increased. Hardly a day passed without the arrival of a special messenger crying for a new pony and a bit of food so that he might thunder off again, his gerfalcon tablet, the symbol of authority, and his wide belt decorated with many small bells, his herald to the next station.

I became more communicative with these couriers, as well as with other pilgrims who stopped. I sought to learn as much as I could about what was happening in Karakorum, and in the lands to the east and west.

In the west, so the travelers said, the Turkomans of the Empire of Kara Khitai, under the banner of Gutchluk, prince of the Naimans, had slain the Khan of Black Cathay and also the Christian Khan of Almalyk, who was a subject of the mighty Genghis.

Angered, the Kha Khan had sent one of his most trusted warriors, Chepe Noyon the Arrow

65

Prince, with two tumans of the army—a horde of twenty thousand—to slay the upstart. This had been accomplished high in the mountains called The Roof of the World. Gutchluk's head, together with a thousand white-nosed horses, had been sent back to Karakorum as tribute to the victorious ruler.

But the Khan was generous following the suppression of the rebellion.

Turkomans by the hundreds rallied to the Khan's standard. From the mighty peaks of the Tian-shan to the seashores of Cathay, there was no lord but Genghis Kha Khan!

But even greater ambition stirred in Karakorum, the travelers reported. The Khan was intrigued by thoughts of still richer lands to be conquered, westward beyond the mountains. Exciting times, and I was seldom free of the feeling that the gods intended for me to be part of them, either as boon or further punishment.

During a midsummer rainstorm I was summoned from the yurt by a clangor of bells. From horseback fell an exhausted courier. His leather jacket, ripped in many places, was blood-stained. Hardly able to stand, he presented his falcon tablet and begged for food.

"I cannot delay too long," he gasped. "Give me your arm and let me rest a little while by your fire." His greased face knotted in pain as I aided his faltering steps.

"How were you hurt?" I asked him.

An expression of disgust convulsed his features. "The gods curse me, but it was the result of my own stupidity. I hadn't eaten much for three days. I spotted a likely-looking bear and stopped to try to get myself a meal. He was small, but fiercer than I'd expected. I stumbled when I was closing with him and he opened my guts. I barely made it back to my horse." His fingers plucked at a leather pouch affixed to his belt. "No more talk. Another pony."

"Of course. But you should rest."

"No. I bear vital dispatches for the Khan at Karakorum, written in person by General Muhuli, the governor of Cathay. I'll be flayed if I fail to make swift delivery. I must mount again the moment I have eaten and—" He stopped, gripping his belly, unable to continue.

"You'd better let me have a look at your wounds."

He yielded. The bear had struck in several places. No single wound was deep, but from all of them together, he had lost much blood riding five leagues from the scene of the attack. It was evident he could ride no farther without endangering his life.

My hands trembled as I dressed the wounds with ointments and bits of sheep wool. Already I knew the outcome of the next few minutes, exactly as if the capricious gods had permitted me a glimpse of the wheel's next turn.

When the courier had gnawed a bit of meat and the dressings were secure, he tried to stand up. Though the courage was in him, the strength was not.

"Clearly you can't go all the way to The Black Sands," I told him. "I have an alternate plan."

A grimace. "What is it?"

"Since you say the dispatches are important, let me take your place and deliver them. I won't stop until they reach the proper hands. I'm a good rider. I was taught by my dead father Kojin, who was a renowned horseman in his younger days."

The courier grew suspicious. "You are not a Mongol. Not with those yellow locks—"

"But I *am* a loyal subject of the Kha Khan. Look, there is no reason not to accept my offer. You can rest here. There's plenty of meat, and dung for the fire. In a few days, when you're feeling better and riding won't be dangerous, you can travel onward a few leagues and locate the road governor. He'll send men to care for the station. You can then follow me to Karakorum and satisfy yourself that I delivered the dispatches."

For a moment the man deliberated. Then he shook his head. "No, I wouldn't dare entrust—" Prevented from saying more by another spasm of pain, he doubled over on the bench, biting his lip. A moment later he gasped out, "Gods yes, take the pouch. I'll surely die if I go on." He raised his head. "But mark me, yellow-hair. Truly I will follow you to Karakorum soon. If you have sullied my name by riding too slowly, you'll be punished. If you do not reach The Black Sands, my search for you will be relentless, and one day I'll find you and kill you. The task of courier to the mighty Khan is not one to be taken lightly."

"Trust me to honor everything you say," I answered, my pulse hammering now. "It's settled, then, isn't it?"

"What choice do I have?" he retorted bitterly. "Yes, it's settled. Now help me stand up so you can bind yourself and prepare."

Chapter 8

A Passage with Bells

I had little time to speculate over my sudden uprooting from the tiny huddle of yurts which had been my home as long as I could remember. In accepted fashion, I wound my belly, chest, and head with bands of cloth, pulled so tight they threatened to cut off my breathing. But in no other way could a rider endure a long, grueling journey.

Over my sheepskins and beneath my leather cloak, I put on the courier's wide belt of bells with its attached pouch. I saddled a fresh pony and placed a generous supply of dried mutton beneath the saddle, where it would be kept soft, warm, and edible.

Taking the gerfalcon tablet from the courier, who was now relaxed by the fire with a sack of wine, I mounted in the pelting rain, spoke to the pony, and galloped off, fully conscious of the terrible struggle that lay ahead.

One hundred leagues to ride. The distance would normally have been covered by two or even three couriers, yet I must go the whole way or lose my chance to enter the gates of the city of which I'd dreamed.

League after league thundered away beneath the flying hoofs of my mounts. Lofty plateaus rose ahead and fell behind; rivers disappeared at my back; rainstorms became dust storms; dust storms became heat, night became day and night again.

The belt of bells worked its singular magic at each yam station, sending attendants running to the quarters of the four winds to provide me with fresh meat, a jolt of wine, a newly saddled pony to replace the one that had likely as not fallen dead or insensible. Pilgrims and travelers heard the jingling of my girdle and fled the sides of the road while I passed. Nothing must delay the Khan's courier!

The hours blended one into another, bringing me few sensations but the bite of the wind or the cut of dust against my greased cheeks. My bones ached and my flesh hurt from the cut of my wrapping-cloths, which kept me erect in the saddle when otherwise I would have fallen from sheer exhaustion.

I passed a dozen ordus—clan villages—where mongrel pups yapped at my pony's heels and awed old men pointed me out to tiny children. Once a family traveling on the road in their kibitka—a rolling cart on which the family yurt is raised and drawn by oxen—made such haste to get out of my path that the kibitka overturned. The children tumbled off the platform and the oxen bolted. I didn't slow down. Though I was sorry I had reduced the family's traveling house to shambles, I was unwilling to stop even for a moment to tell them so. To my surprise, the elders picked themselves up from the roadside and waved to me in a friendly way. Once more I received proof that nowhere in the entire universe did there exist a ruler as feared and loved as the one who ruled at Karakorum.

Drawing within ten leagues of the fabled city and nearly out of my wits with exhaustion, I nevertheless experienced a renewed feeling of wonder. I was actually approaching the throne-city of the almost legendary personage whose name old Kojin had whispered with respect since the days of my earliest remembering. Bits and fragments of all I had learned about the mighty emperor danced in my brain as my pony flew up a treeless, wind-whipped plain on the approach to the wasteland capital of the Mongol empire.

What manner of person was the Khan? The people of the Gobi said he was a bogodo, a true sending of the gods. Some of the Nestorians whispered that he was the regent of Antichrist himself. In hours I might know the answer for myself. I might stand before him!

As if sensing my fear-tinged expectation, my valiant mount seemed to give another burst of strength, carrying us up the long sandy plain. What manner of man? sang my intoxicated mind. What manner of man—or god?

I reckoned the Kha Khan to be in his fifty-fifth or fifty-sixth year, born as was believed in the Year of the Swine in the Calendar of the Twelve Beasts, which equated roughly with the Christian year 1162. His father, Yesukai the Valiant, Khan of the Great Yakka Mongols, had ruled forty thousand tents. Yesukai had been a daring warrior, he had stolen the Khan's mother, Houlun, from the tent of her betrothed on her wedding day. Their offspring Temujin, named, it was said, for an enemy Yesukai defeated in battle, was destined for great things, since his great-grandfather Kabul Khan had once pulled the beard of the Emperor of Cathay, and had bravely drunk a cup of poison rather than be slain by the minions of a foreign potentate.

The Khan's father had been poisoned by enemies when Temujin was only thirteen summers. The boy assumed khanship, sitting on the white skin of a horse beneath the standard of the nine snowy tails of the yak, symbol of his father's clan. But youth had been no measure of Temujin's bravery, people claimed. Though many followers fled from his standard, Yesukai's son successfully defended clan pasturelands between the fertile valleys of Kerulon and Onon against the onslaught of the fierce Taidjut tribe. Neither did youth prevent Temujin from demanding his Khan's tithe of an ox, a horse, a sheep, and a camel from every subject, nor from taking to wife Bourtai of the Gray Eyes, to whom he had been betrothed when the girl was only nine.

With enemies all around—the Merkit barbarians from the frozen tundras of the north, the Buyar Lake Tatars, and the Taidjuts on the east—Temujin's tiny army still turned back thirty thousand of the fierce attackers. He then began to forge about him that corps of great generals, The Kiyat, The Raging Torrents. Their names had thrilled me since birth, and now they rang and echoed in my head as, distantly, the magical outlines of The Black Sands began to rise across the barrens.

The generals were Kassar the Swordbearer, Arghum the Lute Player, Bayan, the Great

Muhuli, Borchu the Bow-Bearer, Soo the Giant Crossbowman, Subotai Bahadur the Valiant, son to the Uriankhi or Reindeer People, Chepe Noyon the Arrow Prince—fabled, godlike men!

Vast stables and granaries bulging with rice, millet, and hay grew visible on the plain, together with black yurt domes, mud and thatch buildings, stone mosques, Buddhist temples, and occasional wooden church buildings belonging to the Nestorians. Karakorum was originally the city of old Toghrul Khan, Lord of Kings of the Karaits, with whom Genghis had allied himself and his hundred thousand tents when he was but thirty years old. Together, Temujin and Wang Khan, as Temujin named Toghrul, had battled enemies in the west—Gurkha and Chamuka the Cunning—in that wondrous battle of which traveling minstrels still sang.

Old Wang Khan was dead now, and his city was in the hands of the Khan. Millions of souls rallied to the yak-tail standard—western Turkomans, Maimans, Ugurs, and Tatars. One man ruled alone as emperor of High Asia.

Could there be any leader greater than this wild warrior of the Gobi who had gone on to conquer Cathay and become the mightiest emperor ever known? If so, I could not pronounce his name.

My exhausted pony bore me into Karakorum itself. The city was a disorderly place, with no apparent plan; buildings and tents and hovels seemed to have been put up wherever whim dictated. The population consisted of persons of virtually every tribe and color save white. I wondered where, among the tents of wives, maidens of Cathay, ladies of Liao, daughters of royal Turkomans, and virgins of the desert clans, I

73

might find beloved Cho Soo. The confusion I saw gave no answer. Across a vast panorama of grazing herds, buildings, yurts, and kibitkas in disorderly rows, I could in no way even begin to identify the tents of Hargoutai.

I had little time for further inspection. A troop of Mongol horsemen clattered out to meet me, drawn by the cries of attention my jingling girdle had roused from the citizenry. I pulled my pony up short, nearly falling from weariness.

Straightening my shoulders, I faced the troop officer. He was a harsh-faced man of small stature. Proudly, he identified himself as attached to the household of Chatagai, the Master of Laws and Punishment—the Khan's second son.

"What brings you to The Black Sands in the guise of an imperial courier, yellow-locks?" the officer demanded. His men kept their hands close to their swords until I explained.

The officer examined my dispatches, then returned them. What he had read obviously displeased him. "These are to be given personally into the hands of the Kha Khan. If you will ride ahead with us to where those two fires are burning, and pass between them to purify yourself of devils, I'll direct you to the royal pavilion." A smile of disdain touched his mouth. "That is, unless being of fair skin means you're too worn out to continue? If so, the dispatches will have to be delayed until you regain your strength." His contempt said he suspected I *was* as weak as he'd hinted.

"No. No!" I said, urging my pony forward. "I've ridden only a hundred leagues. One swallow of wine will refresh me—*after* I deliver the dispatches."

Clattering off, I left the officer to follow,

74

pleased by the murmurs of surprise and respect among those who had heard how far I'd come.

As required, I galloped my pony between the close-set pillars of fire, my cheeks seared by the heat. Having mastered this test without harm, I was led through the maze of close passages which served Karakorum in place of orderly streets. On every hand spread sights and wonders to delight and astonish me. I saw vast caravanserais teeming with camels, wild asses, and other beasts of burden. I heard the fierce din raised by haggling peddlers who looked as though they'd come from all points of the Khan's world. The officer treated me with somewhat greater deference now, pointing out the crowded priests' quarter and the district where structures of every description housed emissaries from a host of tribes which paid tribute to the ruler of all the Asias.

Veiled Turkoman maidens, silk-gowned Cathayan girls, lithe and hot-eyed Naiman strumpets, and countless others roamed between the tangle of yurts and buildings. Many of the women were incredibly lovely. But none could match the beauty of the single girl whose face I sought in the crowds and knew I would not find.

Still, this was indeed Karakorum; I had succeeded in carving out a certain piece of my dream. Already a rough notion of my next step was forming. If I could keep up my courage, that too might be turned into a reality.

The troops belonging to the Master of Laws and Punishment were not concerned about driving ordinary citizens out of their path. Thus a speedy passage was accomplished to the great white pavilion of felt and silk which I had seen gleaming from a distance.

My pulse stirred again. Could I stand straight

in the presence of the person who waited inside that pavilion? If the gods were on my side for a little while, I could.

Dismounting, I walked as erectly as possible toward a small silver table set out by one entrance to the pavilion. I noted another, more ornate entrance, hung with banners and facing south. I later learned it was for the private use of the Khan. No one else could enter there.

The officer turned me over to the captain of the Khan's guard who said sternly, "You will follow these instructions when presenting yourself to the Khan. First, enter and kneel. Do not move or speak until given permission by the emperor."

He searched me swiftly and expertly for hidden weapons, then added, "Also, walk with extreme care. Do not touch your stinking flesh to a single inch of the wall and hangings of the sacred pavilion." He pointed. "Now go in."

I took a step forward, then another. My heart trembled. Though my bones hurt fiercely from the long ride, I went another step and still one more, as though I were climbing toward the seats of the gods on the heights of glory.

One last cloth-of-gold hanging remained. I stepped around it without so much as making it stir and came abruptly into the presence of him whose name must be written in gilt or not written at all.

The Very Mighty King; the Supreme Earth Man; the Finest Steel; the Commander Against Rebels; the Mighty Manslayer; the Perfect Warrior; the Lord Bogodo; the Greatest of Rulers; the Anger of God; the Wrath and Flail of Heaven; the Master of Thrones and Crowns; the Emperor of All Men—Genghis, Kha Khan.

Chapter 9

The Court of the Khan

With a firm step that belied my nervousness, I advanced across the long and lavishly decorated pavilion.

I circled a great blaze of dung and thorn roaring up at the center and prostrated myself before the imperial dais, where the Khan was seated on a wooden bench. I remained in this position for almost a minute, hearing a buzz of voices; my appearance caused comment among the assembled noyons. At last, a pleasant masculine voice said, "The courier may rise."

When I had gained my feet, the Khan extended his hand. "The dispatches from General Muhuli."

I unfastened my pouch and passed the messages to the richly garbed young Mongol noyon who served as the Khan's cupbearer. This person in turn handed them to the Khan who, before he opened them, indicated a table laden with food and wine jars to the right of his dais. "You may refresh yourself while I study the dispatches. When you're finished, present yourself to me again." A quizzical light filled his eyes. "Your peculiar coloring interests me."

He opened the dispatches and proceeded to study them. Then he summoned an Ugur scribe equipped with a roll of hide and an inked brush. The scribe sat at his feet while I retired to the table, helping myself to several chunks of venison which I washed down with sweet white wine. Using these maneuvers as a screen, I studied the wonders of the court.

To the Khan's left, but below the dais, an extremely handsome Mongol woman in robes of white fur sat on a carved bench. From her finely cut features and pale eyes the color of the Gobi barrens, I assumed her to be the Empress Bourtai Fidjen. Though the Khan had many wives and scores of concubines, she and her four sons remained his favorites.

While I was watching her, an angular Cathayan in an embroidered robe was summoned to confer with the Khan at the dais. The man's beard hung nearly to his knees. He would be none other than the Khan's learned advisor, Ye Liu Chutsai. I marked him well. If he proved approachable, he might serve as a means of learning news of Cho Soo.

Around the walls of the pavilion, numerous officers, marshals, and tar-khans of the Mongol army sat on plain benches. Most wore the camp dress of the military: long padded coats and caps of white felt. They ate, drank, and conversed in low tones. A few subjected me to close scrutiny. I ignored them as best I could, concentrating instead on the array of weapons and objects decorating the pavilion's walls. These included a costly silver cradle hung with cloth of gold and a human skull mounted in silver, reputed to be the head-case of old Wang Khan himself.

By now the Khan had finished with the dispatches. Ye Liu Chutsai and the Ugur scribe withdrew from the dais, heads together, discussing the orders their master had dictated. The Khan signaled. I approached, gaining my first close look at him, though I took care not to make my gaze excessively bold.

His frame was spare, his shoulders bony. His face was broad, his skin more tan than yellow, much ridged and creased, like old leather. Even seated, he gave the appearance of being quite tall.

Oddly for a Mongol, his wide-set eyes beneath his sloping forehead had no slant to them. Their greenish irises and large black pupils combined to give him a penetrating stare. Brownish-red hair hung down his neck in braids. Its color matched his mustache.

He was clothed simply, in a sable coat with long sleeves. The waist was bound with a girdle of golden plates. In his right hand he held a small ivory baton resembling a miniature mace of war.

"What is your name, messenger?" he inquired in a not unkindly tone.

"My father called me James the Frank, Lord."

"You are not a Mongol."

"That is true. My real father supposedly reached this land after a long journey from the shores of Frankistan."

"You don't speak in the rude fashion of the desert," he observed. "But how does it happen that you arrive at my pavilion in the garb of a courier, bearing dispatches of the utmost importance, when there isn't a man of your coloring in my entire corps of yam riders? Please illuminate that point." His question was not without mockery.

In polite tones, I first told him something of my background and my life with old Kojin—though I made no mention of how Kojin had died. Then I related the fate of the courier wounded by the bear, altering the story in just one detail: I told the Khan that the courier was attacked on his horse rather than on foot while neglecting his duty.

"He swore he would be but a few days behind me, Lord," I finished. "He will prove the truth of my words."

"The dispatches are the initial proof, James the Frank."

"But I want him to assure you I didn't steal them or appropriate them for personal gain."

The Khan smiled. "I hardly think you would be planting those suggestions if any one of them were true. You don't have the look of a witless man."

"Thank you, Lord. However, I only wished to make clear I promised to deliver them, and I did." I wanted the thought firmly in his mind when I asked my boon.

It seemed he might be willing to grant it, because he continued to look pleased. "Your loyalty and devotion are commendable. Breaking a promise has always been more hideous in my eyes than any other crime. Further, it's always been my contention that an oath sworn by a man is more binding——and more important—than the most exalted prophecy handed down from the gods. What shall be thought of a man making a promise at dawn and breaking it at nightfall?"

For an answer, the Khan shook his head and

looked dour. I sensed he was enjoying his own performance.

To make sure I fully understood his meaning, he put it into a word: "Unpardonable." He smiled again. "Your devotion has gained you a favor in my sight."

"Lord, I am exceedingly grateful."

"Illuminate another point for me, if you will."

"Most certainly."

"You are well built and of good height. How is it that you have not been called to service in the horde?"

I could barely keep the elation from my voice; he was asking a question I wanted to answer, because it could lead to the crucial request I must make of him.

"Lord," I said, "I was very young when the daroga of our province last recruited toward the end of the Cathayan campaign." My throat had a raspy feel as I rushed on. "But I do admit my desire to ride a hundred leagues to The Black Sands was heightened by one selfish wish."

The Khan frowned. "What is it?"

"To serve you in your army."

The Khan's face was unreadable. I was afraid I had been overly bold. But it was too late to turn back. "I hardly dared imagine I would be brought before you in person. But since that's been my good fortune, I'll seize the opportunity and request service with the imperial troops, doing whatever task your officers may find suitable, even the most lowly."

Though the little speech was spontaneous, I thought it a good one, or at least fitting. But that conviction was instantly undercut by a burst of raucous laughter from a bench to the left of the empress.

81

Her face drew into a frown. The man who laughed was a handsome, tawny-skinned Mongol of perhaps thirty-five years. He was robed as a marshal and carried the orkhon's mace of office. He leaped to his feet, still convulsed with mirth. He had an arrogant look about him, and an arrogant manner, too; it made the Khan scowl.

It also drew a smirk from the man's companion on the bench. Younger still, this second Mongol bore a faint resemblance to the one who was mocking my statement. And his expression I liked least of all those I saw. It was petulant; crafty.

At the moment, however, the man standing up was the one I needed to worry about. He confronted the Khan, still amused. "This yellow-locks in *our* army?"

"And why not?" the Khan snapped.

"Just look at him! Now it's true we have men of every bastard blood and hue marching in the horde. But this—this pale-eyed flower would be a joke! The winds of the Tian-shan would turn his blood to water. The snow crystals would pierce his tender hide like darts. On a campaign, I doubt he'd last an hour. Before the gods, father, I think you haven't found a warrior, you've found a clown to keep all the tumans amused!"

"Be silent, Juchi," the Khan ordered in a low voice. "Your disrespectful tongue will one day be your undoing."

So the jester was the Khan's eldest son, Juchi the Guest, Master of Hunting. I wondered at the identity of his bench companion. My curiosity was quickly satisfied when the Khan continued.

"Would that you possessed the restraint of Tuli beside you. Had any person other than one of my own sons spoken as you did, he would have been

82

strangled with ten silken bowstrings and left for the jackals."

Juchi flushed and spun away, a rebellious flame still lighting his eyes. For his part, Tuli, the Master of War, youngest of the Khan's four sons, was content to sit and smile like a fox, delighted by his father's compliment. I liked this Tuli less and less. Juchi, at least, had a certain raw courage, even though it was clear he had no stomach for me.

Suddenly the Khan's voice diverted my attention. "Pay no attention to the crude prating of my eldest, James the Frank. Or may it be my pleasure to call you Nine-Fingers? I see the hand at your left side has one finger missing. Did the gods give you that mystic number of fingers at birth?"

"No, Lord. It—it is a result of an accident." Abruptly I grew conscious of a bleak stare being directed at me by young Tuli. A chill of horror seized me. Did he have secret knowledge of the way in which I had acquired one less finger than ten? If so, he made no mention. But he kept staring.

The emperor continued, "I welcome your ambition to serve in the horde, James Nine-Fingers. There is no more honorable calling. The men who have shared good and bad fortune with me—whose loyalty is as pure as the clearest rock crystal—the men of my armies are, among all men, the ones I treasure most. Over everything that breathes in the earth or above it, I wish them to be raised to power. Often before a battle, standing alone on the top of a hill with my girdles over my shoulders, I have prayed to the four winds and the limitless heavens to send spirits of the upper air to befriend me. But on earth, I pray for strong men to fight beneath my banner. A merchant trusts in his goods for profit. I put my hope of victory in the bravery of my warriors. Therefore, if you honestly wish to serve my cause, you won't lack for a chance. You will be welcomed into the horde. Made a part of it—to serve and glorify your Khan."

"Thank you, Lord," I began, but I had no chance to express my joy.

Juchi reeled from his bench, brandishing a wine vessel. "Serving and glorifying you? My father, the only way this one can serve and glorify you is by sweeping up the dung flakes dropped by the kibitka bulls! It's shameful for an emperor to concern himself with the fortunes of one foreigner!"

"There would be no Gobi but for solitary grains of sand," the Khan replied in a tight voice. "Close your mouth or leave the pavilion."

"In my own good time," Juchi replied, swigging at the wine vessel.

The Khan's knuckles grew pale as he gripped the ivory baton. Rising to his feet, he pointed the baton at his son's head. *"Remove yourself, Juchi the Guest—before I summon men to crack your spine!"*

With a defiant glare, Juchi flung the wine vessel down. It shattered. He kicked the shards aside, then stalked away beyond the blazing thorn fire. Tuli continued to smile, jealous merriment lighting his eyes.

The Khan resumed his seat. He gazed past me in the direction his son had taken. Suddenly I sensed that he must love Juchi greatly; his face was severe, but his eyes were wounded.

Quickly he regained his composure and addressed me again. "James Nine-Fingers, I would like to hear any information you possess about the countries to the west. I mean the countries lying between the Gobi and Frankistan."

Pride lifted his shoulders, turning the sorrowing father of a moment earlier into a warrior again. "Of late I have grown restive in Karakorum. This place with its holy men and temples breeds a mildness of character I dislike. Only the fierce and warlike dominate the race of man. And while savants have often warned me that different nations, like different minds, cannot live in the same body, I find the argument specious as regards nations living within one empire. Witness the example of Cathay. It is my intention to extend my authority over my neighbors to the west. Merchants have brought me word of fertile valleys where snow does not fall and rivers do not freeze. The area is called Ta-tsin, the Far Country. My rash son, Juchi, has reported that two passes lead down to it from the mountain barrier. The land is ruled by one Alaeddin, sometimes called Muhammad Shah, a Turkoman. The country's true name is the Empire of Kharesmia. Did your Frankish father ever speak of it?"

"No, Lord. I was small when he died. But it is certainly possible that he passed through the country on his journey to the Gobi. I regret my lack of knowledge of the subject."

The Khan gestured. "No matter. It is the prize you and all the warriors of my horde may soon take for your own. You see, I dispatched trading emissaries to this same Muhammad Shah, bearing bars of silver, jade and robes of finest camel's hair, together with my invitation to commerce. My emissaries were seized by a rogue known as Inaljuk, governor of Otrar, which is an outlying citadel of Kharesmia. They were slain. Those I

85

sent to protest this action were also slain, and their beards burned."

The face of the Khan had grown stern, almost as though he no longer addressed one man, but all his empire. "I will conquer these men who have shown themselves to be my enemies. There cannot be two suns in heaven—or two Kha Khans upon the earth!"

A feeling of exaltation possessed me when I heard his words. He had spoken of me as part of his horde. My service had been accepted; my petition granted. With this great barrier passed, I felt nothing could stand between me and eventual fulfillment of the vow to Cho Soo.

Though I did not know the exact workings of my destiny, its pattern had clearly taken shape: I would prove myself with the horde when it began the western campaign. Covered with honors, I would return from the campaign a warrior with a reputation approaching that of Hargoutai. I would never be a tar-khan, certainly; I was not Mongol-born. But clearly the way of advancement had been opened to me by the Khan. I would not be barred because of the color of my hair, my flesh or eyes.

Stiff-legged in my pride before the Khan, nearly drunk with the combined fruits of my deeds on horseback and my victory in the pavilion, I should have seen my imaginings for what they were—the witless confidence of a man the gods intend to raise a little, the better to dash him down. But in the pavilion, I lacked the vision to see it.

I lacked it for a few moments, that is. My self-delusion was shattered suddenly as a new arrival strode into the pavilion, moving to a position directly between me and the emperor. A chill seized me.

Over the back of the man's fur collar, I glimpsed a hideous scar.

Chapter 10

The Sentence

"Arise, Hargoutai the Falcon," the Khan said to the prostrate figure. The Khan appeared mildly irritated by the interruption, but I put little faith in help because of it. "Pray speak to me of the pressing matters which bring you pushing and panting into my presence."

My enemy rose and swung half about, so that he could speak to me and to his master with equal facility. I had not laid eyes on him in nearly a year, but his face with its stony cruelty was exactly as I remembered it. I also noted with alarm that young Tuli the Master of War watched Hargoutai in a friendly way, as though the Falcon occupied the position of a favored pupil or attendant.

"Lord Khan," said Hargoutai, with no perceptible trace of malice, "word spreads quickly in The Black Sands. I heard of a most unusual arrival— a pale creature wearing courier's clothes. I hastened to view it for myself, believing that it might be the same creature I encountered last year on my journey from Cathay. And lo, it is so."

Hargoutai's insulting language, referring to me as a sort of sexless thing, made my anger rise. He sensed this and grew amused. He also knew I dared not challenge him physically in front of the Khan.

"You have met the Frankish man before?" the Khan inquired.

"I have, Lord. I gave him those nine fingers in place of his original ten."

Puzzled annoyance darkened the Khan's brow. I was its object. He at once suspected that I had dealt falsely with him. A hush fell over the pavilion. Not one of the assembled officers and marshals made a sound.

The Khan's voice became sweet, all the more frightening for its gentleness. "Come, Nine-Fingers. Didn't you tell me an accident had caused the injury?"

If I showed cowardice, I was doomed.

"I spoke the truth, Lord. The accident was one of judgment. I allowed myself to fall into the hands of the tar-khan, who charged me with committing a crime against his honor."

I gave Hargoutai a stare to show him my words were lies—and that nothing in the universe could make me believe I had done wrong in befriending a slave princess who loathed him.

Hargoutai started to speak, but I kept on hoping to strengthen my position by showing myself unafraid to describe the circumstances of the torture.

"I spoke with affection to a Cathayan maiden brought as a prisoner from Yen-king by the tar-khan. For that heinous deed—speaking!—I was rewarded with this." I flung up my left hand defiantly, scarred nub and all.

"You committed adultery?" the Khan asked me with distaste. "Dallied with a woman pledged to one of the officers of my horde?"

"Lord, I put kisses on her mouth. But I did not claim her virginity."

"That is another lie," Hargoutai the Falcon said. "On the first night away from this clod's yam station, the temptations of the flesh overcame me. I could resist the charms of the princess no longer. I also wanted to learn exactly how he had used her. I took her. And when I did, I found her no longer a virgin."

Hargoutai said it all with an expression of innocence. It became clear that all opinion was in his favor—including the Khan's and that of the sly young Tuli—except that of the Empress Bourtai, who scrutinized me as though she disliked the tar-khan and wished to believe me instead.

Quickly I stepped forward, lifting my chin, risking everything. "Though I be slain for saying so, oh Khan, your officer invents his tale to bring discredit upon my head. Strike me down for my impertinence, but he is not telling the truth. If you need further proof, summon the princess Cho Soo and let her testify."

Hargoutai the Falcon laughed. "You are pitifully lacking in knowledge of Mongol law and custom, clerk. The word of a tar-khan is sacred. Unquestionable."

Raging now, I snarled at him, "With your indulgence, Lord, I call to the attention of the company the fact that I was raised by a wise member of your own race. A man you killed without pity. He taught me a good deal about custom and law.

It is not only the word of the tar-khan which is sacred and unquestionable but the word of *any* man brave enough to stand on his two legs and tell the truth. Under the law, my account is fully as acceptable as yours. Therefore outside proof is the only solution. I demand that the Cathayan girl be brought here to settle the dispute."

Hargoutai's composure dissolved. "You *demand?*

"Exactly." I had him, and he knew it, but he wouldn't give up easily.

Cheeks darkening, he whirled to the Khan. "Lord, the dispute was settled between us when I agreed not to complete the slow torture of Cathay. I stopped when all the joints of his little finger were gone. In return for this mercy, the maid swore enduring loyalty to me. Honoring his demand would in effect cause her to break her pledge. No doubt this clod hopes she'll weaken in his presence—recant—"

"Bring her forward when I am gone from the pavilion, then!"

*"Trick*s!" thundered Hargoutai. "Abominable tricks!"

"I seek only justice, oh Khan. Your justice."

His position weakening moment by moment, Hargoutai glared at me. I glared back, unwilling to surrender though I knew I walked perilously close to death. The Falcon roared at the Khan, "I cast myself upon your mercy, Lord! Must I suffer the jibes and deceits of a herder of sheep? It is not to be borne!"

In an instant, he drew his sword. The curved blade glimmered in the firelight as he shouted, "Permit me to strike him where he stands—removing an abomination from your sight!"

If the worst came, I was ready. I would spring

on him and tear out his throat before the officers in the pavilion could cut me down. The terrible silence was broken suddenly by a clapping of hands.

I spun. Every eye turned to Tuli, who was on his feet and smiling. "Admirably spoken, Falcon! Bravely spoken, too." The crafty-looking youth strode forward to join the group before the dais. He placed his hand over Hargoutai's, gently forcing the sword down. "Your honor has been well defended—if not by blood, then certainly by courage. But I urge you not to bring disgrace on your head by killing the Frank. The revenge is beneath you. *He* is beneath you. As your sworn protector and comrade in arms, I implore you to seek a more satisfactory conclusion to the quarrel."

"Lord Tuli, there can't be any satisfaction until he's dead!" Hargoutai said.

"I agree his manner makes him deserving," Tuli said, taking a full turn about me and giving me arrogant examination. "In fact much of his language reminds me of that of my elder brother."

This oblique thrust was delivered quietly. Its effect, however, was telling. The Khan was instantly reminded of the unpleasant incident before Hargoutai's arrival. This skillful association of my behavior and Juchi's did me no good.

Tuli paced around me, as though I were an animal under inspection. I was ringed by clever enemies indeed, and longed to fasten hands on their throats. Still, unless I played the scene to its end, I would most certainly die.

I waited, tense, until the young son of Genghis Khan completed his second circuit and again addressed himself to Hargoutai. "It would be well for you to know that before your entrance into the pavilion, the Frank man requested the right to bear arms in the horde of our glorious father."

Hargoutai shook his head. "Gods, what insufferable conceit!"

For many moments, the Khan had been silent. Now he raised his head. Every tongue went silent, Hargoutai turned respectfully. But Tuli remained indifferent, watching me, one leg thrust out in an indolent pose, a hand on his leather girdle.

"The tongue of Nine-Fingers is perhaps a shade too bold," the Khan said. "Yet boldness is invaluable in certain circumstances. Without it, I would not be master of the world, nor my generals victorious in battle. I have already given my oath that this man will be welcomed into the ranks. He has the makings of a fighter, regardless of whether I approve or disapprove of his behavior toward Hargoutai's woman. Further, we are now involved in such fine shadings of dispute that it becomes difficult for me to judge whether one man lies and another tells the truth, or whether both lie a little or bend the truth just enough to favor their cause. I'm growing weary of this whole affair. An ambassador from the northern Kirghiz is waiting, so I wish to bring the incident to a speedy close."

He sat up a bit straighter, as if about to make a pronouncement.

"Now this is the law. Although a khan will be forgiven the death penalty nine times, the Frank speaks correctly when he says his word carries the same weight as that of Hargoutai. A man's word, courage, and honor are his only treasures. Also, under the law, I cannot mete out punishment a second time. The alleged adultery was punished when the torture of Cathay was applied, then cancelled by the maiden's promise. I can

93

only caution you, Nine-Fingers, never to cause the princess to break that vow, for it would go hard with her. You would not suffer. The woe would be upon her head."

"I will remember, mighty Khan," I answered, feeling victory very close all at once.

Then he grew stern. I had counted my good fortune too soon. "You have spoken to my tar-khan with extreme disrespect. He holds a position of esteem in my sight and must be treated accordingly, else all disciplines are dust. You deserve a punishment. The fact coupled with my promise to let you bear arms presents a dilemma which I must solve."

The cunning Tuli said, "May I approach your imperial person, oh father?"

"You may."

Tuli the Master of War mounted the dais, reassuring Hargoutai with a comradely clap on the shoulder as he went. I was suddenly mortally afraid, for I thought I detected pity in the way the Empress Bourtai Fidjen looked at me.

Tuli bent to whisper in his father's ear. The Khan threw back his head, slapped his knee, and nodded in delight. Then he beckoned me forward.

"My clever son has proposed the ideal answer to our problem, James Nine-Fingers. You are hereby assigned service with the Mangudai, my most honored corps. You will serve with them during the coming campaign to the west—for as long as you live."

That last had a slight mocking sound, characteristic of the Mongol sense of humor. I did not understand it, though I knew it boded ill.

"May you bring glory to yourself and to the Kha Khan" were the emperor's final words before he waved me off.

"One moment more!" Tuli leaped from the dais to confront me. "From the bewildered look on his face, poor Nine-Fingers doesn't grasp the significance of the honor that has befallen him." In the sweetest of tones he continued, "The Mangudai—The God-belonging—is a picked squadron. They ride first into every battle. Because they are brave, even audacious men, they are glad to forfeit their lives. They heap eternal thanks upon the head of the Kha Khan who has been gracious enough to place them in the front ranks—foredoomed."

Tuli and Hargoutai smiled at one another—and no doubt the gods were amused as well. They had lured me into believing I had won a victory, then showed me the victory was a death sentence. Thus the wheel revolved. Thus pride and defiance and foolish words were punished.

"The envoy of Kirghiz awaits," said Genghis Khan. "Take yourself from my sight, James of Frankistan."

BOOK TWO

BENEATH THE NINE YAK TAILS

Chapter 1

Duel by Firelight

Doomed and damned though we might be, I found the Mangudai a brave and noble brotherhood.

Whereas the main body of the Mongol horde was composed of tumans of ten thousand men each, we of the God-belonging numbered but a thousand, like the Imperial Guards of the Khan. Mostly of Mongol stock, with a number of wild Kipchaks and Tatars thrown in for seasoning, our corps dwelled in yurts of black felt. We owed allegiance to no special lord but were responsible to the supreme commander of the armies whenever the horde took the field.

And that might not be long in coming, if reports could be believed. Already spies were said to be slipping westward toward the mountains of Tian-shan, secretly exploring routes to the fertile empire of Muhammad Shah of Kharesmia, who

99

had dared defy Genghis by burning the beards of his envoys before slaying them.

As for me, the months of late summer and early fall sped by in a round of horse drill and weapons preparation. Soldiers of the Mangudai accepted their fate calmly, even deriving a wild sort of pride from it—and the Khan saw to it that we were equipped in a manner befitting an elite corps: We rode the best ponies in the army, each animal handsomely armored with red and black lacquered leather. Each man carried a stout lance, a light shield, and two ivory bows with a spare bow case from the imperial arsenal.

Gur-khans—lesser officers of the horde—inspected these armaments regularly to be sure we kept them in perfect condition. The gur-khans said we might be using them quite soon; our moment of sacrifice was already being planned.

Rumors flying in Karakorum confirmed it. Couriers galloped to the four winds at all hours. Bearers carried silver tablets to the remotest parts of the Khan's empire, summoning noyons of rival tribes to rally beneath the standard of the nine white yak tails. In this the Khan showed his customary shrewd judgment; the nobles he selected for positions of leadership were the very ones who might grow rebellious once their nominal ruler took the field.

Of Cho Soo I saw nothing and heard little during my first two months in the black yurts.

I had long ago identified the silken pavilions where the concubines of Hargoutai the Falcon dwelled. I spent many a chill autumn night on my pony at the edge of Karakorum, riding beneath the stars and gazing at the distant wink of lamps behind the hangings of those pavilions. I dreamed constantly of her fair face.

I made no attempt to seek her out, however—nor even to ask about her welfare. To have done so might have tempted her to break her vow. Besides, my own destiny seemed clear: I would either die in the first charge of the God-belonging, or—if the hostile gods finally wearied of tormenting me—I would survive and somehow claim Cho Soo honorably. Exactly how I would arrange to set aside the pledge my princess had made to Hargoutai, I still did not know.

Slaying Hargoutai secretly—had I even the barest chance of accomplishing it—would have put an evil stain upon the whole business. So I trusted my luck, my nameless gods, and my own good strength to take care of the future, and concentrated on training myself to be an effective member of the corps to which I had been sentenced.

Because of my Gobi upbringing, I had no trouble mastering the drills and horseback maneuvers. At weapons practice, I made good, and occasionally exceptional, marks. I participated fully in the brotherly festivities of the corps, which included drinking bouts of prodigious length, held, it seemed, every other night, in spite of the Khan's admonition to his people that being drunk more than three times in each moon was less than honorable. We roared and jeered the gods, these destined warriors and I, seated within our black yurts of an evening. During these revels, Cathayan slaves feverishly dressed sheep and horses for the pot and rushed out frequently to pour a draught of wine to the quarters of the four winds. By raging firelight, savage faces twisted with laughter, hands clapped, voices roared. Men danced barefoot to the music of one-string fiddlers and pulled each other's ears in lusty good humor.

Also, a wild band of Kipchak wenches had attached themselves to the troop out of some sort of vague pride, and I did not stay aloof from the women. I took part in dark, drunken couplings which somehow helped still the pain of my longing. Yet even those acts—even the gasps and moans of a lithe Kipchak girl writhing beneath me—left one part of me undefiled. In a cool shrine deep in my thoughts, one gentle, soft-eyed maid of Cathay reigned eternally and alone.

At one of the drunken ikhudurs, an incident occurred which bolstered my courage and cemented me firmly into the brotherhood of the Mangudai. Until this particular night, I had been treated deferentially by the others, yet without special warmth. I felt that my pale skin and yellow hair made the men wary of me. I had wondered what I might do about that but had found no answer until this particular night. When the drunkenness was at its height, a quarrel started between two members of the company.

The first—an innocent—was a gigantic Mongol with shoulders wide as a wooden kang. His name was Bela. Not especially quick in any pursuit except the use of arms, he was nevertheless well-loved among the host and possessed massive strength as well as massive appetites. On occasion he had gone out of his way to be helpful to me, showing me ways to care for my weapons more effectively, for he was by nature open and generous.

Tonight, however, he had taken one draught too many. His last trip outside the yurt to empty his stomach had not restored clarity to his mind or steadiness to his step. As a result, he stumbled about the gathering and fell several times, to the amusement of a solitary group of half a dozen Tatars openly disliked by most of the corps.

Boldest among this group was a slight, wiry fellow with huge arm muscles and a vile sense of humor. His joking was tolerated chiefly because, despite his small size, he was a wrestler of great accomplishment and power. The last man to insult him had died of a snapped spine.

Tonight he made the bearlike Bela the target of his wit and a fight developed. For all his power, Bela was no match for the sinewy wrestler. The Tatar darted in and out beneath the Mongol's flailing arms, raining blows and kicks on the bigger man's belly and legs. Finally the wrestler dipped his hand into the boiling cook-pot. He clenched his teeth against the pain and came up with a handful of stew which he flung square into Bela's face.

The big Mongol danced about, half-blinded and unable to defend himself. In a twinkling, the wrestler had locked Bela's arm behind his back while several of his fellows ran forward to hammer fists into Bela's gut and groin. The big Mongol yelped in pain.

What had started as a brawl was reduced to torture. I had downed enough wine to have no stomach for it. I scrambled to my feet.

"Keep your hand out of the stew-pot and face a man fairly, Tatar."

The wrestler swung around, and his cohorts released Bela, clutching his middle. The Tatars exchanged smirks. Plainly I was a better target for their combined strength.

The wrestler dipped his head, smiling. "As you will, sheep-boy."

I made a gesture as though pushing back his companions. "The rest of you clear away. Brothers, watch the Tatars closely. This is between the little jackal and me."

The wrestler started, enraged by what I'd called him. I laughed at his anger. "The truth doesn't sit well in your belly, does it? But jackal is the right name. And it's time your pack was broken up. Starting with you." I flung aside my sheepskins, took off my sandals and footstocks, and faced him naked.

Uttering growls to intimidate me, he removed his garments. The others drew back to form a ring. In an instant I began to doubt the wisdom of my challenge. Though I outweighed him, he knew a hundred back-cracking tricks that I did not. And there was murder in his eyes.

A few knives flashed suddenly, drawn to hold the other Tatars at bay. The wrestler didn't care for this. In his need for assistance I sensed an inner cowardice; it might be a weakness I could turn to an advantage.

The mammoth Bela was now crouched on his knees at the edge of the ring. He called to the Tatars: "If any one of you so much as blinks, you'll swallow this." Out came his knife. "Let the little jackal and Nine-Fingers go it alone."

I advanced cautiously to the center of the earthen ring. My opponent did likewise. We circled one another like a pair of the wild tigers chased by the horde on its yearly hunt. The Tatar's flesh gave off a stink of grease and sweat. His black locks hung down over his cheeks. Suddenly his mouth split open to reveal filed, pointed teeth.

He was lightning-quick, delivering hard kicks against my legs. In spite of myself, I doubled over. He grabbed me and down we went, struggling violently.

104

One of his fists found my groin, pounding hard. I let out a sharp cry and he pressed his advantage. In an instant, my left arm was pinned beneath my left side, my right wrist was held by his left hand. He hitched himself across my chest from the side, driving his knee into my throat.

Swinging one leg up, I slammed my knee into his back. That jarred his hands loose. My neck and groin burned, but I had unseated him. He tumbled off and dodged the kick I aimed at his own loins: I had determined to pay him in kind.

From the sidelines came shouts of approval from my fellows. Dizzy, I gained my feet. The Tatar lunged with hands outstretched. Fastening a hold on his wrist, I pulled him across my hip. But as he flew past, his fingers stabbed for my eyes. One thumb nearly blinded me before he fell behind me. I staggered away, hurt and blinking.

The cheering died. Cries of warning were raised instead. My sight was slow in returning as I swung around and made out the wrestler's blurred form darting toward me.

He rained blows against my belly. These I returned with a few of my own. He retreated. I did the same, facing him across the human ring and blinking at a furious rate. My chest ached.

The Tatar wiped his feet in the dirt and came on again with a curious side-skipping stride. He was no longer smiling. His furious little eyes showed me again he meant to kill me rather than lose face with the corps.

I fended off his grappling, lunged, wound my arms around his chest, and locked my hands at the small of his back. I squeezed with all my strength. At once he lowered his head—in defeat, it seemed.

Then his filed teeth sank deep into my shoulder.

Blood began to pour down my chest and back, making it hard for me to grip him firmly. He managed to slip away, then rush in again with his thumbs darting. He seemed to prefer attacking the eyes, first Bela's and now mine. Two jabs of his thumbs and I was nearly sightless again.

The battle-ring became a confused blur of leaping flame, yellow faces, and the darting Tatar who danced around me like a wraith. The wound he'd opened in my shoulder bled heavily, smearing my arms and chest. Great slippery patches of blood covered the Tatar as well.

He mocked me from a yard off, making obscene motions. My anger mounted. I ran at him, flinging my arms wide to catch him in a crushing grip. He danced away, caught one of my legs, and gave a yank. I fell.

My skull smacked the earth, dazing me still further. As I floundered on my hands and knees, the Tatar leaped on my back. He applied his strength in precisely the right way, pinning me with one knee between my shoulder blades. He cupped his hands under my chin and pulled my head back little by little.

Frantic now, I reached over my shoulder to grab him. I could find no hold. I tore at the fingers under my chin and couldn't loosen them. His grip was iron.

He kept bending my head backward, backward. . . .

Shadows moved inside my eyes and the fire and the watchers grew dim. The stench of the Tatar's unwashed body mingled with my own blood-smell. In another instant, I knew, my neck would snap and the tengri would claim me.

Desperate, I freed one hand and pressed the fingers into my own wound until the tips were sticky. Then I smeared the blood on the hands locked under my chin.

I felt his fingers slip just a little. I stabbed my hand into the wound again, the pain nearly beyond bearing. Again I covered his hand with my blood and gave a ferocious wrench to the side. One of the Tatar's hands loosened. That was enough.

Like a bear throwing a marten from its back, I threw him off, bringing my heel down on the crook of his nose as hard as I could. He shrieked.

Strength poured into me like wine. I lifted him by hip and shoulder and smashed his back across my bent knee. He screamed in mortal agony. But his cries ceased the moment his spine broke.

I cast him down, limp and boneless carrion. Then I tottered up, drenched in my own blood.

I tried to speak and promptly fell forward on my face, unconscious.

Chapter 2

The Yellow Wolf

I wakened on a soft wolf skin to find half a dozen of the Mangudai bathing my wounds, rubbing on unguents, and sloshing wine down my throat. The huge Bela was among them.

Words of praise for my victory rang in my ears. I could do no more than respond to the compliments with a dull smile; I ached from top to bottom.

"A lance is stuck in the earth point first in front of the yurt tonight," one of the Mongols rumbled with a vast grin.

I managed to ask why.

"To signify that the Tatar jackal, whom too many have feared too long, has been slain by the yellow wolf of the Mangudai. When we gathered at sundown to drink, we were only companions—and your only name was Nine-Fingers. Now you have a new one.

Bela repeated it in a proud way, "Yellow Wolf." It had a pleasing sound.

I asked for more wine, but before I could drink, I fainted again. Through the night I dozed fitfully in the yurt. I awoke at one point in response to someone touching my shoulder. The fires had almost gone out; only a few orange embers still glowed. Most of the men were snoring in their cloaks. When I rolled over, with aching neck, I saw Bela on his knees beside me. His fire-lit face was strangely embarrassed.

"James?"

"I can hear you."

"There—there is something I must say to you."

"Say it."

"Another man—any lesser man—who dared fight my battles for me would have tasted my wrath once the battle was done. But no man could scorn the championing of such a fighter as you." He placed the palm of his hand on the left breast of his tunic. "With my soul as forfeit to the tengri and the beasts of the thunderstorms if I lie, I declare my life to your life and your way my way until the moment we both perish in battle. I entreat the gods to let me die at your side, sharing in your valor."

I thanked him in a drowsy voice. Indeed, I was glad I lacked the strength to say more; I might have accidently debased his offer of brotherhood, and that would have hurt him; the Mangudai were the proudest of the Khan's soldiers.

We clasped hands and Bela crept away. From that moment I became not only a wholly accepted member of the corps, but Bela's virtual master, and god as well. Though I felt decidedly unsuited for the role, I was pleased by his friendship, for he was good-humored, strong-hearted, and one of the most respected members of the company.

Even more important in my long-range plan was the fact that my victory over the Tatar had established me as one of half a dozen warriors among the Mangudai to be treated with the greatest respect.

The honor I had won by killing the Tatar traveled with me throughout Karakorum in the days that followed. The Kipchak girls turned to watch when I went by. I often heard my new name spoken.

I wondered whether word of my feat had reached the tents of Hargoutai; whether Cho Soo's women had told her of what I had done. But whenever I pondered the question, there was pain. The thought of her led inevitably to steamy imaginings, sordid pictures of her body held by the tar-khan while he worked his will. When such images tormented my mind, I forced my thoughts elsewhere; dwelling too long on what might be happening to her roused a hatred of the Falcon that was all but unbearable.

By late autumn of the Christian year 1218, Karakorum was packed with men rallying to the nine yak tails. They came by the hundreds and thousands; great serpents of horsemen twisting across the barrens. Karaits and Naimans, Kirghiz and Tatars—the hoofs of their ponies made clouds boil up on every quarter of the horizon. The population increased twentyfold. New yurts sprang up for leagues around. War was in the air. Daily, the Mangudai stood to horse and rode screaming down the plain in mock charges that were rehearsal for a future attack in which most, if not all, would perish for the Khan's glory.

Our double squadron of a thousand men rode in

ten ranks, one hundred men to a rank. Bela and I occupied positions next to each other in the center of the front rank. Even when there was no drill, we galloped out together to keep ourselves fit, and liked nothing better than an impromptu race run at such speed that the iron-studded leather neck-drops stood out behind our helmets.

The nights grew longer, sharpening with chill. As we sat about the fire tending our various pieces of equipment—pony nose bags, cook-pots, bowstrings—men talked of the Khan ordering a great hunt before full winter descended.

On one such evening, a Cathayan presented himself at the yurt where I was quartered.

"Nine-Fingers, I bid you follow me to the pavilion of the honored Ye Liu Chutsai."

Astonished, I flung on my finest cloak of red leather and accompanied him.

Sweet incense poured its fumes from brass braziers in the pavilion of the learned Cathayan. The prince of Liao himself was resting on cushions, a wooden counting device at his side. His lean fingers toyed with the beads on the rods as I made obeisance. He motioned me to his side, set the counting toy away, and beckoned to a servant who brought green tea in fragile cups decorated with images of birds, rivers, and pagodas. The pictures made me think of Cho Soo. They hurt me sorely.

"Be so good as to sit beside me," the Cathayan said.

I took a cushion, crossed my legs, and waited. I could not read his purpose in his eyes, nor on his lined face.

"Let us first dispense with the courtesies," he began. "By what name do you like to be called?"

Startled, I answered, "By my own, sir. James."

111

Finally he smiled. "James of Frankistan?"

"Yes."

"But you have others now." He indicated my hand. "James Nine-Fingers. And one more recently acquired. Because of your hair and your bout with the Tatar, I am told the Mangudai refer to you as Yellow Wolf."

"That's true, prince of scholars. But James will suffice."

"Ye Liu Chutsai nodded. "Very well. I owe you an explanation for my summons. It's quite simple. You have lately gained a certain eminence among the Mangudai—and I have no great fondness for the tar-khan Hargoutai."

Wondering at the connection between the two facts, I let him proceed at his own pace.

"Though the Falcon's prowess as a warrior cannot be denied, he is a cruel man. Without pity. Without feeling except the basest kind. Without humanity. In privacy, I may say to you that he exemplifies a certain aspect of the character of the Khan himself—an aspect with which I am constantly at odds. Now here is the point. When your name began to be mentioned with great frequency because of the Tatar, certain other details of your background came to my attention." His eyes pierced and held me. "I mean your dalliance with Hargoutai's concubine, Cho Soo."

Wary, I licked my lips, asking myself whether this was some sort of snare the Falcon himself had arranged, and whether the scholar's easy words were all deceit.

"I learned of your interest in the princess," he continued. "And since she is of my own blood—of my own country—I thought I might do you a service by bringing you word of her welfare."

There was no point in dodging the issue. "Solely as a favor to me, prince? Or to spite the tarkhan?"

"Why, for both reasons, if you must know."

I thought I detected a merry malice in his eyes. Although my heart was hammering at the mention of Cho Soo, I still saw a need for caution. "I thank you for your thoughtfulness. However, I think it would be wiser if I did not hear what you have to say."

My response startled him. "What's that? You don't care for word of her?"

"I do indeed. But if it is ugly news, I might be tempted to take action because of it. I—" A moment's hesitation. Then I decided to trust him. "—I like the Falcon no better than you do. I would just as soon see him dead. But not by any rash act of mine, because she would suffer."

"Due to the vow she made to him?"

I nodded. "You know of that, then."

"I know most everything of consequence in Karakorum. I also suspect you love the princess."

The words came out a whisper: "Yes. So tell me nothing that would paint Hargoutai worse than he appears in my eyes this moment. I cannot always control my temper, and I would not want its limits tested."

"It's a wise man who knows his own limits, James."

"Sometimes I do, prince. Not always. But you understand why it might be better if I heard nothing."

"I do. I believe you will find what I have to say comforting, not provocative."

I leaned forward. "There's another reason for my hesitation."

He sipped tea again. "Speak."

"If Cho Soo has asked you to talk with me—

even if she made the request in a most secret way—then she has made light of her vow to Hargoutai. Therefore I beg you to keep silent. I do not want her compromised."

He chuckled, stroking his long beard which lay coiled in his lap. "For a man who is neither Cathayan nor Mongol, you have a nice sense of the intricacies of Oriental honor."

"I was raised a Mongol, prince. I understand the importance of Cho Soo's vow to the tar-khan. It must *not* be broken—she must not be shamed or found guilty—until the hour when I can set the vow aside myself. Legally. Justly. At that time, I'll claim her for my own."

"You seem certain you will."

"I am," I told him, hiding my own doubt.

"Most ambitious sentiments," he said with another smile. "Doubly ambitious, considering the squadron to which you belong, and war all but a certainty when the next snows melt. Nevertheless, put your mind at ease. Cho Soo made no appeal to me. Nor does she know that I have called you here. She will never know. I have approached you of my own accord because—" He hesitated, then gestured in a graceful way. "—because my life is dedicated to the propagation of certain imperishable virtues. Temperance. Mercy. Wisdom. I urge the Khan to practice them whenever he will turn his ear to me. Your love for a maid of my country represents one pole of life—" He lifted a taloned hand. "—at which my cherished virtues repose. At the other pole lies the cruelty of Hargoutai, and, yes, of the Khan himself at certain times." Both hands hovered above his lap, then dropped. "I am, to put it plainer, an aging pedant fascinated with the perpetuation of love and gentleness in any form."

114

"I accept your news gladly, then," I said, sipping my tea. "May I hear it?"

"Certainly. It is scant but not too disheartening. Cho Soo is treated well. She is numbered among the favorites of Hargoutai, probably because he is only too conscious that you still live. A treasure is always more dear when coveted by a neighbor. Cho Soo performs her duties as concubine with the faith and discipline befitting a princess of our land. But from what I hear of the gossip of her attendants, she makes plain she can feel no love for her master. That may serve as a warning. It could stoke the Falcon's hate of you."

"He could hate me no more than he does already, prince."

"It could provoke him to eventual action, however."

I admitted he was right.

"Lastly," the Cathayan continued, "though Hargoutai has an intense desire for it, no issue has come of the union. Many centuries ago Master K'ung wrote that the gods of chance curse a loveless coupling."

He took a sip of tea and lifted a shoulder beneath his robe of peacock-hued silk. With mirth in his eyes again, he added softly, "Though from the way Mongol soldiers sire bastards by the wild Gobi tribe girls, I am compelled to question the wisdom of Master K'ung."

"I thank the gods no child has been born. When first her womb finally bears fruit, I want it to be from my seed."

"Time may or may not bring that to pass," he responded. "Meantime, guard your thoughts as well as your actions. Pursue a prudent course midway between boldness and reticence, and perhaps your wish will become a reality, even though

115

you ride in the front ranks of the God-belonging. Content yourself with the knowledge that the woman you love is as safe and happy as a woman can be when she is held captive in an alien land and forced to dwell with a man she does not, and cannot, love."

Softly the learned Cathayan clapped his palms together. His servant reappeared.

"Conduct our Frankish guest from the pavilion with all due ceremony," Ye Liu instructed, bringing the encounter to an end.

I thanked him respectfully, adding, "It was kind of you to invite me here."

He smiled, and his old eyes showed he was no man's fool. "As I indicated before, kindness was not my sole motive. I would rather see you prevail than Hargoutai. I would always wish mercy and love to prevail over ruthlessness and rage. If the Khan shared my views at all times, I could die a contented man. Good evening."

Walking slowly back to the yurts of the Mangudai, I studied the dark and limitless heavens where countless stars shone. As I watched, a shooting ball of fire raced through the dome of the sky. I took it as an omen. My vow in the sweet-smelling hay of the yam station preceded that sworn by Cho Soo to Hargoutai. As the Cathayan wise man had told me, it might still come true—though how, I did not know.

In the following week, a great review was held on the barren plain to the west of Karakorum. Nearly ten tumans—one hundred thousand men— marched and rode before the Khan.

At this review it was also announced that the great hunt would begin within a few days. The news was greeted with jubilation roared from a hundred thousand throats. We were then informed that Juchi, the Master of Hunting, had already galloped off to game-filled uplands northwest of Karakorum, there to mark off more than a hundred leagues of low hills through which the hunt would range. Riding back toward Karakorum with Bela after the review, I told him that I would welcome a change of scene and a chance to test my weapons.

"And I also," the big Mongol replied, riding easily and with a natural grace despite his size. "Wine begins to sour on my tongue. The caresses of the Kipchak wenches feel the same night after night." A smile lightened his features. "Will we not slay the tusked boar together, brother, once the signal is given?"

"The boar or the tiger," I grinned, feeling a thrill of anticipation.

Bela shook his head stoutly. "No, it must be the boar. He's the most feared of all the hunted creatures. Woe the man who faces him unarmed."

At that instant a halloo went up along the plain behind us. Horsemen scattered, flying from the path of two soldiers who galloped toward us crying, "A path for the tar-khan! A path for Hargoutai the Falcon!"

I reined to the side, Bela close by, and felt a prickling on the palms of my hands. Splendidly cloaked in marten fur, his lacquered breastplates a glitter in the waning light, Hargoutai the Falcon saw me and reined his pony to a halt. While he surveyed me, I fought to keep my face composed, anxious to show neither my fear nor my hatred.

A random evening wind danced the streamers that hung over the ears of Hargoutai's white felt hat. He made a frightening picture, the streamers fluttering and the ringed scar showing red and hideous above the collar of his robe.

"No doubt you greeted the words of our Khan with approval, Frankish man," he said.

I replied politely, "So did all of us in the Mangudai, Lord."

"Yes, yes, but you especially." He was sporting with me again. "Unless my eyes trick me, your head has grown since I saw you last. Probably from your encounter with that weakling Tatar. I ran across him once myself and spanked him when he annoyed me, did I not?"

Half a dozen sycophants in his retinue agreed loudly that this was true.

"Then I must prove myself to you one more time," I responded in a tone so respectful that he could not possibly be angry. Yet his eyes raged. He knew my contempt and loathing; it was as if we two spoke a language unknown to the hundred thousand still milling on the red-lighted plain.

"I will pray for my chance on the great hunt," I added.

"Hear the boaster!" Hargoutai exclaimed. "Mark him well! Spread his promise from one end of The Black Sands to the other. We'll see what great kill he makes, after all the other officers and marshals have their turns. Perhaps a raven or two will be left." More laughter. "Should he kill nothing at all, having made a promise to do so, his foolish boasts must of necessity cease. What a blessing that will be!" He glared. "Stand away, and let me pass on!"

As Hargoutai and his followers clattered off toward Karakorum, Bela looked glum. "He is right, James. You were rash to boast. The tale will spread, and on the hunt, we have last pickings."

118

"The Falcon has put another test to me!" I said angrily. "One way or another, I'll meet it and turn his own jibes back against him!" But I knew Bela was right; I had little chance. This, as much as my hatred, sent me into a rage. Kicking my pony so hard he whinnied in pain, I galloped ahead, cursing the very dust left by my enemy's passing.

Chapter 3

The Hunt

On a bright morning a few days afterward, the horde, one hundred thousand strong, moved north and west from Karakorum toward the foothills Juchi and his squadron had chosen for the hunt.

Never had I seen such a magnificent spectacle as I saw on the barren plain that day. The forces of the Khan, led by Tuli the Master of War and his retinue, advanced with pony armor and weapons glittering in the Gobi sunlight. The noise of the trampling hoofs made a racket loud enough to wake the gods sleeping in the sky.

Our thousand, the Mangudai, occupied a position well to the front and center of the advancing horde. Thus I had an excellent view of the panorama of armed riders sweeping forward like a relentless river. My pulse stirred, and I knew a similar excitement infected nearly every man in our company. After months of camp life, we were tasting the pleasure of conquering the horizon, rolling it backward, and making our marks on the land as we passed. Surely, I thought, no army, not even that of the fabled ancient, Laksander, had ever possessed such might and magnificence.

Each man was equipped and provisioned exactly as though he were riding to engage the forces of the Shah of Kharesmia rather than the creatures of nature. The Mangudai carried the customary lances and pairs of bows, in addition to special hunting shields of wickerwork. Each man had been issued rations of smoke-cured horse meat and mutton, plus small sacks of dried milk curds which could be heated with liquid over a fire to make a warming beverage.

Ahead of the army lumbered ten thousand horses and oxen. Scores of these were slaughtered every night when the main body of the army caught up with the herd, planted the standards of the various commanding officers, and erected the hundreds of yurts carried on kibitkas immediately behind the animals.

After marching thus for eight days, we finally came upon foothills. Here, at the outer limits of the hunting course, were camped Juchi and his squadron. Streamers of the various tumans had been set in the earth along a thirty-league front to mark each tuman's starting point. Again the Mangudai were fortunate in being near the center. The end point of the hunt had also been marked, many leagues away in the foothills.

All through the night we drank and prepared our weapons. Colored lanterns were raised and lowered beside the standards, sending a signal from tuman to tuman that the hunt would begin on the morrow. Rumor said that the Khan and his Imperial Guards, riding swiftly in the wake of the army, would be on the field by dawn.

This proved true. As the sun rose and the morning drum-call thundered along the thirty-league front, the horde assembled itself in a long line that was deepest at the center. The flanks of the line—lost beyond the horizon to the right and left—curved forward to form a bowl-shaped rampart of soldiers and mounts. The cattle had been pastured behind us, near the yurts which would remain standing until the hunt came to an end.

The cool air nipped our lungs and stung our cheeks. Weapons winked up and down the line. Long gilded horns, cymbals and kettledrums began to sound, a savage music.

From the rear thundered the thousand of the Khan's Imperial Guards. These gigantic soldiers were armed with the axes and swords of heavy cavalry. The horde parted, making a path through which the Guard galloped in a swirl of dust. Genghis himself was in the lead, riding a white stallion.

I marveled again at the sight of the great warrior. Though middle-aged, he rode like a young man on his high, peaked saddle, his legs drawn up into short stirrups. Eagle feathers and red streamers stood out behind his white felt cap. The girdle of beaten gold plates, which he wore over his sable robe, caught the sun and threw off a thousand dazzling reflections. Mounted on a black pony at the Khan's side rode a lad of six or seven years. Bela said the child was Kublai, son of Tuli, the favorite among the Khan's grandchildren.

The Imperial Guards halted. A long horn blew. The Khan raised his arm, held it high a moment, then let it fall. As far as the eye could see, thousands of warriors in ranks ten deep booted their ponies forward. Again the clatter of hoofs shook the earth. Again my heart beat hard. The hunt was on.

We rode with our weapons sheathed; none could be used while the game was being flushed, a process which would take several days.

Bela called to me through the dust: "Do you begin to regret your boast, my brother? There isn't a man among us who doesn't have the same hope as you—to cover himself with glory. Most have hunted with the Khan before."

"I have no regrets," I shouted back, though I was lying. I knew well that odds against fulfillment of my boastful vow were staggering.

Bela laughed, though not unkindly; he recognized my deception. "Come, brother, you can admit the truth to me. Doesn't your gut churn at the prospect of the challenge you've set for yourself? Doesn't your head reel a little? Doesn't doubt nag at you when you speak of it?"

"Yes, that's true," I admitted, marking him more perceptive than I'd thought.

"Then you have a chance!"

"Why do you say that?"

He grinned. "Because only the hunter who tastes failure in his thoughts develops the will to prevent such failure from happening. I know of what I speak, brother. Unlike you, I'm always convinced that covering myself with glory is an accomplished fact."

I did as he counseled. I imagined scenes in which I saw myself without a kill at hunt's end. I saw myself jeered at by the tar-khan. My resolve mounted as the ranks of the horde swept forward.

By dawn of the second day of the advance, we

sighted our first animal, a tawny gray wolf loping away over the foothills. The individual horsemen immediately drew closer together, like links in a human chain. Disgrace would be the lot of any two men who let even one beast slip between them.

This barrier was maintained even during the hours of darkness. Along a thirty-league front, watch fires burned at close intervals. Guards were changed every hour, so that each sentry was fully alert at all times. No one could go through the lines without speaking a password. After several nights of such wariness, our pride was up and our appetites whetted, for not a single beast had escaped. And ahead in the dark beyond our encampments, animal eyes glowed from time to time; wolves howled mournfully; leopards hissed and spat. There was a great rustling in the air those evenings; the sound of trapped beasts on the move. Much game would await us on the killing field which we were scheduled to reach in a few more days.

My anticipation mounted as the final hours crept by with maddening slowness. But at last the circle began to close. On the second to last day, ten thousand beasts raced before us, growling and crying in terror, leaping and running and raising a mighty cloud of dust through which I occasionally caught glimpses of leopards and tigers, wolves, bucks, bear, antelope, wild asses, and countless smaller creatures such as martens, sables, and wild dogs. Others said they had spied the tusked boars, but I did not. Overhead, screeching ravens wheeled through the dust clouds.

At last we reached a long valley, broken by trees and rock formations. On the far slopes fluttered the banners of the gurtai, marking the limit of the hunt.

The horde blackened the skyline and soon encircled the valley. Below, more animal life than I had ever seen or imagined screamed and roared and dashed to and fro; the beasts seemed to know they were caught and as good as dead. On closer inspection, the valley itself proved to be an ideal location for the hunt. The groves of trees and the rocks, which were broken by gullies and pierced by cave-mouths, offered hiding places for the quarry—and thus greater sport.

The horde gathered on the shoulders of the hills in ranks three deep. All at once a mighty shout rose as a single figure on a white horse descended toward the valley floor. Drums rolled and brazen cymbals crashed.

The Khan was armed with only a bow, a quiver of arrows, and a bare sword. In the first hour every eye was trained upon him as he sought out a tusked boar, then a wild wolf, and lastly a raging tiger—and slew them all.

On the crest of the highest hill, his pavilion had been erected. There young Kublai waited. Presently the boy's grandfather returned to the pavilion and disappeared inside, having left his kills below on the valley floor. Moments later, Juchi the Guest rode down the hill while an attendant blew on a long horn. Suddenly Juchi screamed and gestured. Horsemen broke from the ranks. As the princes and tar-khan rode down to the valley, I looked for Hargoutai but did not see him.

The noyons enjoyed only a brief advantage over the common warriors, for the Khan believed in fair treatment of the men who fought and died for him. As soon as the noyons reached the floor of the valley, another double burst of the horn was sounded. Bela shouted, pounded my shoulder, and peeled his lips back in a wild grin.

We went forward. One hundred thousand warriors, blades bared and arrows nocked, at last reached the field they had sought for two long months.

Chapter 4

The Kill

Dust clouds soon billowed in the valley, and the ground began to darken with the blood of the slaughtered game. Within moments of reaching the base of the hill, Bela and I became separated. I let my pony take me where it would—though for almost half an hour, I was discouraged by the poor pickings: two wild dogs, easy to kill, and no prize to be proud of. If they were the sum of my efforts for the day, Hargoutai would laugh long at my pretensions. And with justification.

Soon I was dust-covered and in bad spirits. I had left the dead dogs in a grove. I would go back to claim them if I found nothing better, but I hoped that would not be the case. The pony carried me between high slabs of rock marking the entrance to a crooked gully. There, screened a little from the melee behind me, my luck began to change.

The change was not immediately apparent,

though. The pony clopped through the gully, rounded a sharp bend, and stopped suddenly. Directly ahead, a huge pile of boulders—from a slide—blocked the passage.

Disgusted, I started to rein around and ride out. Then I heard a wild snorting from the far side of the boulders. My belly grew tight as I flung myself out of the saddle and clambered to the top of the slide, armed with my sword and wicker shield.

From below, a gigantic tusked boar glared up at me. He charged at the rock on which I lay, then turned and ran back off up the gully, which opened onto the valley floor at the other end. Since there was no way for me to get my pony past the rock fall, I scrambled down and went after the boar on foot.

Out on the plain, a dozen hunters milled about and a tiger screamed. The boar was running toward them, in plain sight if only they would look. I prayed they would not, for I wanted the tusker for myself.

While my attention was momentarily diverted by the hunters, the boar vanished.

Cursing, I searched both gully walls. Had my quarry been taken from me by magic? I howled in anger, in good Mongol fashion. Then my eyes lit upon a dark place a short way up the gully wall, hidden somewhat by a growth of shrub.

I advanced, filled with a renewed excitement. Brushing aside the branches, I peered into the opening. It turned out to be a cave entrance—the boar's lair.

Crouching in front of the opening, I laid aside my shield, carefully lifted a branch, and studied the dark interior. I heard the boar shuffling. I had trapped him.

I considered my best course. Since I had left my bow and quiver with my pony, I could not fire arrows at him. I would have to kill him with my short sword. This required goading him to a charge, so that I might impale him as he came charging out.

The cave mouth was narrow. I would have time for one good stab; two, if I was extremely lucky. Chances were good that I might miss altogether and be gored by his tusks. Still, I refused to be frightened off. He was truly a kill worth having.

I lowered myself onto my belly, preparing to crawl a short way into the cave, when suddenly I became aware of a dim light at the far end. I had cornered the boar not in a cave but in a sort of natural tunnel through the rock. The lair had two entrances, and I could easily lose my quarry if he chose to flee the other way. He hadn't yet. I could still hear him moving inside.

My hands were cold with my own sweat as I regained my feet, hunched over, and lunged straight into the mouth of the lair.

I found that I could stand nearly erect. I stumbled across something. In horror I picked up a richly carved blade. Had another hunter been here before me? And why didn't the tusker charge? He certainly must have scented me.

Astonished, I heard someone breathing hard at the far end. A bow string twanged. The boar trumpeted in pain.

I sought to see beyond him to the other hunter, but my eyes had not yet grown accustomed to the darkness. I could see little more than a blur of light at the other entrance. Suddenly the boar came charging at me, an arrow-shaft in his flank and dumb fury in his small eyes.

I made ready to meet his charge when he wheeled without warning and went plunging back toward the unseen bowman in the shadows. A voice cried out. The squeals of the great beast grew louder. Its cloven feet crashed on the floor of the lair. I moved forward swiftly, my sword held well ahead. Drawing close to the site of the struggle, I perceived that the beast had his snout down and was worrying the fallen hunter with his tusks. The man twisted one way, then another. I smelled blood; the boar had wounded the bowman and was trying to finish him, prevented only by the sheer bravery of the fallen Mongol. The man lashed out with his small sword, hacking the animal's snout but unable to deliver a killing stroke because he could not stand and defend himself properly.

Running up behind the boar, I rammed my blade into the boar's side, then tore it free. The tusker staggered. He crashed against the cave wall, snapping off the arrow still imbedded in his flesh. Then he swung back toward me, stamping and bellowing. Death was on him, but he was determined to vent his wrath on his latest tormenter.

I retreated a step. My sandal struck a rock slicked with the boar's blood. I yelled, tumbling. My sword clattered out of my hand.

The boar charged. His cloven hoofs trampled my leg. His head dipped. One of his tusks grazed my face and tore a long gash from chin to ear. Blindly, I reached for the hilt of my sword, found it, and brought the blade over and down, driving it halfway through the boar's neck.

Blood poured over me. The maddened animal gouged and stamped. A tusk gored my shoulder. I could see his immense hairy snout, his nostrils daubed with a mixture of my blood and his. He was staggering, but there was strength in him for one more onslaught. His head lowered. His tusks pointed at my throat.

I thrust upward with both hands on the hilt of my sword. I drove clean through the boar's neck, releasing the handle at the last instant and letting the beast tumble against the cave wall, dying.

Finally I stopped panting and clambered to my feet. I wiped my red hands as the boar's flanks heaved one last time. I wrenched my sword out of the boar's neck and tottered forward to see whether the other hunter was dead.

He wasn't; I heard him coughing. Neither of us could speak. I knotted my fingers in a cloak of what felt to be rich fur and dragged the wounded bowman bodily along to the light at the tunnel mouth just ahead. There I lowered him and knelt beside him, turning back a fold of his gory cloak to get a look at his face.

The wounded hunter was Juchi the Guest.

Horrified, I leaped away. I was afraid I had desecrated his person by laying hands on him. He panted and struggled to raise himself on an elbow. Then, while I gaped in confusion, his forehead wrinkled in anger. "Must you stand there like a brained pony? Help me—" His speech was punctuated by a sharp groan. "Help me to sit, can't you?"

I propped him up. He proceeded to tear his clothing aside and examine the wound along his ribs. He stuck a finger into it. His head went back; his eyes closed. For many moments he simply swallowed air, holding his palm tight over the wound.

My own hurts made me dizzy and lightheaded.

I could not speak. Finally Juchi's eyes popped open. He regarded me with a degree of calm I found surprising in one so badly hurt.

Bracing himself against the cave floor, he glanced out to the noisy plain, where the hunt still went forward. Then he shook his head in a bewildered way. A smile leavened by pain twisted his mouth. "So, Nine-Fingers. You're the slayer of the rogue boar, eh? He almost had me."

"I would not knowingly have deprived you of your prize, Lord Juchi."

"No?" he mocked. "Would you have let him deprive me of life and breath instead? I think not. Gods, I didn't dream when I first set eyes on you in my father's pavilion that the gods would ever make you my benefactor. And I called you unfit! Should you spread the tale of this encounter, my fame will be eclipsed."

"My lips will be silent forever, Lord Juchi."

"Don't be a fool. I was joking. Well, joking a little anyway. I envy you the kill, but I wouldn't wish for an instant that you hadn't made it. Accept my gratitude," he added gruffly, as though embarrassed about finding himself in my debt.

I kept silent. He grimaced again, then went on: "Since your quick work has granted me a few more years of life, I owe you a boon. Bend your shoulders forward."

This I did, greatly puzzled. Juchi toyed with the hem of his sable cloak. Much daubed with boar's blood, it still shimmered in the weak sunlight filtering into the mouth of the cave.

"This cloak was given me by my father the Khan when I was first old enough to ride beside him. It's my most valuable possession. Unless I can wash it clean, I suppose it will be marked with that tusker's blood. No matter. He lifted the edge of the sable cape and touched my shoulder with it. "By the sign I give you now, and by the oath I take on this garment which has been blessed by the touch of the Lord Bogodo, Genghis Kha Khan, I name myself your protector from this hour forward. Should the day come when you have need of help greater than that which can be given by your own strong arm, you may call on me and I will intercede. This I vow in the name of our father the Kha Khan, who is the Lash of the Gods and the ruler of all creatures upon the earth."

At once he drew the cloak away. Throughout his speech, I had sensed that his references about loyalty to his father rankled him, though I couldn't mistake the love and affection which underlay the rebelliousness. He coughed in an embarrassed way, hitching himself toward the cave mouth and peering into the dust clouds where ponies galloped and animals bellowed.

"And now you may serve your protector by finding some members of my squadron to come and fetch me away from this scene of disgrace. There'll be no great kills for me today. The red slop pours out of me like wine from a stuck bag. Go—go!" He gestured in an angry way. "Haven't I acknowledged the error of my original thoughts about you? What more do you want? *Move along!*"

"Yes, Lord Juchi," I stammered, too overcome by my good fortune to make proper obeisance. I hurried from the cave, heedless of my own wounds, staggered to the end of the gully and began calling for an officer of the squadron of the Master of Hunting. When at last one turned up and I told him why I sought him, I was treated to a glance of astonishment, then of disgust. A short time later, I stood to one side while Juchi was dragged forth, placed upon a litter, and carried away.

As the group departed, I heard one of the officers say to Juchi, "Shall I have your kill brought to your pavilion, Lord? Truly, the boar's tusks are magnificent and should be preserved as trophies."

"The carcass belongs in the camp of the Mangudai," came Juchi's grumbled words. "The kill belongs to the man of Frankistan. Yonder. Were it not for his skill with a sword, my soul would have departed this earth."

Over their shoulders, the litter-bearers subjected me to further scrutiny. Some were awed, but more were clearly displeased. Too weak to care, I sat down and began stuffing bits of wool into my wounds. Then I retraced my steps through the cave, passed the stinking remains of the boar, and emerged at the point where I had first entered.

Clambering across the boulders in the gully, I mounted my pony, circled the hill, and returned to the other entrance. There I hitched my lariat to the boar's four legs. I dragged him away from the cave mouth and back through the tangle of hunters, searching for Bela or others of my troop.

The swollen sun was lowering over the valley and its pall of dust. The air reeked of slaughter, a hot, strong smell. In the distance a long horn pealed. I recognized the meaning of the signal. As tradition demanded, a grandson of the Khan— such as Kublai—had approached his grandsire and requested that the remaining animals be given back their life. This request was always granted.

The long horn's blast ended the hunt. From every quarter of the valley, ponies thundered up the hillsides, officers and warriors alike dragging slain animals behind them.

As night fell, the carcasses were cleaned and hacked apart. Cook fires blazed up. Men dug their teeth into haunches of bear and buck while seated on bodies of leopards, tigers, and boars. The jubilant Bela, who himself had slain a good-size brown bear with his arrows, dressed my wounds and welcomed me to the fires of the God-belonging. Already the tale of my saving Juchi's life was flying from tuman to tuman, and my comrades could not act quickly enough to satisfy my every request, whether it was for a drink of wine or the tastiest gobbet fresh from the fire.

Surely my destiny was now being woven into a pattern of good fortune. To have the first-born of the Khan as my personal protector was a victory of which I had never even dreamed. Yet it had come to pass. Word of it kept circulating through the horde on the long journey back to Karakorum, lending me for a time the stature of a hero. While I heard nothing in the way of commendation from the Khan, I did not expect it. I felt certain the Khan knew I had inadvertently saved his son's life. That in itself was another boon.

Cho Soo, beloved—with the gods smiling on me at last, it cannot be many more seasons before I come to claim you, set aside the vow made to Hargoutai the Falcon, and ride with you across the face of the world to seek my birthplace in the land of the Franks.

Of my promise to Hargoutai the Falcon about a noble kill, little was said apart from good-humored jests among the Mangudai. I did not see the tar-khan on the whole long journey home-

135

ward to The Black Sands, nor in fact throughout the winter which soon closed down. I imagined Hargoutai was avoiding me. My good fortune on the hunt had undoubtedly humiliated him again.

I had proof of that one snowy winter night. Near a Nestorian church in Karakorum, I was fallen upon by a band of ruffian soldiers and beaten nearly insensible. They used no weapons, so I decided afterward that they had not meant to kill me, only to hurt me—which they did. I was barely able to crawl back to the yurts of my comrades. I suffered one broken bone, which required the rest of the icy season for healing.

Of Cho Soo I also saw nothing. Nor was I summoned again by Ye Liu Chutsai. From an officer who had taken a Cathayan girl as concubine, I heard that my beloved remained in good health and poor spirits in the tents of Hargoutai. She had still not conceived a child, for which I was thankful.

"The beating was salve for Hargoutai's wounded pride," Bela mused one spring night as we lay near a dung fire on a plain twenty leagues to the southwest of Karakorum. The horde had been ordered forth toward an assembly point, for the Khan had at last decided to strike west against the Shah of Kharesmia. Bela went on: "But you haven't seen the tar-khan for a very good reason."

"What's that?" I asked.

Looking rather mournful, he answered, "The Falcon has no need to taunt you further. His hour has come—or should I say yours and mine? The Mangudai don't have many more months to live, James. Chances are good that the enemy will cut all of us down in our first battle."

The barrens echoed with muffled sounds of horsemen moving in the night, the long columns illuminated by torches and their passage marked by the strident beat of the kettledrums of war. A cold wind touched my cheek. Bela was right.

"That's a hard truth to face."

"I'm not a clever man, James, but I learned long ago that the truth about this life is never soft."

I said nothing, depressed all at once. We of the Mangudai would soon charge a foreign foe, blades bared as we rode to meet our high destiny—which was to die.

How could I possibly better my fortune? I saw no way. I saw, in the dance of the fire, only certain death.

Chapter 5

The Charge of the God-belonging

The time had come. In a narrow valley walled by forested slopes of dark green, our horde of four tumans prepared for combat on a late winter day in the Christian year 1220.

At the far end of the valley, weapons gleamed and pennons fluttered in the army of Muhammad Shah of Kharesmia, a horde of eighty thousand, twice our strength. The enemy force was personally commanded by the Shah and his son Jelal ed-Din, a famed drinker and swordsman.

The heavens rumbled, black with an impending storm. This was the season for heavy rains on the western slopes of the Tian-shan. With each thunderclap, the Mongols around me cast frightened eyes upward, afraid that the tengri would soon be flying. No true son of the Gobi wished to be abroad, let alone fighting, while a storm raged.

The weather seemed to bring no fear to our

foe, however. I could easily see the eighty thousand Turkomans and Persians of Khorassan preparing for battle.

All along our lines, warriors made their weapons ready. Bela and I sat our ponies in the front rank of the Mangudai, near a hill where Juchi the Guest and Chepe Noyon the Arrow Prince watched a portly, gray-gowned Nestorian take the omens beneath the lowering sky.

The priest chanted a mysterious litany, read from a tiny scroll, then cast two little canes to the earth. Juchi's name had been inscribed on the head of one cane, the name of Muhammad Shah on the other.

Juchi leaped from his saddle and picked up the cane which had fallen on top of its mate. He raised the cane over his head, shouting, "The tengri fly. But my cane fell atop that of the enemy. Though the gods of the sky are angry, we will bring our father the Kha Khan a victory!"

Thunder crashed. The first drops of rain spattered my cheeks. Men cringed from the noise in the heavens. Cries of fear erupted in the ranks, but Juchi's shout drowned them out. "Let your weapons be thirsty! Remember our brother Chepe Noyon met the Shah on the Roof of the World not a week ago, and the Muhammadan showed his contempt for the Mongol by refusing to fight. Today he cannot refuse." Juchi flung his arms wide. Rain struck his face as he screamed, "Attack! Attack and *slay*!"

He mounted, conferring quickly with Chepe Noyon on the route of charge down the valley. If we hurried our charge, we could still strike the Shah's army while its ranks were yet incompletely formed.

With my left hand I lifted the reins of my

pony, carrying my sword in the same hand. With my right I clasped the arm of my brother Bela. Then I pulled out my lance.

"We've ridden far to reach this dark ground, Bela. Should this prove our final resting place, I can only tell you that my days have been brighter with you at my side."

"And mine also, James."

"I can't believe everything will end for us today."

"No man ever believes he will die," Bela said sadly.

"I suppose that's true. Still, if it happens, let it happen honorably."

"Aye," he agreed. "I swear that before death takes me, many a Turkoman will perish from my blade." He hefted his lance in a last salute. Above the shriek of the rising storm, Juchi the Guest ordered the Mangudai forward.

My pony responded eagerly. Our double squadron, a hundred across and ten deep, began its descent to the sloping floor of the valley, gathering speed until we rode at full gallop, yelling at the top of our lungs. Behind us came the heavy cavalry, ten thousand Mongols wearing iron chest plates. Behind them, thirty thousand more streamed out, lances and bows at the ready. The whole mounted horde, front to back, covered almost a league of ground. Ahead on the plain, the Shah's army milled, trumpets braying and cymbals crashing alarm. Scattered squadrons of Turks and Persians raced out to meet us, though it was plain that their coming was disorganized, and that we had already won a brief advantage by our swift start. I saw that our line and the enemy's would meet near a shallow lake.

Sword in my rein hand, lance in my right, I

rode like a storm-demon, marveling at the turns of the fated wheel that had brought me here. The past months of hardship had a dreamlike quality. Yet the agonies of the long road from Karakorum had been all too real . . . .

In the spring of the foregoing year, 1219, the quarter-million men in the Mongol horde had gathered on the pasture lands southwest of The Black Sands. Throughout the summer months, the cattle fattened and Tuli drilled the tumans. In early autumn, the Khan journeyed out from Karakorum and we began our advance into the eastern ranges of the great mountains of Tianshan.

We rode into a land of such chilling cold and icy waste that it seemed we traveled through the very home of the winter-demons. Snow came down from the northern skies well before the appointed time, frightening the learned astrologers. When the Khan demanded the meaning of the omen, the learned Ye Liu Chutsai could only say it signified that the master of the cold Gobi winters would win over the lord of the warm places.

Was there ever such a season of toil, suffering, and despair as that one? Ever such a feat of heroism and daring to match the journey across a barrier of mountains none had ever crossed before?

The horde stretched out for leagues and leagues. The great Khan rode in the van, surrounded by a thousand Imperial Guards on matched black horses.

Behind him came Tuli, commanding more than a hundred thousand. The right and left wings numbered fifty thousand each, and the rear guard another fifty.

Fifty thousand cattle and oxen preceded us. We had ten thousand Cathayans, the Kopao-yu, who were masters of artillery. Their siege engines were carried disassembled on kibitkas. We had interpreters from every tribe, merchants to serve as spies, mandarins to hold office as governors in provinces which we passed through and claimed for our own.

We advanced into the Tian-shan, encountering terrible blizzards, and traversed snowfields where horns of dead wild sheep stuck up like grim warnings. Full winter closed.

The herd was soon slaughtered. The hay ran out. The fodder carts were burned. The camels fell by the hundreds, lowering their spent bodies into the snow with a queer, awkward dignity.

And still we marched and rode, a quarter-million of us, up toward the peaks.

We passed the last growth of mammoth pines and larches, reaching the empty, frozen plateaus —a region of unbearable cold. The ponies, their hoofs bound up in yak skins, were all but starved. With bleeding muzzles, they rooted beneath the snow for bits of moss.

We slept under leather cloaks and awakened covered to our own height by fresh drifts. We cut open the veins of animals and drank their blood. We crossed gorges on bridges of logs, dozens of men dropping off and screaming away to their death far below.

But then, at last, we could go no higher; we had broken the world's back. We had only to go down. Down into the rich lands of Kharesmia. . . .

As the Christian year 1220 began, Juchi the Guest and two tumans, of which the Mangudai were part, dropped away on the left flank to the south, leaving the mile-high snowfields and riding toward the Pe Lu, the Great North Road. The land grew warmer.

Meeting Chepe Noyon and his two divisions, this left wing of the horde advanced through a long chain of valleys along the Pe Lu. Meantime Muhammad Shah and his forces came out of their walled cities along the River Syr, to the valley through which I now rode. Again I looked on the past months as an unbelievable dream. With the horde, I had crossed the very heights of creation to a new land. It seemed a great waste, that effort, if death was its only objective. By the gods, I swore, as I rode, I would *live*!

Signals from the officers were flying through the ranks of the Mangudai as we hammered even closer to the shallow lake and the forces of Muhammad Shah coming to meet us. Bela and I read the signals and headed our ponies around the left side of the lake. The other half of the Mangudai thundered in the opposite direction. This was the first time I had seen the favorite Mongol tactic—the sweep, or tulughma—executed. I marveled at its effectiveness. The Turkomans and Persians had been advancing in a single central force. We fell upon them from two sides.

The first moments of battle were pandemonium—plunging horses, thrusting lances, hacking blades. A squadron of Turkoman cavalry descended on us, then another. I took a cut on the head and a sword thrust through the calf. I lost sight of Bela almost at once.

Moments after the battle began along the shore of the shallow lake, the storm broke in full fury. My pony took a lance through its throat and I tumbled into the water. The valley resounded

143

with cries of fury from thousands of throats as the forces of the Shah began to rally and race to the support of the troops which had been caught between the charging wings of the Mangudai. But we were quickly reinforced by Juchi and Chepe Noyon. They brought up the Mongol heavy cavalry, slaying ruthlessly.

All this I saw while floundering, hurt and weakened, in the water at the edge of the lake. The lake was already tinted red and full of floating corpses. Suddenly two robed brown Turkomans rushed at me. My lance was gone, but my sword remained. I lopped the head from one of the Turks and watched it sail away through the rain, just as the other man stabbed his blade into my thigh. I rammed his throat and heard him wail to his Allah for mercy before he dropped, bubbling his last breaths beneath the surface of the lake.

Dizzy and weak, I fought my pain and tried to stay on my feet. Overhead, flights of arrows hissed. I saw that the remaining Mangudai had ridden out of the way to permit the heavy cavalry to sweep through, followed by the lighter horse, all plunging ahead along the valley. The forces of the Shah had already turned and begun their retreat. They apparently intended to defend the hilly heights whence they'd come. It was also clear that they'd never met warriors as fierce as the Mongols before.

Loss of blood was weakening me moment by moment. I had survived the charge but might not survive the aftermath. I tottered up the shore of the lake, put my sword through the breast of a Persian still twitching among the reeds, and began to wander among the dead, seeking a face I knew or a pony I could ride. Here and there among the tangle of corpses, a few others of the Mangudai arose. When we had all gathered in a group to watch the conflict raging up the valley, we numbered but thirty. We stood in the rain with our uniforms slashed and our limbs washed in blood.

Thirty from one thousand. And Bela was not among them.

We remained near the lake until a squadron of cavalry came galloping back, bringing spare horses captured from the herds of the Shah. But we did not leave the field because Juchi and Guest had not withdrawn the standard of the nine white yak tails borne up the valley by his bearer; The Yassa forbade soldiers to retreat until this standard had been carried to the rear.

We occupied ourselves by hunting for weapons among the dead, most of us insensible from our wounds. Now and then a man discovered a comrade still living and lifted him to horseback. It was also forbidden to leave an injured brother behind.

One of the injured proved to be Bela. He was unconscious, a great hole torn in his belly. But he appeared to be sleeping peacefully in spite of his wounds.

Groaning and lightheaded, I practically fell off the pony I had been given. I knelt at Bela's side, touching his face. "Bela? Brother? Again the gods have smiled. We both did not die. But I fear my time has come. My head is buzzing strangely, I..."

Those were the last words I said. I pitched forward across his body.

Chapter 6

Gur-khan

What transpired in the following two nights and days I cannot precisely record, for in that time I slept on the edge of death, tended by my companions in Juchi's victorious horde.

When I did waken and beg for wine, in a camp in a valley far from the scene of the battle, my heart burst with joy at the sight of Bela lying near me, his cuts bound up and his eyes clear.

My own wounds stank of the herbs brewed by the Nestorian servants among us, and though I was still in considerable pain, I felt reasonably whole and curious about the fate of the army.

My comrades told me the wounded had been borne from the field once the Shah was in full retreat. With ten thousand Mongols lost in the struggle, the remaining thirty thousand had climbed the forested slopes of the valley in the storm, marched two days' distance in a single night, then marched the same distance the next day and night, to camp at last in a range of low peaks leading into the very heart of Kharesmia.

We had won a great victory.

Hearing this, I managed to rise, drink, and salute my brethren by the fire. Truly, as the Khan had promised, we were the scourges of the earth.

"But that's not the only achievement in which we can take pride," Bela informed me from where he lay. "Thirty-and-six warriors of the Mangudai are still alive. To them, a special honor has been given—bestowed by our Lord Juchi himself."

"Tell me about it."

Swelling with the grandeur of his news, he went on: "No longer must those who survived the charge down the valley take their places among the tumans as mere soldiers. No, James Nine-Fingers—now we may wear insignia of authority. We are gur-khans of the horde! Don't look so disbelieving, brother! I speak the truth."

His teeth gleamed as he grinned. Around the snapping fire, murmurs from the other soldiers who had shared the first charge told me that I had heard correctly.

"Lord Juchi himself published the petitions of rank!" Bela rushed on. "And the tidings have been carried by couriers to the ears of our father the Kha Khan, together with news of how Muhammad Shah ran with tail hanging before the might of the Mongols."

"Where is the Khan's army now?" I asked.

"It has passed through the Gate of the Winds out of Tagh-Dumbash, and is marching around Lake Balkash to the hills of the Kara Tau. Our glory and prestige will go with us to the heart of Kharesmia. Think of the spoils to which we'll be entitled!"

147

For some reason, I had reservations. "The news is indeed good, brother. But it's not as wondrous as you'd have me believe. True, a gur-khan is an officer. But not a high officer."

He bristled: "High enough to make Hargoutai the Falcon burn with rage, isn't it?"

Swiftly I glanced up. Long tatters of flame whipped out from our fire. The wind from the hills touched me, cold. I nodded slowly. Bela had put words to what had been troubling me. "Exactly right. He expected me dead, and here I emerge covered with honor, small though the honor is. It can't fail to start him plotting again."

Bela's brief frown showed he did not particularly enjoy my pessimism. Yet it was on me like a disease, or the formless fears a man feels when he wakes before the break of morning, terrified without knowing why.

Perhaps I felt it because I had arisen too quickly and taken wine. My forehead was slick with sweat; details around me none too clear. Whatever the cause, I said, "It's not because of Hargoutai alone that I worry."

"Gods, what a time for bleak spirits!"

"I have reason."

"*What* reason?"

"I don't know that I can properly describe it."

"Having raised the subject, at least have the decency to try!" he snorted.

I hitched closer to the fire, feeling the intense heat fanning my cheeks like the breath of a demon. I was not entirely sure I could explain my foreboding. But to placate him, I made the attempt.

"You know I'm not of Mongol blood, Bela. But having been raised among your people, I have a healthy respect for those powers we never see but only call gods—"

"They favored us in the battle!" he cried.

"You, perhaps. You're one of their own." My ears rang as I sensed the presence of powers I feared. "By rights I should have been struck down beside the lake where we met the soldiers of the Shah. Yet out of a thousand, I was one who survived. One who was allowed to live."

"Be grateful!"

"Yes, I should be, but—"

"You question too much, James. You think too much, that's your trouble. There's nothing so extraordinary in what happened. You handle a weapon well, and the gods of chance ordained that your time to ascend to the heavens hadn't yet arrived, that's all. Who knows when it will happen? Perhaps a jackal will leap at your throat and tear it out next time you squat to relieve yourself—the manner of the coming of death is different for all men. Different and unpredictable."

"Sometimes I think I can predict mine."

Disbelieving, he said, "You pretend to know the place? The very hour?"

"No, no, not that. But I think your gods have reserved a special dying for me."

"Endless mysteries!" he complained. "Now you speak of the Mongol gods as if they aren't yours."

"They are—that is, sometimes. At other times I think I have Frankish gods, too. But their names are unknown to me, and they may never reveal themselves. It's the Mongol spirits I fear most. I fear they plucked me back from the black brink in the battle for a purpose."

"What purpose?" He was angry now.

"I think it's to lift me higher than I have a

right to expect. First they let me survive the battle. Now they permit me to be raised to gur-khan. That way, when they choose to take me, it will be all the more painful because they tricked me into false confidence. Into thinking I might outwit them. Outrun their reach—"

Bela shook his head. "I'm certainly thankful no one ever taught me to think so much! I tell you, brother, *all* you need worry about is Hargoutai the Falcon."

Thus he ordered the universé with a few simple words.

You don't understand, I thought in a helpless way. *You didn't see me kill the roebuck. You don't know I broke the Khan's law, and laughed at the gods when I did it. You don't know I am* marked *for punishment!*

Was it the truth? Or was it the delirium of the wounds and the wine? I had no idea.

Bela did not care. "It's Hargoutai, I tell you. Worry about him and nothing else and you'll be fine. Carry your blade ready at all times, keep a watchful eye out, and you'll come through safe and smothered with honors. Why, with your luck, Hargoutai will probably fall in battle—you'll never see him again—and when we ride back to The Black Sands, your sweet little Cathayan will be waiting for the claiming."

"No," I persisted. "It's not to be done so simply. It's not over—"

"What's not over, James?"

The way I'm to be scourged for scorning the gods in which I only half-believe. They refuse to be regarded so lightly.

While he stared at me, half in anger, half in puzzlement, I closed my eyes. A painful throb had started behind my forehead. The glow of the fire

150

became so bright, I had to shut my eyes. *Am I mad?* I thought.

The pain beat in my temples. Then, slowly, it began to diminish. My forehead cooled. I gulped air. Bela repeated his pronouncement: "You think too much."

"Perhaps," I whispered. Then, louder, trying to summon conviction, "Perhaps."

But I couldn't convince myself the gods were done with me. Still, *he* was done with me, especially if I kept on. So I put on the best smile I could, saying, "But we've exhausted the subject."

"Thank heavens! You're a gur-khan. Be content and stop borrowing trouble. Enough will come our way without begging for it. We aren't through fighting, you know."

"You're right. Forgive my ramblings. Is there wine enough in the skin for me to have another drink?"

"Aye."

"Then pass it here."

"Gladly!" Bela grumbled. "You're trying to take all the joy out of our promotion. Gods, James, say no more about these black powers of yours. Drink and enjoy your good fortune!"

I only wished that I could.

Wine scalding down my gullet helped quell the gloomy forebodings, and I managed to pass the next hour in boisterous conversation with those gathered at the fire. A dozen times we recounted each passage at arms in the battle beside the lake, growing thoroughly drunk and thoroughly swelled with confidence during the retellings. For a while, I was able to forget the throbbing of my wounds and my certainty that the game was not yet played out.

In the morning this heady mood of assurance

still possessed me. As the dawn drum-roll beat out through the foothills, I felt the kiss of a sun warmer than any I had known for months, warmer even than the pale radiance of the Gobi. I knew that we must not be far from the low, fertile plains of the Shah's country, and I was stirred by the thought.

We had lost close to a tuman in the valley battle. I heard reinforcements were on the way from the main body of the army. We should have an additional five thousand with us when we reached the lowlands of Kharesmia. The whole army was heartened by the news. There was a prevailing mood of good cheer as we made ready to march.

Juchi the Guest galloped up, his prized sable cloak flying behind him. He paused to ask about my condition. I assured him it was good. The feigned disappointment I had seen on his face in the boar's cave shone there once more.

"I swear you shame me more with each day that passes," he said, pulling a long face and pretending dismay. "Why, before long, my father will no doubt name you his eldest son and set me a task as your cupbearer! Already your fame must be circulating among the main army—James Nine-Fingers, savior of the Khan's son and bearer of a charmed life! Your reputation will soon be enhanced in Karakorum, too."

"How is that, Lord?"

"A full report of our victory is being dispatched to The Black Sands today. I have no doubt you'll be mentioned," he added wryly.

Then Juchi's eyes glowed with mocking humor. He was familiar with the tale of my love for the Cathayan princess. "I'm sure there is one in Karakorum who'll delight at the news. She's probably prostrate with grief, believing you dead." Then, more soberly: "I say this next as your protector and friend. Hargoutai's eunuchs may not permit a *full* account to reach her ears. If you wish to be certain it does, you might want to make an arrangement with the Nestorian friars traveling in the courier group. Just a suggestion, of course." His massive shoulders lifted under the folds of sable, leaving the decision to me. With a sharp order to his retinue, he continued on.

I wasted no time in following his hint, for it was a wise one. I would have to be cautious, though, and make sure that in seeing that news of my safety reached Cho Soo, I did not in any way cause her to violate her vow. I thought I could do it.

Quickly I located a pony and clattered off among the crowds of men preparing for the day's march.

"Which way to the yurts of the Nestorians?" I shouted as I rode. At each camp circle I was waved on.

If Lord Juchi had made his sly suggestion the night before, I might not have responded to it so eagerly. This morning, with the sun sparkling and a feeling of exaltation running through the ranks, I called myself a fool for fearing the gods. Had I not survived the battle? Was I not a gurkhan? I had an obligation to tell my beloved of my good fortune, to give her hope and proof that I was moving slowly but resolutely toward the fulfillment of my vow, made more than two long years before.

Leaping from my saddle at the camp of the Nestorians, I sought out the leader of the band who would be returning to Karakorum. He was a robust, gray-gowned Karait priest from whose shoulders hung a gray stole painted with hideous images of scarlet devils. "Good father," I began, "I would call on your generosity and ask you to carry a private message back across the Roof of the World to our city on the Gobi."

"Well, if you must," he sighed, fiddling with a string of holy beads. "Already I'm burdened with a squadron's worth of messages. Everything from complaints about incompetent officers to a warrior's wish to tell his favorite concubine the thrilling news that the upland air has a healthy purgative effect!"

The worthy father's eyes gleamed merrily. "But I surmise from the eager look on your face that your message concerns nothing so trivial."

I smiled. "I hope not."

"Let me guess its subject. Could it be the one most important to men who've been away from home a long time? Namely, love?"

"You've guessed correctly, good father."

"Then to whom shall I deliver the tidings that you lived through the battle, Nine-Fingers?" he asked. When I gaped at the use of my name, he said: "Come, don't be so modest. I'm well acquainted with your reputation. Who isn't? Your condemnation to the Mangudai back in Karakorum was noted and much discussed. In fact, my brothers and I said a prayer for your squadron, even after the omens of the canes showed favorably. A man can never have too many prayers to support him! So tell me—what's the name of the wench to whom I must speak?"

"The lady is called Cho Soo. She dwells in the tents of Hargoutai the Falcon. But you mustn't speak to her directly. Nor allow her to hear about me from any of your fellow priests. If you know something about my history, perhaps you also know she's sworn a vow of faith to her lord." His suddenly stoic expression and somber eyes told me he did. "I must not be responsible for any violation of that vow, father. It must not seem as if she asked about me."

"The news must reach her as if by accident, then."

"Yes. If you can locate a trusted handmaiden and perhaps repeat the information to her, together with a word of caution, the handmaiden can then introduce the news in the guise of gossip picked up in a public place."

A frown creased the holy man's brow. "Isn't your devious method the same thing as a direct message?"

"I don't believe so or I wouldn't send it. Public news is not personal. At least I hope I judge the difference correctly. I want her to know I'm safe, yet not in a way that might be misconstrued."

"You have a nice understanding of the intricacies of Mongol protocol, Nine-Fingers."

"I don't care about protocol, father. I care about her plight."

He pondered, then nodded: "Very well. Your consideration for the lady prompts me to help you. Your message will be delivered, and in the manner you specify."

"Thank you, father. May the gods accompany you on your journey," I said, mounting my pony.

A tranquil expression spread across his face. "My god is never away from my side."

Silently, I wished that I could say the same. I did not know whether I had one who stood beside me, but I had no doubt a great many were ranked against me and might make their vengeance felt again.

As the tumans mounted and moved forward into valleys green with vegetation, I struggled once again to throw off my mood of pessimism, and gradually succeeded.

The sun grew hotter hour by hour. Foragers and scouts galloped out ahead of the army. The horde rode proudly—lords of the earth.

Only once more that day did I have misgivings. I saw a wild falcon wheeling high in the blue, some smaller bird helpless and dying in its talons.

I shivered and wondered whether I had seen an omen.

Chapter 7

War in the Warm Country.

"Yonder!" the cry rang from squadron to squadron. "*Yonder*—Kharesmia at last!" With the armies of Islam and its protector, Muhammad Shah, fleeing before us, we entered the abundant and dreamlike country in the early spring of the Christian year 1220.

We descended from the white mountains into the golden radiance of the Shah's domain virtually unopposed. The Shah and his warrior son Jelal ed-Din had fled to rally their forces along the banks of the swollen River Syr, which flowed westward from Lake Aral. Also springing from the great lake, but curving in a more southerly direction, ran the fabled River Amu. These two rivers formed natural defense lines in the Shah's kingdom and stood as barriers between the hordes of the Khan and the rich walled cities of Khorassan to the south.

When we came down from the peaks in our

sweltering cloaks and sheepskins, Juchi's force was divided; twenty thousand thundered south with Chepe Noyon the Arrow Prince bound for Samarkand, while we continued our march to the Syr. There the five thousand promised reinforcements would supposedly be waiting.

Our spies traveled far ahead of us, followed by the foragers and advance points of the army—two hundred warriors riding in pairs. Bela and I were chosen as one such pair. Thus we had a matchless opportunity to gaze on the rich countryside long before our fellows did.

The Mongol battle plan was masterful. The Shah had separated his forces, leaving forty thousand men in the cities along the River Syr and another thirty thousand behind the walls of Bokhara near the Amu while he led the balance toward Samarkand still farther south. The sons of the Khan—Ogotai, Master of the Council, and Chatagai, Master of Laws and Punishment—marched against the Syr citadel of Otrar where the traitorous Inaljuk was hidden. Smaller forces descended upon Tashkent and Jend. And as Chepe Noyon aimed at Bokhara from the east, the mighty Khan himself led his troops in a circuit through the Desert of Red Sands to surprise the same city from the west, thus confounding the armies of Islam by means of the tulughma.

Our part of the horde had as its goal the walled city of Khojend on the Syr. After subduing it, we were to proceed south to aid the Khan. But we soon knew that the walls of Khojend, center of the Khokand district, would not be easily breached. Spies reported that while Khojend's garrison was small, its leader was one of the mightiest among the Muhammadans. He was called Timur Malik and known in Islam as the Iron Lord.

Still, Bela and I had much to see before the fighting began—and we took full advantage of our good fortune in being posted out ahead of the army. We drank in sights as a man with a parched throat gulps water. We rode near pale, beautiful villages with all-white walls, strange minarets, and lofty watchtowers. Cattle grazed placidly in the fields around these villages, or took their rest in the shade of poplar and willow trees. Pomegranates and melons grew in abundance. Some of the latter were as large as Bela's two huge fists held side by side. The melons made excellent refreshment as we scouted the country.

But never had we experienced such intense heat. All day the sun flamed in the sky, and I suspected the weather must sometimes be like this in Frankistan. The warmth was not unpleasant, at least not to me. Bela detested it. But I had never quite accustomed myself to the Gobi's chill, and basking in the clear, bright sunlight strengthened my resolve to one day return to my true father's country.

Together with the other advance riders, Bela and I sent back reports on the exact locations of the Khokand villages, after which Juchi's commanders descended upon them, stripped them of grain, wine, and horses, and promptly set them afire. Robed Muhammadans were taken as hostages, and all officers of gur-khan rank or higher were required to spend time with these captives every night, learning their language. In two weeks I had mastered the rudiments. In four, I became proficient.

Islamic women found their way into our camp

also, wailing piteously when the Mongols tore off
their veils and took pleasure from them. Though
I found the women not unattractive, something
held me back from dallying with them more than
once. On that occasion, I was drunk and imagined
I saw the face of Cho Soo instead of that of the
Turkoman girl. Afterward I felt much ashamed.
My companions in the horde laughed at my sentiments. Were we not conquerors, entitled to all
spoils?

Thus did the district of Khokand feel our
wrath, and the smoke of sacked and burning villages cast a pall over heaven after we had passed.

The weather grew still warmer with each new
day. Many a soldier found himself riding with
only sandals on his feet, a sheepskin about his
middle, and lacquered breastplates on his chest.
Some even tried the silken robes of the Muhammadans, but I found them uncomfortable. We
met no organized resistance as we advanced. We
took what we needed for food and savored the
feel of full bellies again. Whatever we did not
need, we killed, burned, or destroyed.

Finally the day came when the spring-swollen
Syr lay before us. The walls and towers of
Khojend rose on its far banks.

We had now been joined by the five thousand
soldiers promised by the Khan. They brought
with them a detachment of officers of the
Cathayan Kopao-yu, together with a host of carts
bearing the various components of their siege engines.

Khojend drowsed in the morning sun, oddly
quiet for a city confronted by an enemy. Although its parapets were lined with frightened
Mussulmans watching our encampment, not a

soldier could be seen. Had the defenders and their leader Timur Malik fled without a fight?

"Something is wrong, but I can't reckon what it is," Juchi the Guest growled to his assembled gur-khans on the bank of the swift-flowing river. The sun stood high, casting shadows on his moody face. "Except I suspect this much. There's a trick in the air."

Sharing his puzzlement, we studied the broad river, the city, and the thickly forested island lying square in midstream. Juchi shielded his eyes against the glare. All along the bank, ponies pawed and thousands of warriors awaited his command. From behind came the thud and clatter of the war machines being assembled.

Juchi spat into the reeds. "Very well. Tricks or not, we will go ahead. We will lash the city and see whether Timur Malik comes out of hiding with a squeal."

That night the army camped along the river. Each man looked to his kit in preparation for the crossing on the morrow. Lanterns burned on the parapets of Khojend, but in no other way could we tell the place was inhabited.

I found myself nervous that evening; there would be another battle before the sun went down again. I finally managed to fall into a restless sleep, dreaming of Cho Soo.

"Get up, James. Quickly!" Bela exclaimed, hitching on his breastplates. "Lord Juchi's in a fury. We've been foxed."

"How?"

He pointed to the wooded island in the middle of the murmuring Syr. Torches gleamed among the trees.

I rubbed sleep from my eyes. "Whose fires are those?"

"Not ours!" Bela growled. "The wretched Timur Malik and a thousand Turkomen boated over from some hiding place in the city. And while we slept! Now they're ready for battle in a position that's all but invulnerable. It's clear they mean to die rather than surrender. A Kipchak who chanced near Juchi's yurt told me he'd never seen the Khan's son so filled with wrath."

"But it looks as if Khojend is ours for the taking," I protested.

"Khojend be damned! Timur Malik is held in such high esteem that if we capture the city but leave him jeering at us from that island, we've won nothing at all!"

Before dawn, colored lanterns beside Juchi's yurt summoned his gur-khans to his side. Naked to the waist and dragging a wine sack on the ground behind him, the Khan's son was truly in a towering rage. He tramped back and forth, peering at the black river and the island in the center.

The island was dark now. All the torches had been extinguished. The lanterns along Khojend's parapet had gone out as well. Night birds cried in the heavens, an eerie sound.

At last Juchi exclaimed, "When the light breaks, each gur-khan will gather one hundred warriors and ride back through the district. You will bring to the bank of the river each human being—man, woman, or child—who can walk or crawl. But do not bring them empty-handed. Each must carry a stone of this size—" Juchi spread his hands. Then he glanced at a Cathayan officer of the Kopao-yu seated near the entrance to the hastily erected yurt. "Am I correct in the size?" Juchi snapped to the officer.

"Slightly bigger would be better, Lord," the Cathayan murmured. "So large."

162

Juchi expanded his hands to match the Cathayan's estimate: "So be it—this large, then. When a captive puts down his stone, he is to return to the countryside and find another, and then another, and another, until he falls dead of exhaustion. In the event someone refuses to help in this fashion, he or she is to be slain."

Quietly, a man asked, "Not children, Lord?"

"*Anyone* who refuses. We'll drag Timur Malik off his cursed island by the very hairs of his beard. Now make ready and begone by daylight!" Swinging about, he disappeared into his yurt, taking a long drink from the wineskin as he did. Those of us assembled—nearly two hundred gurkhans—scrambled to obey his orders.

The river-bank camp was soon roused. As I rode away from the river with my own hundred hammering behind, the dawn sky was lit by the red glare of fire-pots arching over the Syr and trailing tails of flame. The fire-pots were shot from siege-engines that stood in the stark silhouette against the pink and pearl radiance of the heavens.

Pot after pot of the hellish fire went flying beneath the paling stars. But as my troop mounted a low hill in search of captives, we could see that the flaming destruction could not possibly reach Timur Malik's island. The pots fell into the Syr and disappeared beneath its foaming surface. Still uncertain as to why Juchi wanted stones—if fiery missiles would not reach the island, surely rocks wouldn't either—I nevertheless urged my men forward.

A league from the Syr, we came upon a small village. We galloped into it at full speed while the inhabitants wailed and fled before us. We dragged them forth from every dwelling and alleyway, but there was little bloodshed, so greatly did they fear us. For this I was grateful. I lacked the stomach for the useless slaughter of conquered peoples, a practice advocated by the Kha Khan to prevent resistance once the horde had passed. With the exception of a venerable sayyid who cursed us from the steps of the village mosque, no one offered resistance. The sayyid died with a bone arrow in his breast.

By midday, the several hundred villagers had trudged back to the Syr, a long, woeful procession winding like a serpent over the countryside. Tiny children rolled rocks before them. Even old men labored in the sun-baked dust, adding their feeble strength to the task of moving stones they could not carry alone.

Turning the captives over to the care of officers at the river's edge, I gathered my warriors and rode off again, glad to be away from the sorrowful sight of prisoners bending under the whips of their conquerors. Although there were many qualities of the Kha Khan which were admirable, including his military genius, some of his methods, and those of his sons, were far from humane—just as Ye Liu Chutsai had once said.

Hardening my heart as best I could, I returned to the task of carrying out my orders.

After three days of combing the countryside, the River Syr's bands teemed with humanity working among great piles of stones. Juchi's purpose became clear at last. Boulder by boulder, a wide stone causeway leading to the island was being constructed by the captive Muhammadans.

Now and then one of these slave workers would refuse to continue with the task, whereupon he was immediately shot down by a handful of arrows. The River Syr soon turned red.

Bloated bodies floated away on the torrents. Yet the causeway went forward. On the island there was frenzied activity and the constant crash of toppling trees.

On the fourth day, Timur Malik's resistance made itself evident. As the captives wailed, cried out to their Allah, and labored to extend the causeway, twelve log barges were hurriedly carried from the woods on the island and launched into the water. Several hundred archers swarmed aboard, including a figure in dazzling white robes who was identified as the Iron Lord himself.

From the barges, the Turkomen began to rain showers of arrows upon their own people working on the causeway. The Cathayans wheeled up the rumbling siege engines and began to launch boulders at the barges, but the Muhammadan steersmen seemed particularly adept at avoiding the hurtling rocks.

Fresh bowmen climbed aboard the barges at nightfall, but Juchi refused to halt the construction, which continued by torchlight. Those working at the extreme end of the stoneway were automatically doomed, presenting clear targets. The number of bodies in the river Syr increased to horrifying proportions. Although the Muhammadan arrows flew three days and nights, the causeway crept forward. And Juchi himself did not avoid danger. He drove his pony up and down the causeway, dodging arrows, caning the naked backs of the Cathayans, and cursing their slowness. His Mongol overseers took some comfort from his courage—they could hardly hide themselves when he exposed himself to death—but many of them died in the performance of their duties.

When the stones of the siege-engines proved

futile against the barge-borne attackers, jars of flaming sulfur were tried again. To counter this measure, the wily Timur Malik overnight added sloping walls as well as roofs to his craft. All exposed surfaces were covered with sod, rendering the barges less vulnerable to burning. His archers continued to shoot through numerous ports.

I was constantly sickened at the human cost of the causeway. At least a thousand Muhammadans dropped into the Syr every day. Dead eyes stared from the rushes. A maid's dark hair floated on the surface. A child's arm bobbed white and lifeless.

Yet the causeway went forward, soon reaching nearly two-thirds of the way to the island.

Again there was a midnight alarm. The River Syr gleamed with torches as the gur-khans rushed to answer the summons. We soon learned the disheartening reason for the alarm. Timur Malik had recognized at last that the Mongols could not be turned aside. He had abandoned his island, audaciously floating his thousand warriors down the river by torchlight, while Juchi ranted and howled.

Bela and I and the other gur-khans formed a small company which rode swiftly down the Syr with our leader, pursuing and soon passing the torch-lit barges of the Iron Lord. Outriders were left along the bank to follow the progress of the escaping Muhammadans, while Juchi and the rest of us galloped ahead of those in flight. The remainder of the Mongol force was to follow, save for a small detachment left behind to slaughter all the captives who had worked on the now-useless causeway. I was thankful I was not there to witness the unholy spectacle.

We covered three days' distance in a night

166

and a day. The second dawn found us flinging ourselves from horseback at a great bend in the river. In an hour, a thousand men in a special force had joined us, bringing axes and a dismantled stone-caster carried in twenty carts.

We plunged into a nearby stand of timber. By nightfall we had constructed a bridge of logs across the place where the Syr narrowed at the bend. During the night, the stone-caster was erected at the center of this shaky, creaking structure. Timur's escape route was formidably barred.

A day passed, a pleasant, bucolic day. Fat clouds sailed in the sky. The river bubbled. We peered upriver but saw no sign of Timur's barges.

Nightfall again. Juchi summoned Bela and me to his quarters. Of late we had become his favorite message-bearers. As the Khan's son put it, "I feel you will succeed where many others could not. Killing one of you would require a miracle from the sons of Islam. Killing both would demand that Allah himself came down from his heaven."

Juchi issued brief orders. We were to ride back up the Syr and learn what had become of the army, of the barges, and of the outriders sent to keep watch on them.

We had ridden a good distance by the time the sun rose, so we halted for a short rest in a grove of willows among some hills near the river bank. There we pulled bits of warm meat from beneath our saddles and wolfed them down.

As I tore at the tough meat with my teeth, Bela suddenly raised his hand. He squinted at the crest of a hill where the rays of the breaking sun radiated. "Quiet, James! I heard something."

"Is my chewing all that noisy?"

"I said *quiet*!" He listened, then jerked out his sword. "Horsemen!"

I still heard nothing. "Probably our outriders," I began.

"Let's take no chances."

I threw away my unfinished food and vaulted into my high saddle. By then I heard the riders. Bela had sighted them on the sunblazing crest of the hill.

I shielded my eyes and saw half a dozen black figures etched against the skyline. Then the mounted band plunged down the hillside, riding straight toward our willow grove. It was clear they had not seen us.

Robes flapped as they approached. "Muhammadan dogs!" Bela cried softly. "But riding Mongol ponies!"

I needed no further prompting. I seized my bow, readied an arrow, and with my comrade's blade glinting in the morning sun, we rode forth to attack.

Chapter 8

Dangerous Mercy

We kept behind a screen of willows, riding to within an arrow-flight of the enemy before they sighted us. A moment after one Muhammadan raised an alarm, my arrow knocked him from his saddle.

Bela urged his mount on with a fierce scream. Charging through a wash, we struck with surprise still in our favor. I claimed two more with my bow, while the swinging arcs of Bela's blade hacked down another two. The remaining pair rode off up a hill. I put an arrow through the throat of one of their ponies. The rider fell. His companion wheeled back, dismounted, and tried to lift the fallen man to his saddle. The unhorsed Muhammadan had apparently wrenched a leg; he could not rise. His comrade, dressed in a brilliant white robe oddly patterned with scarlet, struggled to get him to his feet. By that time, Bela and I reached them. We held them at bay with Bela's sword and my nocked arrow.

"Do you give yourselves into our hands, or is death your wish?" I asked them.

The deeply tanned faces of both men burned themselves into my mind, perhaps because both were so lined with anguish and despair. The man with the wrenched leg wore a head-cloak and elaborate silver breastplate. His companion, much older, had no scarlet pattern woven into his white robe, as I had imagined. The pattern was formed by bleeding wounds.

He took four steps to his saddle, laid his hand on his bow, and said, "I still have one arrow shaft in my quiver. I will take one of you before you kill me."

"Kill us and be done," cried the younger Muhammadan on the ground.

"Hush, Hamid!" the other ordered. He was obviously in great pain but refused to show us how much he was suffering. "There's something odd here. That one—" He pointed at me. "—isn't a Mongol. To judge from his eyes and hair he might be a Frank. And he speaks our tongue, though not well."

"Enough!" I shouted. "Did you come from the barges on the river?"

"Aye." The wounded man nodded. "But we heard your horsemen pass in the dark, and we suspected a Mongol trap, so we fled to the bank under cover of darkness. There, more of your men fell on us. But we matched our thousand dead with three thousand of yours before we left the field," he finished, a fierce look in his eye.

"Then your commander Timur Malik is indeed a brave warrior, as we have heard," I told them. I expect I gave them the compliment to salve my conscience about their coming execution.

The fallen Hamid didn't care for compliments from men of the horde. He screamed at me: "Lumps of cow dung! *Barbarians*! You stink with insolence! How dare you speak of bravery? You know nothing about it! You permit old men and children to die for you—!"

"Hamid! Be still," the older Muhammadan warned, clutching at his robe. Fresh spots of blood kept appearing.

But the fiery Hamid struggled up on his knees, refusing to keep silent. He pointed to the older man. "*This* is a brave warrior! Fall down and pay homage to a man worth ten thousand of your Khan! Don't you know the Iron Lord himself, the great general and atabeg of Islam, Timur Malik?" With this revelation, Hamid let his arm fall, breathing hard.

Timur Malik watched me; he was tense. I was stunned by the revelation of his identity and truly impressed by his courage. I could find no words adequate to pay tribute to a man who still had the spirit to fight even while he might be dying on his feet. Except for those dreadful spots on his robe, I would never have known he was hurt, so proud and calm did he look. Truly he was the Iron Lord.

Bela had not mastered the Muhammadan tongue as well as I, and I suspected he did not yet know the identity of our captive. I turned to him and explained in Mongol. His eyes grew large. He treated the wounded man to a stare of wonder.

Carefully, I said, "We are comrades in all things, Bela. Of a single mind. So I'll tell you the thoughts of my head and heart. We have captured a noble tiger but an injured one. We have the

171

choice of slaying him or bearing him alive to Lord Juchi. However, the ride to our lord's yurt might prove too hard. He could die on the way. Left here, he might recover." Watching Bela's expression, I continued, "The truth is, brother, I can't find the courage to slay him. He fought nobly on the island at Khojend. He has plainly fought nobly again. In short, I would rather let him go than kill him or take him prisoner. If we let him go, men might think a little better of the Khan's soldiers."

"But if we release them," Bela stammered, "and it is discovered by our master Juchi—"

"It need never be discovered," I said quietly.

Again his eyes widened. He pondered, testing the point of his blade with his thumb. "We're brothers of the heart, James. My life is yours. But I really can't fathom why you don't want to kill him and thus bring glory to yourself and me as well. It must be some strain of your Frankish blood emerging."

"I would hope it's a strain of ordinary humanity," I said. "If you can find it in your soul to put up your sword, they'll be free men."

A moment of silence. Then, with an explosive curse, Bela flung his sword on the ground. He wheeled his pony and rode off a short distance, signifying his reluctant assent.

I waved to Hamid, who had gotten to his feet at last. "No word of this meeting shall pass from the lips of my comrade or myself. If you die on the other side of the hill, the guilt is no longer ours."

Timur Malik inclined his head—his only sign of gratitude. Lurching clumsily, he and his officer succeeded in mounting the remaining pony. Hamid's face, so alive with loathing only a moment ago, now showed less enmity. "We owe you royal baksheesh—" he began.

Timur Malik shook his head. "Unless I misjudge him, the Frankish warrior has already gained his reward—the deed itself. Allah be with you, soldier." He lifted his hand in a salute. Then the horse bearing Hamid and the Iron Lord started forward. Soon they were out of sight.

I went to Bela, who admitted that he had bowed to my will only because we were so close; he was enraged at the loss of a prize as important as Timur Malik, but what concerned him even more was Juchi's anger should the act of mercy ever be discovered.

"It must not be," I said.

"But I might accidentally talk of it sometime when I'm drunk!" He was quite serious.

I shrugged. "Therefore you have to stop drinking."

He was not amused.

I laid a hand on his shoulder, trying to show him how much I appreciated the way he had subjugated his altogether understandable desire to take an important captive. "If I never knew it before, I know now you're my brother."

"Sometimes it's a damned painful relationship, I don't mind telling you." But after one more stern stare, his annoyance moderated a little. "I really didn't want to kill those two, only capture them. I wouldn't reveal this to anyone else, but sometimes I don't have the stomach for the Khan's butchery either. I don't mind losing Timur Malik—well, I only mind it a little."

"Good. Now let's ride back toward the river and see whether we can find the army. If we're questioned, remember that we saw no riders. *None.*"

"Believe me," he declared with fervor, "*that* I will never forget. While I'm sober anyway."

When the army reformed at the bend of the river, Juchi's wrath knew no bounds. The Iron Lord had escaped him. But for once I rejoiced in the misfortune of my protector.

Fortunately he was soon cheered by good tidings from the south. Bokhara, with its learned academies and its twelve-league wall, had fallen. All its treasure had been delivered into the Khan's hands, but the Khan himself had paused only two hours in the city, hurrying on with his army to Samarkand.

It was to Samarkand that Muhammad Shah had retreated with his corps of nobles, his war elephants, and his household. But the prince of Islam had not lingered long, fearing the city would be razed and burned just as Bokhara had been.

Dispatches brought us the story of Bokhara's sad, gory end: The Turkoman officers in charge of the city's defense had viewed their situation as hopeless and fled by the water gate to join the Shah who was hiding somewhere along the River Amu. Bokhara's gates had then been opened by its judges and imams. Only the governor had fought a last stand from his tower, but fire-arrows had burned him out.

Thus the spoils of Bokhara were delivered into Mongol hands. Rich merchants, called upon to bring forth their treasure, did so—and were immediately slain. Mongol horsemen galloped through the mosques and libraries, lighting fires. On the plain before the city, every male citizen was killed. Every female was ravished and then killed. Only a few artisans were spared for slave labor.

As had happened before, the Khan left desolation in his wake, and the world trembled before the Wrath and Flail of Heaven.

I should have been proud. We, the barbarians from the high Gobi, were rapidly becoming masters of the richest quarter of the earth. It was brave news—except for the unremitting bloodshed which had brought it about. More than ever, I was glad I had spared the Iron Lord and his man Hamid. I think Bela was too, though he never again said so aloud.

Fortunately, Bela abstained from heavy drinking when we rejoined the horde, and no hint that we had freed Timur Malik reached the ears of Juchi the Guest. I was uncomfortable while we lingered in his camp though.

The stay was not a long one. Bela and I were chosen as the couriers who would deliver word of the Khojend campaign to the Khan at Samarkand.

Immediately on receiving our orders, we gathered our provisions, saddled, and rode out within an hour. I was happy to be free in the starlight with only the wind and Bela for my companions and the dispatch pouches safely tucked away.

Happy, that is, until I thought of Hargoutai the Falcon. So far as I knew he was with the Khan's force, and I would surely meet him again before much more time had passed.

Chapter 9

Siege at Samarkand

Not many days after our departure from Juchi's encampment, I presented my dispatches to Genghis Kha Khan in a white silk pavilion on which the standard of the nine yak tails fluttered in a warm breeze off the Amu.

Although the pavilion was considerably smaller than the one in which I had first gazed upon The Emperor of All Mankind, it seemed far more splendid. The simple and primitive weapons of the Gobi which had decorated the walls at Karakorum were gone, and the pavilion was filled by glittering towers of treasure from the Shah's kingdom, heaped higher than a man's head in many places.

I saw dozens of fine scimitars with gleaming blades a man could bend almost double without breaking. I saw a pile of shields bearing Islamic crests flung atop a peacock's array of bolts of silk—vermilions and scarlets and deep blue-greens and turquoise. There were heaps of leather slippers with curled toes; caskets full of little ivory figures; and a shining sea of silver chain mail in the midst of which a golden chest had been overturned spilling out rubies big as eggs and red as the first morning sun.

Strange, sweet smells arose from the treasure, filling the pavilion with a heady scent wholly in keeping with the warm, indolent world of Kharesmia.

The great Khan sat alone amid all this splendor, save for his Ugur scribe and a lesser officer seated on either side to protect his person. I prostrated myself, arose on command, and presented my messages.

He read the dispatches and passed them to his scribe with a slight frown of annoyance. Long horns sounded in the distance. The clatter of the army drifted to my ears. Presently the gaze of the Khan returned to me.

Until that moment, I might have been merely another courier plucked helter-skelter from the thousands who served him, but all at once a gleam of recognition fleeted across his face. He gathered up the folds of his sable robe and stepped down from his dais. I stood aside for him to pass, noting that despite the availability of rich apparel from the conquered kingdom, he still preferred the simpler garb of the Gobi.

Raising his right hand as he went by, he crooked a finger. "Walk with me to the door of the pavilion, Nine-Fingers. Much time has passed since last I saw you, but your name has been in my ears many times."

"Fortune has chosen to smile favorably on me, Lord. I was spared in the first great battle against Muhammad Shah—spared so I might continue to fight under your banner."

"I expect that fortune may have had some hand in it," said the Khan as we reached the door by which I had entered. "But I don't doubt your courage played an important part, too. When you first came before me, I reckoned you to be a man who wouldn't allow himself to be lightly treated by the fates. There's a fire in those odd-colored eyes, not unlike that which I've seen in the eyes of my beloved and adder-tongued eldest son."

Lifting aside a hanging, which I dared not touch once he had done so, the Khan walked into the sunlight.

"I am angered by the messages you bring me," he said. "The head of Timur Malik would have been a great prize and that a thousand Turkomans should outwit a far larger force of Mongols is galling. I am not accustomed to such defeats," he finished in a soft voice.

A shudder crawled along my spine. For a moment I imagined he was truly a god—a bogodo— with the mystical power to peer inside my skull and learn that I'd released the Iron Lord. I struggled to keep my face expressionless, though my hands trembled at my side. Gradually his face became less severe, and my fright waned as the Khan adopted a more pleasant tone.

"Your elevation to gur-khan pleases me, however. It demonstrates that my first opinion of you was correct."

We had passed between officers of the guard and a silver table of wine and fruit, and now stood on the crest of the hill where the pavilion had been raised. The hill was about a league from the walls of Samarkand. Below on the plain, a spectacle to stir the dullest heart unfolded, bathed in the brilliance of the sunlit day.

In the foreground spread the horde, one hundred thousand strong, sweeping from one end of the plain to the other—a veritable sea of ponies and men interspersed with great numbers of towering siege engines larger than any I had beheld before. These giant machines were hurling gigantic boulders and pots of fire toward the most powerful of all the Shah's cities, Samarkand.

The city itself was lovely, its white spires and minarets contrasting with the grays and blacks of its high wall and twelve massive iron gates. Its ramparts swarmed with defenders.

At the foot of the wall, countless squadrons of Mongols worked to raise and climb great wooden ladders that would reach the parapets. The men above hurled down boulders and vessels of fire. Hundreds dropped from the ladders every moment, while hundreds more fell victim to the arrows which rained down on them. But as one Mongol pitched off a ladder and fell into the writhing mass on the ground, another went clambering up to take his place, blade in hand.

Within the city, several large fires burned, belching black smoke into the heavens. Shouts rose from the siege engines as the Cathayan engineers urged their workers to redouble their efforts. These voices blended into a roar that seemed to shake the very foundations of the world.

While I gazed at this awesome sight, Bela approached. He had been waiting nearby; now, trembling, he took his place at my side. Never before had he stood so close to his Khan. His eyes rolled as though he might faint at any moment.

"My son Tuli has done well in arranging the horde for the siege," the Khan remarked with a gesture at the field below. Then he said to me, "We are evenly matched, Samarkand and I. The city is defended by slightly more than a hundred thousand Turkomans and soldiers of Khorassan. The walls are strong. Twice we've assaulted them—without success. But we will prevail. The strength of a wall is neither more nor less than the bravery of those who defend it, and none in the whole world is braver than the Mongol." Bemused, the Khan shaded his eyes and studied the battlefield. "Ah," he murmured, "Ah! When the scholars ask what is best in life, I can quickly answer them. To crush your enemies, to see them fall defenseless beneath your feet, to take their horses from them and all their goods and treasure, to hear the lamentations of their women—that is best upon the whole earth."

Screams drifted from the walls. The Khan's face drew into cruel lines. I knew he must be thinking about the hundreds of soldiers dropping from the ladders.

"They cannot hold out long," he said with quiet fury. "My will prevents it! The merit of any action lies only in the conclusion. The wall shall be breached before many more suns fall down the sky."

Bela and I exchanged baffled glances. Had he forgotten us? We couldn't withdraw until he gave us leave.

As if sensing our discomfort, the Khan broke out of his reverie and turned to us. Bela found that too much. He moaned and collapsed on the ground, prostrate before his emperor. Impatiently the Khan told him to rise, then summoned one of the officers on guard outside the pavilion.

"See that these gur-khans are rewarded for their efforts with food and wine as well as with two blooded stallions apiece from the stables of Bokhara." A smile touched his lips, lifting the ends of his drooping moustache. "There is method in my gift. Good horses will carry you swiftly back to my son Juchi tomorrow, with new instructions.

The Khan raised his hand to dismiss us, then had another thought. It was directed at me: "Frankish man, I will give you one more boon for good and loyal service. Tar-khan Hargoutai has spoken to me concerning your successes. Spoken angrily. He considers you an upstart, but I see by your face that you know this. I have told him that I can't remove you from the rank bestowed by my son Juchi, though young Tuli, who champions the Falcon, insists I have the power should I wish to exercise it. I do not. Your bravery and loyalty to the standard of the yak tails is commendable. Therefore I am deaf to the pleas of Hargoutai. But since you will remain at Samarkand overnight, I advise you to keep yourself hidden, thereby preventing the Falcon from suffering further abasement of his pride."

Uneasy, I said, "Thank you, Lord. I will heed your advice."

He was pleased. "Retire," he said as he spun around and returned to the pavilion.

I helped poor Bela to his feet; he had nearly swooned at being so close to the imperial presence.

"No glory for us at the walls of Samarkand, brother," I joked as we walked along. "Just a good night's rest—and perhaps a Muhammadan

181

wench for you. Then horseback again. Gods, my butt's weary of that!"

He didn't hear me.

"*I have stood next to the Emperor of the Earth!*"

"Come, brother, he's only a man like us, with two legs and aches and children who vex him."

"He is the sending of the gods!"

I clapped him on the shoulder. "If that's all we're going to discuss today, we're liable to forget his warning to avoid Hargoutai. I choose to heed it. Hargoutai slew my father at the yam station. But I don't think the hour has quite come for me to repay him. So we'll find a likely tent, with meat and a couple of jugs of wine. Then we'll ask about for a captive girl. We'll spend a safe, pleasant night slumbering or tossing—or both."

But that was not to be. Although the morning sun burned and the sky was clear, the tengri were aloft, beating their dark wings to warn me of coming danger. I did not hear.

Shortly past the hour of noon, a roar from the plain drew us from the shadows of the tent in which we had been resting. We rushed to the lip of the hill to learn the meaning of the alarm. Below, we saw two long lines of robed Muhammadans winding through the milling army. Officers on horseback rode along the fringes of this unhappy procession, whose like I had seen at Khojend. All who moved too slowly were whipped.

Soon the captives were dispersed. Groups of several hundred were put to work on siege engines, pulling and winding the great cables. Thinking no more of it, Bela and I retired to our couches, talking of our interview with the Khan, of the prospects for the summer in Kharesmia, of the day's enervating heat, of a dozen things common and familiar to soldiers. As we talked we drank wine. By the time the sun fell, we were thoroughly out of our heads. Thus, when a renewed racket reached our ears from outside, we were slow to react.

Bela turned to listen and fell off his couch, sprawling on the costly Bokhara carpet.

"James?"

I belched. "What?"

"The walls of the tent are bright."

"So they are. It must be noon."

He scratched his head. "I think it was noon several hours ago." He blinked. "Wasn't it?"

"I can't remember."

"James, you have two heads."

I took hold of my jaw. "I do? No, I only feel— where are you going?"

He was crawling on all fours. "Outside. To tell those fools to stop their shouting so a gur-khan can rest peacefully."

Quite dizzy, I rose to follow him. Once outside my head began to clear. The plain of Samarkand was aflame. The bellies of clouds which had closed over the heavens shone scarlet in the glow of countless burning towers. Confusion reigned. Men ran screaming among the tents. A horseman approached, riding furiously. Bela and I blocked his path. Since we were gur-khans and he was but a common soldier, we chose to exercise our rank and haul him bodily out of the saddle. Somewhat incoherently, we demanded to know what was happening.

He wailed miserably. "Please don't delay me, Lords! I must join my squadron and pursue the

Muhammadan dogs. The Khan has given orders that none must escape."

"One word more and you may be gone," I told him, sobering. "Has the city fallen?"

"It has, Lord. The elders opened its twelve gates from within. When they saw the great numbers of their own recruited from the country-side and put to work on the machines, they grew sickened and fearful. The first gate opened an hour ago. The Turkoman warriors who defended the walls are escaping on the city's far side. Half the Khan's army is being sent to slay them. Noble Lords, please don't force me to stand here any longer! The penalty for a man caught wenching while his squadron's going into battle is the worst of all possible deaths."

"Be off! Our thanks and good wishes to you," I said.

With cries of gratitude, the soldier mounted and sped away.

I stood a moment letting the hot evening breeze wash the wine fumes out of my head. I studied the spectacle of torches winking among the orchards surrounding Samarkand—did those lights belong to the pursuers or the pursued?

Abruptly I felt a hand on my sleeve. "Don't move or make noise, James," whispered Bela.

"What is it?"

"Men. Behind us. Coming with great stealth."

"Let's walk slowly to the tent. Our weapons are inside."

Feigning unconcern, even allowing a drunk-sounding laugh to rattle from my lips, I faced about and linked my arm in Bela's. Our tent looked peaceful enough, one or two lamps gleaming through the silk hangings. I was ready to curse Bela for a wine-bibbing dreamer when a flash of silver burned in the passage between our tent and the next.

A massive figure ran out from the shadows.

"Good evening, my Frankish friend," said Hargoutai the Falcon, executing a sardonic bow.

Chapter 10

The Gifts of Hargoutai

"It has taken me a good while to find your hiding place," he went on. "Word of your arrival reached me this morning. Of course I couldn't let you sojourn here without a proper welcome. Without calling on you."

"I can imagine your purpose," I said, aware that I was going to have to fight him to survive.

A stunning smile disarmed and confused me. "Why, no, I don't think you can. I came to present you with gifts befitting your new-found station in life." Above his breastplates of silver Islamic mail, the hideous scar on his neck mocked me like a second smile.

Before I could move or answer, shadows stirred in the passage between the tents. My intention to fall upon him and fight for my life and Bela's was quickly put to rest by a stirring in the passage. Hargoutai stepped forward to provide room for a dozen of his followers who came slipping out of the dark. Each man was armed with an axe, mace, or sword. Behind them I heard the snort of tethered ponies.

Moving with the litheness of an animal circling its prey, Hargoutai lifted a yellow drapery aside, then gestured to the interior of our tent: "Step in, noble gentlemen. Go ahead of me—after all, you are great warriors! You've eluded death in the ranks of the Mangudai and risen to heights of eminence."

Each vicious syllable was an unspoken curse. Yet I couldn't believe he'd dare to slay me outright thus risking disfavor with the Khan and Juchi the Guest. I decided to make no sudden move to provoke him. Instead, I nodded in response to his invitation and started forward.

Bela growled in rage. I laid a hand on his arm and shook my head. He followed me, but not willingly.

Once inside the tent, six of Hargoutai's men took places behind him, and the hangings were let down. Hargoutai picked up an oil lamp and held it high, as though to examine the changes in my face and form since we last met.

"A prouder light does shine from your eyes these days," he said. His voice was calm, that unholy calm I had come to associate with his periods of most intense wrath. "And there's a lift to your shoulders—a cocky stance foreign to you before. Why, yes—you're indeed a gur-khan now."

"Don't mock me too much, Lord Hargoutai," I said. "Though I'm still of lesser rank than you, I'm not the clod whose hand you cut at the yam station." I stared straight into his eyes. "I enjoy the favor of an imperial protector whose position is equal to that of yours."

"So you do, young master," he responded. "But

my protector, Lord Tuli, rides on the plain of Samarkand, while yours is many leagues from here. Thus that factor is cancelled."

Amusement showed on the faces of Hargoutai's men. I felt a stab of terror in my bowels as the tar-khan added, "Protector or not, the months haven't mellowed your tongue." A muscle near the scar on his throat pulsed and beat. He flung the oil lamp down, bursting out, "Frankish offal! Your name and your deeds have mocked me too many times! That is not to be borne."

Little tongues of fire licked along the Bokhara carpet at his feet but were quickly stamped out by one of his soldiers. The Falcon too damped his anger just as quickly; as if the buried fires of hate could be controlled by his will alone. He once more became the Hargoutai I feared the most, a man of frosty calm and measured words.

Taut at my side, Bela noticed this sudden change, too, and smelled the danger of it. I heard the sharp intake of his breathing.

A smile touched Hargoutai's lips. "Abomination though you are, Nine-Fingers, I am not so witless as to attack you here. No, you're much too famous for that. So, as I mentioned, I've come to you with two gifts, which I trust you'll receive with proper thanks and gratitude."

"I see no treasure casks, only weapons, Lord. Let's have an end to clever talk of gifts and rank, and settle our differences like men."

Hargoutai shook his head. His voice dripped contempt again. "A nice attempt, but futile. Don't think you can stay me from the presentation of my gifts by suggesting we brawl like common soldiers. No, we must deal with each other as befits our stations! I must give you the gifts—two of them." He smiled. "The gifts of death and life. You shall receive them in the order named."

"A strange order, Lord. Considering your feelings about me, I would think it would be the other way around."

"I'll give you credit for putting on a brave show," Hargoutai remarked with what I thought might be a veiled glimmering of admiration.

Little good it did me! My own sword rested out of reach across the tent. Still, the game was not played out yet, and I sensed that the gods, mine and Hargoutai's both, hovered near, perhaps to take a hand in the final outcome.

Hargoutai began pacing back and forth in front of me, much as he'd done during our initial encounter at the yam station.

I struggled to keep from showing my fear, and Hargoutai perceived the effort, pointing and saying to his companions, "Look—there's not so much as a flash of feeling on the young Frank's face. Perhaps I can produce one with the first gift."

Bela's breath whistled through his teeth. I sensed rather than saw an increased tension in his great body, matching my own.

"Let me tell you a tale," Hargoutai began in a gentle tone. "A tale about a Nestorian priest who traveled with couriers to Karakorum, bearing news of Juchi's defeat of Muhammad Shah in the western Tian-shan. When subjected to questioning later by certain eunuchs and household persons, this holy man revealed that a Frankish lord with yellow hair had charged the priest to carry a message—a message about the Frank's fate. It was to be delivered by indirect means to a certain concubine dwelling in the yurts at Karakorum. Does the tale interest you thus far, Lord?"

Now that I heard his words, I knew I had defied the unseen Mongol gods once too often. I had been spared from death among the Mangudai so I could face this moment.

"Yes," I whispered. "I beg you to continue, Lord."

"Very well. Now this Nestorian, it seems, was instructed to deliver his message through the mouth of a prudent handmaiden of his own selection. Thus the message would be received as a scrap of public news. The handmaiden carried out her part of it. But there her prudence ended. She described her curious instructions from the priest—described them in detail to another of her number, whom she thought worthy of trust. That trust was misplaced. Those in charge of the household, knowing the nature of a vow sworn by the ultimate receiver of the news, took it upon themselves to question the Nestorian. Question him vigorously, I might add. Thus they discovered the truth. What they learned was communicated to me before the gates of Bokhara. I sent back my own instructions by the next courier. They have been faithfully carried out by this time, I expect. It was necessary—oh, yes, quite necessary. By allowing herself to receive news of her Frankish lover, the concubine who swore the vow broke it. She listened when she should have turned away."

"Tricks!" I screamed, hurling myself forward. Hargoutai's followers dragged me back.

"You're the trickster, I think," he chuckled.

"Liar! You twist the law—and words—to suit yourself. Yes, I sent her news. The crime is mine! Listening to another is not a sign of breaking a—"

"Yes, she *broke* the vow!" Hargoutai cried in

return. "She broke it when she welcomed the word of the lover she swore to forget."

In mounting terror, I exclaimed, "What have you done to her? What punishment have you laid on her because of your hate for me?"

"The penalty for breaking vows," he shrugged. "The death of retribution. The pouring of melted silver into her eyes and ears."

This time my scream was like an animal's. I wrenched myself from the grip of my tormentors and seized Hargoutai's throat to strangle him. The effort was doomed. His men fell on me, tearing my hands free and kicking and pummeling me. I made a desperate lunge for my blade, which was lying behind a couch.

"No marks upon him!" came Hargoutai's shout, which I did not understand. With my hand just a short way from the pommel of my blade and its promise of retribution, I was plucked back by the crew of burly officers and struck time and again before I fell. A black pool seemed to open beneath me.

Through a haze I saw brave Bela fall, beaten and kicked. One final time my hands reached for my dimly glimpsed tormentor. My fingers formed claws. High above, Hargoutai's jeering face with its scar-collar floated like a visage of the evil gods.

Too weak to reach him, I sprawled on the Bokhara carpet. Hargoutai stamped on my hand and laughed.

In the swirling cosmos of my mind, there was no longer light.

Wakening slowly, I was conscious for a time of a swaying motion. I fainted again. When I opened my eyes, I found myself seated on the ground with my arms lashed behind me. I was tied to the trunk of a tree in a dark orchard.

Bela was similarly bound to another tree nearby. The night resounded with the hoofbeats of flying ponies and strange cries in a tongue I recognized all too well. Hargoutai's minions moved like shadows across my field of vision.

"Lord?" one of them called urgently. "We must flee this place. The Muhammadans are all around us. If we're discovered in the midst of them by our own brothers. . . ."

In a moment, Hargoutai appeared with a flaming brand in his fist. Its glare was brilliant compared to the smoldering spires of Samarkand distantly visible through the lacework of trees.

It took only a moment to guess our situation. Hargoutai the Falcon had carried Bela and me around the great city on horseback, straight into the path of the Islamic army which was fleeing pell-mell through the darkness.

Cho Soo lost. My comrade and I delivered into the hands of our sworn enemies. Surely the gods had taken a sweet revenge for my presumptions.

With a savage motion, Hargoutai the Falcon rammed the butt of the torch into the earth. Then he stepped back to admire his handiwork.

"One light in all this dark glade!" he chuckled. "Good for warmth, eh, Nine-Fingers? And useful as a beacon to lead the men of Islam to your side. I hope the Muhammadans will comfort you, but I doubt it. I'll say this much more before I go: It's not that your dreams were too proud or lofty. It's only that you entangled me in their fulfillment. Not the wrong dreams but the wrong enemy— that was your mistake."

"Lord!" cried a frightened voice. *"The Muhammadans!"*

"Bare your swords in case we meet them as we ride out," Hargoutai ordered. He swung up on his pony, lifting one hand in salute.

Never would I forget him, proud and vengeful, his silver mail ablaze with a thousand reflections from the sputtering torch. Around his throat— the scar. In his eyes—triumph.

"You see?" he laughed. "I didn't kill you, Nine-Fingers. I left you with the gift of life!" He galloped his pony away.

The gift of life. . . ." His cry echoed and died. He and his men vanished. Bela and I were left alone, bound face to face, with the torch flaring between us.

We both knew our fate. Not many moments would pass before the torch-glow would bring a curious member of the escaping army in our direction. No words passed between us. We were both too sickened in heart and soul.

The night rang, thundered, hammered as the Muhammadans went riding by like dark ghosts. Then I heard a man cry out, and another. The cry was taken up and repeated. The hammer of hoofs changed pitch. Horsemen were coming toward us—

I struggled against my bonds. They held and would not give.

My vow is worthless, princess of Cathay!

My promises are not gold but dross.

And molten silver has laid your beauty to rest forever . . .

On my cheeks I felt the scald of raging tears.

A voice cried out, "This way! Yonder by the torch. I see a man. No—two—"

BOOK THREE

THE CHAINS OF KISMET

Chapter 1

In Bondage

Over a jade-veined marble floor of the palace of Merik, the royal governor, sounded the leather-slippered feet of a eunuch.

"Come forth, oh Mongols, despised of Allah and lower than street dogs. The esteemed wazir of Nishapur sits beside his most excellent highness, Merik, in the royal hall and would gaze in wonder and astonishment upon two barbarians from the wild steppes."

Thus, six months after our capture by the warriors of Islam, Bela and I were summoned to exhibit ourselves before the highest officials of Merv, the pleasure city of Khorassan, the white-walled, rose-scented Jewel of the Sands.

Hot sunlight fell through latticework, forming delicate patterns on the polished floor of our apartment in the slave quarters of the governor's palace. The sun gilded the bare shoulders of the huge eunuch who had come to fetch us.

He clapped his hands impatiently while we adjusted the voluminous pantaloons which were the only garments allowed us save for our heavy collars of gold alloy. These had been sealed about our necks by fire soon after our arrival in the swarming pleasure-city beside the Murgh Ab—the River of Birds—in the very heart of the empire of our enemies.

The not unkindly eunuch, Rashid, smiled when I finally said we were ready to accompany him.

Rashid, who was about ten years older than I, wasn't a bad sort. Of Arabic stock, he said he came from a village near the sacred city of Mecca.

An attendant produced gilded chains, which he hooked to rings on our collars. The eunuch gathered the end of each chain into one of his pudgy hands, and with our chains jingling, we set off down the corridor toward the hall of the governor.

The procession had become an almost daily occurrence during the past weeks. Bela and I were more highly regarded at Merik's court than the tigers and wild elephants the governor kept in his menagerie.

But Bela didn't care for the chains. "Must we constantly be bound by these clattering chains?" he complained. "The collar is bad enough! It dishonors a man who once roamed the Gobi as freely as the hawk flies."

"But the wings of the hawks were clipped in an orchard at Samarkand," Rashid joked. "Be thankful for your blessings! Weren't your lives spared when it was decided that you be the first minions of the accursed Genghis ever exhibited for the pleasure of the nobility of the Shah's empire?"

With the windy rhetoric that I had come to find typical of the sons of Islam, Rashid continued to enumerate the various highlights of our debatable good fortune.

"Weren't you transported here without a mark being made upon your flesh? Given the finest quarters of all the slaves of his highness, as well as good food and your choice of slave girls? In return for such mercy, you suffered only to the extent of having the golden collar put about your throats, and being required to promise you would never seek escape so long as the collars remained in place. In truth, Allah has favored you! Allah has smiled on you! Redeemed you from the dead! For this you should thank him whose spirit still lives within the black rock beneath the velvet curtain in holy Mecca. Yet your protests are endless! When will you show gratitude for your fine apartments? Your schooling in the tongue of my fathers? Your free run of the house of the governor?"

"Never, old Rashid," I said with a weary sigh. "Cut the hawk's wing and leave him helpless on the ground and he'll sicken and die."

Rashid sniffed disdainfully. "You appear to be sound enough—except for your battle scars, of course."

"A man doesn't always show his worst scars on the outside."

The eunuch sighed. "Ah yes, you're thinking of the Cathayan girl again. You told me about her the night you and I drank the wine of Shiraz."

"She's dead, Rashid. I don't want to talk about her. That I did so on the night in question was the fault of the wine."

"Still," Rashid argued as we reached a turn in the cool corridor, within earshot of flutes and muted drums, "it's plain you think of her a great deal. Frankly, that's a wretched waste. There are many among the slaves of Merik who are fair to look upon. Chief among them is the Circassian girl I've mentioned before. You know she's expressed interest in you. Since she has hair and eyes much like yours, I can't understand why you won't avail yourself of the delights of her flesh. Your beloved has passed through the veil of the immortals. You owe her no more debt."

"Wrong, I owe her a great debt. It'll be paid when I kill her murderer."

"But that you can never do while you wear the gold collar. Ah, well, I'm almost convinced it's futile to argue with you."

I nodded. "It is, I—"

"Hush," he said. "We're approaching the hall. Jingle your chains for me like a good fellow. Give me a struggle. Gnash your teeth together and roll your eyes. After all, a barbarian holds no fascination if he speaks in the measured tones of a scholar."

I sighed and said I would try to give a good show. Bela muttered in disgust.

Accompanied by the piping of a flute, we entered the hall of the governor, clashing our chains as Rashid had asked and capering from foot to foot while uttering growls at the assembled company.

Arrayed on the divans in jeweled robes was a group of ambassadors from Nishapur, together with their grizzled wazir, who was seated cross-legged beside the portly, teak-faced Merik. The governor wore satin and a headdress decorated with jewels and plumes.

Bela had little heart for the performance, but I put my best into it. Doing so fulfilled the bargain

I had made one night in the camp of a Muhammadan officer not far from the orchard at Samarkand.

At the time the bargain was struck, I was in despair. But the tug of life proved stronger than that of death. Alive I still had hope, albeit a small one, of one day slaying my betrayer. So I promised the officer good behavior and accepted the gold collar which was eventually clamped about my neck. The officer transported us to the city of Merv on camel-back. Bela and I thus became the only two creatures in Merik's menagerie who roamed about on two legs.

Once our brief show for the governor's guests drew to a close, an officer of Merik's guards leaped forward and laid a whip across my back, ostensibly to subdue my hostile tendencies. I collapsed on the marble, whimpering. Bela accepted the lash with less grace, snarling in genuine anger. But soon he too was whipped to his knees.

The visitors shivered and buzzed in astonishment. The wazir expressed his wonder: "Indeed they have a barbaric look and manner," he said, popping a juicy purple grape into his mouth and dabbing his lips with a snowy napkin. "The larger appears to be a true Mongol. The other, though, is a truly puzzling specimen. He growls and grovels like a Mongol, yet he somewhat resembles the pale Franks who have plagued the borders of our empire for years."

"His origins are unknown to me," answered Merik. "On the other hand, he was taken into captivity at Samarkand. There is no doubt that he came from the horde."

"Can't you question him?" the wazir asked. "Won't he tell you about himself?"

"Not a word," replied Merik with that perfect

Muhammadan guile which had no doubt helped him rise to the governorship of a great city. "The brutes are unable to learn our language. They do nothing but sulk about all day, rattling their chains and gnawing on wild ass meat, which they prefer above all else."

"Most curious," was the wazir's final opinion. "Pray Allah such terrible creatures never threaten the walls of my beloved Nishapur."

"They may," Merik advised dolefully. "The warrior Genghis has a madness that drives him to do battle, no matter what the cost in soldiers lost or maimed. I'm of the opinion that he is indeed what the shamans tell us—a supernatural visitation sent by Allah as punishment for our sins."

"Frightful!" cried the wazir, raising his hands to show his dismay. "Not since the days of the courts of Jamshid and the throne of Mahmoud of Ghazna has Islam stood at such a peak of power. It's a cruel kismet that we should now be menaced by a horde of creatures little better than animals!"

"But we are," the governor told him. "My own soldiers are on constant alert against an attack."

"Surely in the Holy Book there must be a prophecy to solve this dilemma."

"If there is, the sayyids can't find it," Merik said unhappily.

At this point in the conversation, I received a nudge in the ribs from Rashid. I uttered another growl of rage, slinking forward a step toward the trestles bearing every conceivable kind of food and drink: whole sucklings, fruit, vessels of wine almost beyond counting.

Merik clapped his hands, signaled to Rashid, and explained to his visitors, "The brutes grow hungry for their ration of ass meat. They must be fed promptly lest they tear at their own flesh."

The wazir shuddered. "Terrible. *Terrible!*"

This last indignity heaped on us, we were led from the lofty marble chamber where sunlight fell through lovely walls of latticework. We were herded back along the corridor through which we had come.

At a safe distance from the hall, Rashid took off the chains and complimented us. "Surely if ever a pair of actors deserved a reward for a good performance, you do." He chuckled. "Didn't you notice the delight in the eyes of His Excellency when you made the lunge toward the food? Oh yes, he was pleased—particularly with you, James. You're entitled to a reward! Let me send an houri to your side. Perhaps the Circassian girl. She inquired about you again just this morning."

"You nag worse than an old crone," I said as we entered the apartments. "I don't want a woman."

"I don't believe it," the eunuch said with bland certainty. "No man can live long without food and wine in his belly—or the caress of a maid to relieve the burdens of the day. I should know, since I can feel no such desire and can therefore objectively assess a normal man who denies the basic needs of his flesh."

"Well, I don't have any reservations like my friend here," Bela said, flinging himself down on a divan and running a finger around the inside of his collar. "Send me that dusky little one."

"Ayesha?"

"Is that her name?"

"If you mean the dark girl with the breasts like small melons, it is."

203

"Send her!"

Rashid bowed, smiling. "It shall be done before the moon rests tonight. What answer do I give the Circassian girl about you?"

I took a flagon of sweet wine from a table. Swallowing a draught, I snapped, "Rashid, why do I constantly find myself the object of your concern?"

"Because Allah gave me a sentimental nature when he took my manhood! I meant no harm."

"No, of course you didn't. I simply find it astonishing that a slave girl whom I never set eyes on until a month or two ago should be panting after me like a heated bitch."

"It's not so difficult to understand, James. Like you, the Circassian girl finds herself a stranger in Merv. Like you, she is a different breed, a curiosity to be exhibited—and sampled—by the governor and his guests. She wears no ring about her throat, but she is still a captive and far from her homeland. In you she's seen a man whose flesh is like her own. Isn't it natural that she'd seek your company? And yet you shut yourself away, lying on your couch night after night, staring at the stars and cursing your kismets. I tell you as a friend, such bitterness poisons a man. Destroys him! You're not a barbarian, as you must pretend to be in front of Merik. You're a man. Men— whole men—must have women, or they become as crippled in the mind as I am crippled in—well, you get my meaning."

I nodded. He spoke a truth I had tried to hide from myself far too long. "Send her, then," I said. "When the moon's up."

"You will help yourself by your decision, James," the eunuch said.

"I'll help myself to get rid of your incessant fretting about my welfare, anyway."

"Gods!" cried Bela. "Such learned disputations over a simple matter like taking a wench!"

"Simple?" Rashid returned. "Why, love is the most mysterious phenomenon in Allah's universe! Not to be undertaken lightly."

Pleased at the outcome, he smiled and left.

Chapter 2

Lilith

For almost an hour after the sun went boiling down behind clouds of scarlet and saffron in the west, I stood staring out across the perfumed rose garden of Merik's palace. The wail of the muezzins crying prayers from minarets died away. One after another, tiny white stars began to glow in the darkening blue heavens. Many a night I had stood in the same way, swearing in silence that I would never break faith with my dead beloved, and calling on those god-eyes in the sky to witness my declaration.

Yet tonight I was tempted to forget those promises. Rashid knew my state better than I knew it myself. When I heard stealthy sounds from Bela's chamber, followed by giggling, it was as if the heat of the day returned to my body. The sweet odor of a thousand roses began to work on my senses.

Was Rashid right? Had I wrapped myself too

long in the winding sheets of my own misery? I still lived. Blood still coursed in my body.

With a guilty feeling, I soon found myself awaiting the rising of the moon. When its white face showed at last over the shadowed garden, my heart was thumping in my chest for the first time in many a night.

The moon climbed higher. No one came. I began to doubt my own sanity—or, more accurately, Rashid's sincerity. The Circassian girl wanted no part of me. Or the eunuch had been pretending.

Still, wasn't that a lusty slap from Bela's apartment, as though a hand had been laid on shapely buttocks in the play of love? There were squeals of pleasure, muffled moans that quickened in frequency, then silence.

Confused and bitter, I returned to my couch and at last managed to doze a bit. I woke with a start. Someone was in the room! I groped along the couch for a weapon that did not exist.

Suddenly a girl whispered, "Don't be alarmed, master. It's only me—the slave you bid come to you. I've brought a jar of wine."

I relaxed, but just a little. I no longer even knew how to talk to a woman. Awkwardly I said, "Come sit near me." I touched the couch and moved to make room.

Her answer drifted through the perfumed dark in tones I found incredibly sweet. "No, master. Rashid has told me of the state of your heart. He has told me how you loved a princess of a land far to the east, and how she was taken away from you. I only came to talk, not tempt you to forget a true love."

Small white hands seemed to float in the moonlight which flooded through the lattices. Those

207

hands pressed a small jar into mine. Then she added, "I'll sit at your feet. It's close enough for speech, but not too close."

So saying, she stepped out of the darkness. I caught my breath in astonishment. She was indeed fair to look upon.

She paused for a moment in the place where the moon's rays made a pattern on the marble floor. She was taller than the maids of Islam, with a wild look about her. Slimly built, she had certainly not passed her twentieth year. But the ripe breasts of a woman were clearly in evidence beneath her moon-silvered veils. High cheekbones gave a slight harshness to an otherwise well-proportioned oval face. Her mouth was generous. And never in my life had I seen eyes of such startling blue. Not the blue of sunlit ice, but the warm blue of the smoke of a summer campfire on the Gobi. As Rashid had often said, her hair was nearly as fair as my own.

Overwhelmed by the picture she made, I gestured clumsily to the carpet beside my couch. She sat down gracefully. Tilting the jar to my mouth, I took a drink. A part of me long dead came to life for a moment. It too told me I remained a man.

When I passed her the jar, she declined it, saying she had taken wine with her evening meal. Though her polite tone befitted a slave girl, a certain huskiness in her voice hinted at hidden warmth.

"Tell me your name," I said after a second drink.

"Lilith, master."

"And you're Circassian?"

"Yes. My parents were slain when I was in my twelfth year. Their murderers were Muhammadan slavers. They carried the girls of our village to market in Baghdad. There Merik's head eunuch chose me for this household."

"Have you found life in the harem difficult? From your looks, it would seem that you haven't been ill-treated. In fact the sun of Khorassan seems to have enhanced your beauty."

Though my compliment was awkwardly said, she smiled. "You are kind, master. And it's true Merik is benevolent. He doesn't treat his concubines unkindly. He sees to it that they're bathed daily, well rested, clothed in fine apparel, and given food for the mind as well as for the belly. I have learned to make rhymes, and even to draw a little. Still—" A gentle sigh escaped her mouth. I felt its warm touch on my cheek and was roused again. "—still, no chains are as strong as the chains that bind the heart. My own heart is bound to the earth where I was born and lived free for twelve years. Since first I attained the age of which I could properly fulfill the duties of a harem girl, I have longed for the—" A pause. "—for the sight of a person of my race."

"Circassian blood doesn't run in my veins, Lilith. I was born in the country of the Franks. I don't know exactly where, though someday, if my neck's ever free of this cursed collar, I intend to make my way westward and live among my own people. Perhaps before I die. That's the one dream left to me now."

She said lightly, "Still, you and I are closer in kind than each of us is to the people of Merv. That's a kind of bond between us, whether we wish it or not."

"Why, yes, you're right," I answered, amused at her artful ways. "Wouldn't you like some wine?"

"Yes, I believe so. My throat has grown dry. The night seems warm."

While she tilted the jar, I studied the pale column of her throat and the soft thrusting of her breasts. I found myself wanting to touch her.

As she returned the jar with murmured thanks, her fingers brushed against mine. The contact sent a pulse along my nerves. Guilty thoughts of my Cathayan princess struck me again.

For a while I kept silent, struggling with my conscience and, at the last, losing. The spell of the moon-flooded evening and the sense of warm flesh near mine brewed a potion I could not refuse.

Somewhere a flute began to pick out a tune, melancholy and sad. Lilith laid her hand across mine. "Master, have I offended you in any way? If so, tell me so I can go away and return another time."

"No, Lilith, I'm not offended in the least. In fact, your presence has brought the first real happiness I've had since I came to Merv. I'm sorry I was silent so long. There's a reason for it."

"The woman you once loved?" she asked softly.

I had to be truthful with her. "Still love, Lilith."

"Tell me about her."

"What? No woman wants to hear about another."

"No, that's right. But from what Rashid said, her story is part of the story of how you came into captivity. That, I want to hear, master— even though some of it's bound to make me jealous," she added in a teasing way.

I laughed, my dark thoughts disappearing. She squeezed my hand. "Tell me now. I'm good at listening—that brings me favor in Merik's eyes.

He's bored by the others chattering and vying to amuse him. So let me share your past. Secret grief once spoken is no longer so painful."

What she said was true. But somehow the prospect of sharing the story still seemed a betrayal. I was silent again until she spoke one more word.

"James?"

It was startling to hear my own name pronounced with such tenderness. At first I was surprised. Then I realized that of course Rashid would have told her the name. Hearing it, I felt something break inside me, and I spoke.

I told her almost the whole story, ending with an account of my betrayal and capture. As she had promised, the telling seemed to lift a burden, as though I had been freed from one of the wooden kangs of the Gobi. By and large, the story had been a grim one, so I tried to soften it at the end.

"And now you have a perfect right to leave, because I've committed two unforgivable sins. On a beautiful night, I've spoken of ugly things. And even worse, I've said a good deal about another woman."

The moon had gone dark; the distant flute as well. I couldn't see her face as she answered, "Why, James, I'd think it odd indeed if a man of your years and strength hadn't loved someone else. Besides—"

A rustling of her garments; she was kneeling before me, her palms resting on her thighs. "— only those with narrow hearts have room for just a single love. Love takes many forms, you know. There's the love you have for a fight well won. The love you bear for your friend Bela. Perhaps your heart's open to another kind as well."

"What kind, Lilith?"

"The freely given affection of a woman who could never take the place of your best beloved, but who would care for you, comfort you, if—" Her voice grew hoarse, as though she were embarrassed, but something—the wine, the darkness, or hunger of the same kind I felt—made her finish. "If you only asked."

"It would be unfair to ask that of any woman."

"No," she said firmly. "She would rejoice in the greatness of her man's heart. Rejoice that he found room for her beside another when she was lonely, when she wanted—"

Suddenly, with a little cry, she broke off the speech and rose up on her knees, her body between my legs and her mouth pressed to mine.

The guilt flooded into a terrible crest—and fell back as I tasted of the tongue that came slipping between her open lips and mine. She thrust herself deeper into the cleft of my legs, uttering a little cry of delight at what she felt.

Still awkward with her, I reached for her breast, fondling the veils and feeling the tip of one breast growing hard beneath the fabric.

Yet I couldn't continue without being fully honest with her. So I broke the embrace and cupped her chin in both hands. "Lilith, listen carefully. I understand what you've said, and I value the gift you're willing to give. But I can't take it unless you understand—"

"That you don't love me the way you love her?" She kissed me again, her wine-scented lips gentler this time. "I do understand. I don't ask that you love me more than you love her. We're both far from our homelands. We're both captives. The nights are too long and too lonely for me, James—and who can say how long we'll be in Merv together? Perhaps years! There's ample time for love to come. I ask only that you give it a chance."

"I will," I whispered. "The gift is accepted. Come up beside me."

I gathered her in my arms, kissing and caressing her as she stretched beside me on the couch, the veils tumbling aside so I might touch my lips to the sweet, hard flesh of her breasts.

We laughed at each other's clumsiness, for we were eager all at once; it seemed an age until we were free of our garments and touching, while the heat of an unseen sun poured between us, melting us, joining us—

There was a wildness in her, as I'd guessed. It showed in the rake of her hands on my back when I took her, and the quickening rise and fall of her loins when I plunged deeper. Her kisses drove out loneliness and defeat; for a few ecstatic moments when we could not get enough of one another, I even forgot the collar on my neck.

Finally, with a happy gasp, she rolled from beneath me and we lay side by side upon the couch, her hair a soft fan on my bare shoulder.

That night I learned a great deal about Circassian girls—or one, anyway. She had the strength and appetite of the young, and it wasn't long before she stirred me again.

At last, pearl gray light began to brighten the latticework. Birds set up a chirping in the rose garden, and Lilith and I fell asleep together.

She had given me a greater gift than she knew.

She had brought the miracles of happiness and even hope back into the bleakness of my existence.

Chapter 3

· The Face from the Past

In the months that followed, my soul leaped up toward the sun in a manner foreign to it in times past. The performances at which I was expected to snarl and caper became almost enjoyable. On occasion, Merik summoned his favorite harem slaves to sit among his guests during a feast, and thus I had opportunity to gaze on the Circassian girl for one more hour.

At such times, I liked to posture and cavort more fiercely than usual. Even Bela joined in the spirit of things, lurching his chains right and left with a horrendous clatter and requiring three or four cuts of the whip before he would pretend to give up. All the while, my eyes would dart to Lilith's, and we would share secret mirth. Now and then my outrageous leers and grunts proved too much for her, and she would have to avert her head and use her hands to muffle outright laughter.

The good eunuch Rashid was happy to arrange frequent meetings in my apartment during the evening hours. He superintended the whole affair with considerable relish, since he noted a marked improvement in my attitude as a result of my liaison with Lilith.

I found her a companion of untold delights; not only of the flesh, but of the intellect. She was bright, and full of the wit so pleasing to the Muhammadan mind.

One day, however, Rashid darkened our horizon.

"Word of your affection for her has reached Merik's ears."

I frowned in alarm. "Does that mean punishment for her? If so, take me to the governor. I'll ask him to punish me instead."

"Bless me if those aren't the words of a man whose head buzzes with love!" he exclaimed, smiling in a way I found ill-suited to the delivery of bad news.

"You're right," I admitted. "I think I am falling in love with her. At least a little. But I want an explanation of that smile of yours. You've just said Merik knows about Lilith and me. That ought to rouse him to anger."

"On the contrary!" Rashid declared like a cat pouncing. "It delights him. Especially since a wise member of his household pointed out that your demonstrations have become much more lively as a result. Besides, Merik has nearly as many wives and virgins at his call as there are grains of sand in Khorassan."

"This wise member of the household you referred to—would his name be Rashid?"

He laughed. "It would. I told you once that my

head was stuffed with romantic notions. You doubted me."

"Never again! May Allah forgive my foolishness. I wish that I could give you baksheesh."

"No reward necessary," he said. "It's enough to see my little intrigues bear fruit. There's another reason why Merik is unconcerned. The Mongols are loose in the north again."

"I didn't know that, Rashid."

"Haven't you noticed the change in the court?"

I admitted I had. There had been restlessness among the nobles lately, and frequently a scowl on Merik's face.

"I have even heard," Rashid continued, "that the fears of the worthy wazir of Nishapur have been realized—that your brothers of the Gobi have devastated his city. Further, the warrior Alaeddin is dead."

Bela, who had just entered from his own apartment, gasped in amazement. "Muhammad Shah is dead?"

"Aye. Word came to Merv at nightfall yesterday. Once the walls of Samarkand had been breached, the mighty Muhammad fled like a frightened calf before a Mongol warrior called the Arrow Prince. This Arrow Prince was ordered by the Khan to pursue our holy leader to the ends of the earth if required. But he didn't have to go that far," Rashid added with a trace of sadness. "Merely to a fishing village on the shores of the Caspian. The Shah set sail for an island. The Mongols, it is said, tried to follow him into the water, shrieking and howling for revenge. Many horses and men on both sides perished. The Shah had only three followers with him when he was killed. His jewels, his armored elephants, and his household troops were all gone.

While pursuing Muhammad, the Mongols razed Balkh and Nishapur. Now the army that dispatched him has turned northward into the country of the Circassians and the Kurds. Surely the Khan intends for them to ride to the end of the world. They'll probably plunge their mounts off the edge in order to conquer the nether regions!"

Bela's eyes shone with fierce pleasure. "Perhaps one day the Khan will knock at the gates of Merv."

He couldn't anger the eunuch. "I think it likely," he said sadly. "I know you'd like your brethren to liberate you. But I tremble at what might befall our beautiful city. The thought has also crossed the mind of the governor. Haven't you heard the clatter of the garrisons drilling? The governor is too worried about the Khan to be jealous of you, James. Nothing else will matter if the horde marches this way."

Later, Bela and I speculated about the possibility Rashid had raised. It so excited us, we lurched about our quarters shouting and hugging one another. That night, when Rashid again arranged for Lilith to come to me, I put off her kisses—which piqued her not a little—and told her the news of Genghis Kha Khan, some of which she'd heard.

"The whole of Merv mourns the passing of the Shah, right enough. They say his son Jelal ed-Din is somewhere in the northern wastelands beyond Lake Aral gathering an army. The main part of the Mongol horde withdrew to the cooler ranges above the Amu, to hunt during the winter. But now the outriders and advance parties are moving again. Two sons of the Khan, one named the Guest, the other—"

"That is Lord Juchi, the Khan's eldest and my protector," I interrupted. "I spoke of him."

She nodded. "Together the Khan's sons destroyed Urgench which was a great shock for the inhabitants of Merv. Urgench is considered the natal city of all the people of Kharesmia. They say the siege was long and terrible. Jelal ed-Din barely escaped with his life. No lady in the harem speaks of anything but the possibility of being ravished by the barbarians now—they expect the Khan to invade Khorassan in the spring. However, I've told them barbarian caresses were just like Merik's—" Her eyes twinkled. "—only they last longer and give much more pleasure."

I laughed, then said, "You've brought more news than gossipy old Rashid."

"In the harem we hear a great deal." Her eyes grew somber. "No one else but your friends would repeat it to you, since the Mongols are your brothers. They—" There was a catch in her throat."—they could free you to return to the land of your birth. Free you to seek revenge against the slayer of your father and your best-beloved."

"I've thought of that," I said, instantly regretting the words. Her blue eyes were sorrowful. I clasped her hands in mine. "We must make plans."

"*We*, James?"

"Yes. Since Rashid spoke to me this morning, I've thought of nothing else. Perhaps I can never escape from Merv, nor Bela, nor you. Perhaps Merik himself will have Bela and me slain if the horde comes to the gates. On the other hand, that won't prevent me from preparing myself as best I can. I—I have something to ask you, Lilith."

Apprehensive, she said, "Go on."

"Lately I've come to think I've shed enough blood to last a lifetime. In a choice between a black road of hatred and a bright one of hope, the wise man will choose the latter. What lies westward in Frankistan, I don't know. I don't even know whether I can reach it. But if I'm freed, I'll return to the Mongols no more. I'll ride toward the land of my own people. Bela will go with me, I think—a valuable second sword-arm on what will surely be a long and dangerous journey. I would ask you—will you go with me to Frankistan, too?"

Her glad cry told me the answer. I kissed her fervently.

The days began to fly at a rapid pace. Each sunrise produced new rumors and alarms, brought in secret by Lilith or the eunuch.

Like a ponderous beast, the army of Khan was stirring in the Amu highlands. In the bitter north, Chepe Noyon the Arrow Prince had devastated the salt steppes above the Caspian, hurling back armies of wild Kipchaks and Alans, and advancing through Laksander's Iron Gate to defeat the almost legendary lords of the Georgias.

Then came more grim tidings. Chepe Noyon had been slain in battle. But his army was being drawn back eastward under Subotai Bahadur the Valiant, to rendezvous with the forces of the Kha Khan which were rolling southwestward from the Amu under the banner of young Tuli. The movement surely signified an invasion of Khorassan—and a threat to Merv. In that case I had less time than ever to think about gaining my freedom.

How it was to be accomplished had baffled me until the night on which Bela and I were summoned before Merik to perform for the officers of the city's garrison. Merik hoped to brighten their spirits, which were sagging with each new bit of information about the Khan's advance.

There was little enough to distinguish the exhibition from any other until close to the end. I was on my knees, taking the captain's lash across my back, when one watcher's face seemed to leap out at me. I was sure I recognized him. Although Rashid led us swiftly from the hall and I had seen the face only for an instant, I knew it to be that of Hamid, companion to Timur Malik.

Scarcely an hour afterward, while the military feast continued in the great hall, Hamid presented himself in my quarters. He wore an officer's garb and was as stern looking as he had been in the willow valley where he and Timur Malik had escaped death.

I salaamed properly, then said, "Greetings, warrior of Islam! I thought perhaps your face was a hashish-vision when I saw it in the hall. But now you stand before me. Be so good as to grace my humble couch while we talk a while."

"I can't spare more than a moment," he answered, remaining on his feet. "My commander is drunk, and I'm charged with seeing that he returns safely to quarters when the feast ends." Briefly, the harsh planes of his face were softened by a half-smile. "You talk of hashish-dreams. I thought I'd chewed it when I saw you grunting and slavering before Merik's guests. Could this be the same Mongol soldier who gave me back my life beside the Syr? Yes, I said to myself, the same yellow locks and only nine fingers. I compliment you on your skill at acting like an illiterate brute, though I confess your rigmarole wasn't completely convincing. Some in the

220

audience have encountered Mongols in battle. They may be crude, but they're not animals. Your clever performance leads me to think the blood of a good, conniving Mussulman runs in your veins."

"No," I said, "I've just studied the ways of my captors."

At that he laughed aloud. "How Timur Malik would have enjoyed seeing you caper—you, the Samaritan who spared us!"

"Is the Iron Lord in Merv? I didn't see him among the guests."

"Search for him among the dead instead," Hamid replied, his smile gone. "He fell before the onslaught of the Mongol squadrons at Urgench. When Jelal ed-Din fled into the wilderness with his retinue, those officers who had managed to stay alive dispersed with small groups to strengthen the defenses of the cities of Khorassan. I was sent here with one such contingent."

"You think the Khan will strike, then?"

Hamid nodded solemnly. "But I came to talk of your future, not his. My conscience reminds me that I must repay your boon in kind or suffer eternal torment."

All at once my stomach tightened, and my pulse beat hard. How steadfast was Hamid's feeling about owing me repayment? I decided to find out.

"Honorable Hamid, there is but a single boon that could satisfy my heart. I want to return to the land of the Franks and seek the people of my birth. But I can't do it while this collar stays on my neck. Throughout Islam, it marks me as a slave. I could never travel safely."

He shook his head. "I don't have the authority to set you free, nor the influence to persuade the royal governor to do it. Name another boon, Nine-Fingers—one within my power to grant."

"This one *is* within your power to grant, Lord Hamid. Beyond the walls of Merv, none would know that I am a slave—*except for this collar*. Suppose the Khan knocks at the gates in a few weeks. The city and the palace will be in confusion. I am not asking you to set me free *legally*, you see—" I left it there, watching his face.

He frowned. "I am told you promised Merik you would never flee."

"Not while the collar is on. Removing it removes the vow also. Take the ring from my neck—and the one from the neck of my comrade, Bela—and the debt's cancelled." I paused a moment. "That is the *only* way it can be cancelled."

He didn't like it, but he bent to it. "Very well. It shall be done. When you judge the hour to be right, send a message to me in the quarter of the Prophets. If I can't come myself, I'll send a trusted man in my stead." He clasped my arm. "You have colossal nerve, Nine-Fingers. But it's admirable, too. Would that Allah had willed you for my brother in arms."

"Your kismet would gladly be mine," I responded politely, trying to conceal my jubilation. "Then, by emulating your example, I would truly heap honor upon myself."

"Allah be with you," he repeated, bowing formally. "Allah accompany you both day and night."

So saying, he left the chamber.

With a whoop, I ran to rouse Bela from the pallet in his apartment.

"Waken, brother! A visitor has come to us tonight bearing the key to open the hawk's cage. Pray for all you're worth."

"Pray?" he mumbled. "Pray what?"

Laughter came easily then. "This prayer: Oh mighty Khan, anger of the Heavens, send your horde against Merv, the Jewel of the Sands! Send it soon, so my brother and I can ride to Frankistan!"

Chapter 4

The Shadow of the Khan

Bela was exceedingly cross because I'd disturbed him. "I take it you're trying to tell me some bit of luck has befallen us?"

"Marvelous luck!"

"Can't you convey the news quietly?"

"The news that you're going to be free? No! Of course it's not entirely luck. We had a hand in it long ago. The wheel always comes around, they say—"

"In the name of the gods, James, what are you prattling about?"

I hooked a finger in his collar. "This. Before long you may not be wearing it."

At last he was pleased. "You mean no more disgraceful performances, rattling those gilded chains?"

"Not if our luck holds."

"Well, I imagine that's worth being wakened for. Nothing would make me happier. I wasn't

224

born to sleep in buildings raised by man, no matter how beautiful they may be. I prefer the blanket of heaven."

"And you'll sleep beneath it again, and soon! Remember how I told you I saw Hamid among Merik's guests this evening? While you slept, he came to me . . ."

Quickly I described the meeting. Bela's eyes lit with an enthusiasm matching mine, and he lost all desire for more slumber. We drank wine until the sun rose, making such a racket that Rashid came to see whether we had lost our wits.

As it turned out, our prayers of entreaty to the Khan were hardly needed. The court of Merik became more and more disorganized. The feasts at which we performed grew less frequent and finally ceased altogether. A feeling of doom descended upon the household and the city.

One hundred thousand of the horde, led by Tuli, Master of War, were marching forth from Balkh. Merv's streets swarmed day and night with soldiers and anxious citizenry. We could not see them from our apartment, but we could hear them every waking moment.

In the palace, eunuchs and slaves scampered frantically about stripping tapestries from the walls, swooping up golden goblets and silver urns, and carting His Excellency's treasures away into hiding.

But suddenly the frantic preparations came to an end one night when the whole sky seemed suffused with a ruddy glow. Screams, howls, the crash of boulders against masonry, and a roar from a hundred thousand throats told us the horde had arrived outside the walls. The shadow of the Khan lay across Merv now. The household settled down to a dreadful period of waiting.

On the eighth day of siege, Rashid came to us with the news that he was being sent to the walls, and that it might be our fate to join him there eventually. He brought Lilith with him, deeming it prudent for her to stay with us since the harem was in a state of panic. We bade him a sad farewell, for in his foolishly romantic way, he had bestowed many a kindness upon us. I would not soon forget the stately salaam he gave us just before he departed. He did not owe it to us; we were slaves.

As he turned to leave, he added a final word. "Your message to the quarter of the Prophet will be delivered by an esteemed distant cousin of mine. The lad's only nine, but he's brave and dependable."

With that he turned, gazed sadly about the airy apartment he knew so well, then withdrew, passing out of my life forever, doubtless to be slain on the parapets.

He was a good friend.

The siege continued for fourteen more days and nights. It raged in a distant clangor whose fury we could only imagine. Lilith stood beside me for hours on end as we watched dust and fire rising from the walls. I tried to comfort her, because she'd convinced herself we would all be slain.

She might be right, I admitted to myself. No one came from the quarter of the Prophets to remove our collars.

Food was seldom brought to us any more, and when it was, it was poor fare. Merik's house lay silent, entombed. We were seemingly forgotten in its vast maze of passages. Would the walls never crumble? Would no one ever arrive to fulfill Hamid's vow? Bleakly, we watched the little rose garden below our windows, our only view of the outer world apart from the constantly shimmering dust clouds in the heavens.

Then on the twenty-second night of the Mongol fury, a sound we had not heard in many days came from the streets; pony hoofs clattering. We heard women scream. A man's voice shouted in a tongue I knew all too well.

Bela leaped to his feet, shaking the latticework. "The gates are open! Our brethren are in the streets!"

"Woe is our lot—and may Allah have mercy on us!" rumbled a new voice, whirling us around.

Lilith uttered a cry of alarm. But I saw we had nothing to fear. The burly Muhammadan who stood there carried the tempered rasps, chisels, and mallets of a smith.

"My name is Ali Zoar and my trade is iron-working," he said, wiping sweat from his face with the hem of his robe. "Your message reached me many days ago, but I was taken to the wall to defend it."

"Why have you come back?" Bela wanted to know.

"Because the wall has been abandoned. We were evacuated the instant the gates were opened. I'd rather be on my way out of Merv, but I swore a vow to the officer Hamid to complete a task he wanted done—a criminal task. Well, no one will pay much attention now that we're invaded, so let's get it done."

Nervously, he studied the furnishings and finally pointed to a low marble bench. "There. You first, Frankish man. Kneel down with your head turned sideways, your cheek on the marble. And prepare yourself for pain. I have no time to remove your collar delicately. Already the Mongols

227

have begun evacuating the city, driving the people out onto the plain at the point of a lance. On your knees and hurry about it!"

I knelt and laid my head on the bench. Swiftly the Muhammadan applied the rasp to my collar. Because of the angle which he was forced to work, my skin was soon gouged and bleeding.

Ali Zoar complained constantly, damning Merik for cooperating with the Mongols in order to gain promised mercy for the people of Merv. "I doubt there'll be any mercy. Most likely we'll get death instead. The commander of the Mongols is a cruel beast who imprisoned six hundred of the richest citizens when they went to him in good faith. Brace yourself, Frankish man! This blow will tell the tale."

He grunted with effort. Down came a mallet on the butt of a chisel—hard. The blow blurred my mind for a moment, but all at once I heard a wondrous clanging sound.

When I tottered up so Bela could take my place, I saw on the floor my bloodslimed golden collar, broken forever.

As Ali Zoar labored to free Bela, I questioned him. "Did Merik willingly surrender the city to Tuli's forces?"

"What else could he do?" the big man growled. "The alternative was slaughter. He sent out an imam with silver vessels and jewel-decked robes. The fellow returned with assurances of the governor's safety—and promises that the people would be treated mercifully. You know how much faith I have in *that* statement. By Allah this metal's stubborn! Merik's already had a hint that your brave brothers have deceived him. He went out to sit beside Tuli at a feast in his tent. Merik wrote down the names of the six hundred I mentioned. A Mongol officer at the gates asked for them. They came forth to Tuli's tents in good faith, but they had no sooner sat down to parley than they were set upon. Now I suppose they're being tortured to reveal the hiding places of their wealth. The first Mongol officer who brought the list was reinforced, the gates were held open, and that finished it. Don't grunt so, elephant!" he snarled at Bela. "One last strike . . . *agh!* There."

Finished, he flung aside his tools and fled, crying, "Allah be your guide and companion—if he has not already abandoned this accursed place!"

Distant footfalls in the palace indicated a mass flight had already begun. I drew Lilith and Bela to my side.

"We must leave now and keep together until we're on the plain outside the city. Bela, fetch the burnooses Rashid left for the two of us. Our safety lies in not being discovered as Mongols— you in particular. When we reach the plain, we'll make our escape on foot—we'd be stopped instantly on horseback. Once out of the vicinity of the walls, we can search for mounts and food. But above all we must stay together."

"I'm frightened, James," Lilith said as I threw on a dark burnoose.

"Keep your hand in mine and your face veiled. All will be well." I wished that I believed it.

Bela rushed back from the lattice. "We'd better go now. It sounds like there are already mobs in the streets."

"Lead the way," I said.

Thus we began our exodus from the palace of Merik.

It was desolate, empty, gutted by fear. In one shadowed corridor we came upon an officer of the royal guard, spreadeagled with a Mongol lance through his breastbone.

We descended through the various levels to the slave gate, which stood open. In the dark streets, the terror-stricken people fled toward the walls. Panic drove them; many were almost hysterical, thrashing and shoving and kicking to move a few steps forward. Occasionally a Mongol officer on horseback beat a path through the mob, lashing about with a braided rope until the way was open. It was a scene of horror. I saw a veiled woman drop the babe she carried in her arms. She screamed as the crowd pushed her forward. She tried to struggle back to find her child, but the crowd refused to let her pass. At last she fell, trampled like her child.

Bela and I struggled on, protecting Lilith between us. She clung fiercely to my arm. Ahead, at the end of the avenue, I glimpsed open gates but a nameless dread filled me. The memory of the dead soldier, lance in his breastbone, danced in my head.

All about us, the crying crowd surged onward, bearing us through gates that rose ten times higher than our heads. We stumbled out onto the plain of the River of Birds, to whatever might lie in wait for us in a world turned mad by the howling of the frightened souls fleeing from Merv.

Chapter 5

Red Exodus

No other night of my life had ever been so ghastly as that night when the teeming thousands poured out of the once-proud city.

All about us we heard the weeping and the lamentations of Muhammadan householders who had gathered a few precious articles in small ass-driven carts. Once the mob broke from the gates and began to spread out, running, the carts were overturned and smashed. Nor were carts the only casualties. I saw a dozen people step on the head of an old, injured holy man. I wanted to strike at the wild, thoughtless Muhammadans—and at the haughty Mongol officers who galloped up and down, jeering and striking the fugitives. I wanted to tear the whips from their hands and give them a taste of their own brutality. This aspect of the Khan's warfare—this goading and harrying innocent people—filled me with a fury. I would have fallen on the soldiers but for the

231

prompting of my reason. I knew I must not lose
sight of my two companions for one moment.

So we staggered on, clinging together and
keeping our heads down to hide our faces. Behind
us, new light spread across the sky as the horde
thundered into the city and began to put it to the
torch. Flames soon leaped up from the loftiest
minarets until it seemed the fire would scorch the
very stars.

Such a scene of misery and destruction could
never have been captured by an artist unless he
had seen it himself—or gone mad. The ragged
column in which we hid ourselves rolled onward
half a league, given direction by the Mongol officers who turned it in a great curve out toward
the rim of the plain, to make room for the thousands still fleeing the city. As the column curved,
we came within sight of the pavilion of the commander of the army.

Tuli was seated in the open, in a carved chair
set on a dais of gold. He was surrounded by fifty
of his private guard and a hundred flaming
torches stuck in the earth. While the ranks behind us forced us ahead, I saw part of a grisly
display on the dais.

Muhammadans wearing the military garb of
Khorassan were made to kneel one after another.
Their heads were lopped off and thrown into a
growing heap at which young Tuli gazed with
pleasure and satisfaction. Seeing the barbarity,
Bela glared like one deranged. I thought that per-
haps for the first time, he was regretting his
Mongol birth.

I placed myself between Lilith and the ghastly
spectacle.

Bela had been craning to watch the executions
at Tuli's encampment, which was now behind us.

He swung back. "James, unless my eyes were deceived, I saw someone we know standing near the Master of War."

"Who?"

"Hargoutai. Gods! To be so close to him and not be able to repay—"

"Another time," I panted as we were shoved and buffeted toward the shouting officers. "We have problems enough staying together."

In truth I had missed seeing the Falcon in the confusion. Even if I'd seen him, I doubt if it would have made much difference. He stood for death, while my immediate concern was life. I slipped my arm around Lilith's waist and felt her shudder. She was more important to me than vengeance now.

"Bela," I said, "can you make out what the officers are yelling?"

"Not well. Something about left and right—"

Abruptly, above the crashing of the Mongol whips, I made sense of it: *Men to the left! Women to the right!* Children through the center. . . ."

Dread took hold of me again. The column was being split into three parts, and in another moment or so, we would be at the turning, the point of separation.

Bela's reactions were faster than mine. He swept off his burnoose and began to drape it over Lilith's head and shoulders, a hard task to undertake while trying to keep from being trampled. Before he had quite finished, we reached the officers. I pulled Lilith's head down on my shoulder.

With her trembling form between us, we staggered to the left. We had gone half a dozen steps when a hand grabbed my arm and pulled me from the ranks.

A greasy Mongol face loomed close to mine. With one sweep of his hand, he tore back Lilith's cowl. "Aha! I thought I saw a glint of gold hair! Let her go, you Muhammadan dogs."

Two of his companions rode over to aid him. Lilith screamed as they laid hands on her.

I leaped at them, trying to drag the nearest one from the saddle. His comrade whipped my throat. I yelled. The lash wound around my neck. I was jerked backwards.

Bela's shriek of rage roared out somewhere. Excited Mongols identified him as one of their own kind. I tried to tear the strangling whip from my throat. Another lash was laid on, tearing the back of my robe and cutting my shoulder open.

Lilith disappeared. Bela too. Dazed, I dropped to my knees as a Mongol pony reared over me. The hoofs slashed down. I covered my head, rolled aside, and missed death by a hair's width. When I staggered up, another whip cut my forehead open.

Blood streamed into my eyes, blinding me. All around, Muhammadans rushed on, desperate to avoid the kind of punishment being given to me.

"Take the traitor to the commander," a voice cried. "I'll swear he was born on the Gobi."

"Bela?" I screamed, for it was he they were taking. I didn't see him anywhere—nor Lilith either.

A kind of madness gripped me then. I clawed my way into the mob, struggling to open a path. The mongols whipped me back. I fell and would have been trampled but for the hand of a man I never saw. He was behind me, and he held my neck, shoving me along until I untangled my feet. I heard him whisper, "You have little enough chance to live as it is. Don't throw it away! Stand up. Keep walking!"

Bumped and buffeted, my unseen benefactor suddenly let go. But I managed to stay upright. In the confusion, I never glimpsed my benefactor's face.

Once more I tried to break out of the crowd. Three Mongol horsemen converged to drive me back again.

Nearly out of my mind with rage and despair, I stumbled on, bleeding and gulping air.

Bela and Lilith were gone.

How long I walked I can't precisely say. My next clear memory is of a section of plain I did not recognize. Mongol officers were ordering us to lie down on our bellies with our arms behind our backs. Too weak and weary to protest, I obeyed without thinking. Fresh wailing went up from the hundreds of captive men around me. Then, dimly, I sensed the horrid truth. The soldiers of the Kha Khan were repeating a practice begun outside the walls of other captured cities of Kharesmia—namely, the slaying of every single inhabitant.

Mongol officers worked their way along long lines of prone figures in methodical fashion. They knelt, seized a Muhammadan's throat, and choked the victim until he lay still. Then, as each murderer finished his chore, he moved on. Others of the horde worked with swords, dispatching the men of Merv with quick, efficient thrusts.

I was too spent and sick to care. Everything I held dear had been taken from me. In a moment the breath of life would be taken as well.

Chapter 6

Dark Reunion

The thought goaded me. It forced desperate strength into me. I raised my head a little and looked about, trying to shut out the screams of the dying.

Off at an angle, away from the fast-approaching slaughter crews, I spied a mammoth heap of corpses, doubtless the result of the first stages of the mass execution. That corpse-hill might offer hope . . . .

Slowly, I raised myself to my knees. Down the line, the protests of an old man resisting his killers diverted their attention for a moment. Without thought I began to crawl.

I never believed I could make it. The Mongols would see me at any instant. Yet they didn't, because the elderly man was flailing and kicking like someone half his years. A sword ripped his throat open just as I reached the fringe of the mound of the dead.

I fell against that loathsome peak of corpses and began crawling around to the opposite side. Possessed of a madman's power, I burrowed my way into its ghastly confines, tearing with my hands and pushing with my head until I carved a sort of quivering cave within that putrefying charnel hill.

I closed my eyes. I opened them a second later and nearly shrieked. In the last spasm of death a hand twitched against my cheek. I sunk my teeth into the flesh of my wrist to keep from crying out. The hand grew still.

In a while, the sickening reek of dead flesh became almost bearable. The distant cries of the dying captives reduced themselves to a singsong music. If the swirling confusion in my brain signified the coming of death, then let it come.

Distorted memories flitted in my head:

Lilith screaming; being torn from my grip; thrust into the column of women—

I saw Bela, too. I saw him fall under the lance butts of his attackers—

I could stand no more. My brain went blessedly dark . . . .

Miraculously, I awoke.

I had no idea how much time had elapsed until I saw gleams of sunshine filtering between the twisted puzzle of bodies all around me.

A hot stench plagued my nostrils. Insects buzzed. One fat fly went crawling down my nose. I shifted my shoulders. The mound of dead flesh moved a little. The fly crawled away.

Clenching my teeth, I heaved backward, then forward. The corpses shifted with a slimy sound.

At once I knew the sunlight must be softening them; the stink was overpowering. I tore my way forward until I was free of that grisly hiding place.

I sucked great gulps of hot desert air. I burrowed my head into the sand because the sun's light blinded me. I still didn't care whether a Mongol officer came striding up to deliver the final stroke.

Long moments passed. A flap of wings sounded close by. I put my palms in the sand, raised my head, and looked around.

Streaming and rotting in the sun, a field of corpses stretched to the foothills. Beyond, gray smoke climbed heavenward. I realized that what I saw was no illusion. The city of Merv had been leveled overnight, its walls knocked down by siege engines, and the whole of its former loveliness burned away. Nothing remained but a square league of smoldering ruins surrounded by thousands of dead bodies. The River of Birds ran a reddish color.

I pondered what to do. I decided I would search the whole of Merv's desolation, if necessary, until I found a sign of the fate of the two who had fled with me. Gathering the tatters of my burnoose around me, I began to walk, my head thrown back as I gulped the desert air to wash the foulness of the corpse-heap from my lungs.

No one disturbed me. There were no Mongols on the plain. With its dreadful task finished, the army of the Khan had melted away with that swiftness I knew so well.

Overhead, the vultures wheeled, flocks of them dipping down to pick at the bodies. I kept walking, my step unsteady and my vision blurred again. I tried to gauge the location of the imperial dais of Tuli. In its vicinity I hoped to find Bela's remains. Having been identified as a Mongol, he would most likely have been taken before the Khan's son. Perhaps I could discover his head in the pile I had observed on the way from the city. After orienting myself a bit more, I sighted what I thought to be the approximate location, about a league distant. I began to make my way there.

During this unhappy pilgrimage through the ranks of the dead, I saw I was not the only person left alive. Now and then an injured Muhammadan moaned as I passed, and I paused to give what comfort I could, cleaning and binding wounds with scraps of garments taken from nearby bodies.

Perhaps a dozen men wandered about as I was doing, black stick figures in the midst of hot silence.

None of the living hailed me, or even came close; I might turn out to be the enemy. I did not approach them for the same reason.

At last I arrived at my destination. The tower of heads had grown to stupendous proportions. The burned, blackened shafts of the hundred torches stuck up from the ground.

Suddenly one of the still-living reeled from a hiding place behind the pile of heads. My breath caught in my throat—

"Bela?" I raced forward. "Is that you, brother?"

"Who calls?" came the answer.

The shambling figure stopped and swayed, arms outstretched toward me. Then he took a step and stumbled over the heaped heads. Sprawling, he cried, "Who is it, I say?"

"Me, Bela. James."

Floundering among the heads, he called, "Don't mock me, Muhammadan. Go away and leave me to my misery. If you come too close I'll get my hands on you and crack your spine."

"Bela, listen to my voice. It's me!" I reached his side. "Look at my face! You'll see it's—"

I was stricken dumb as his head lifted. His eyes were gone. Dried blood and dirt clotted the sockets.

Like some hurt beast, he lumbered to his feet, his great hands reaching toward me. I could barely speak.

"Brother of my life, I'm not a Muhammadan, but your comrade. Take my left hand—there. Run your fingers over it. You have five and I have four." Misery and joy mingling in my words, I cried softly, "Can you doubt me, Bela?"

"*James?* James—"

"You know me now?"

"Aye." The blind head bobbed. A heart-rending sound came from his parched, blood-stained lips. He fell against me clutching my shoulders and crying like a child. With my back to the grisly mound, I bade him lie down so I could examine the ruins of his eyes. I had been given a purpose again.

"Rest here, Bela. I'll go to the River of Birds and fetch water."

"Fetch a sword instead, James."

"We don't need a sword. The soldiers are gone."

"Use the sword to kill me. What good is life if I have to live it in pitch darkness?"

"What good?" I repeated. "Why, there are a thousand things for a blind man to enjoy." Full of despair myself, I tried to cheer him. "There's wine to be savored on the tongue, and the kisses of maidens for your mouth. There's the plunk of a one-string fiddle to please the ear. Speak no

240

more of misfortune. Rest. Be glad you can't see the sights I do. Of the two of us, you're by far the luckier."

I made him promise he wouldn't try to run away. Then I went among the dead until I found a small leather pouch on the body of a bearded man. This I took down to the banks of the river, filling it with red water.

Bringing the pouch back to the site of Tuli's chair, I bathed Bela's ruined eyes as best I could, then bound his head with a long strip of reasonably clean wool taken from another dead man. At last he sat up.

He confessed to feeling good, though only his great strength permitted him to say that; he could not help but be in terrible pain. Yet he refused to show it. He did admit it would not be easy to get used to his new condition. Then, licking his cracked lips, he said, "James, I must tell you sad news. The one who betrayed us in the orchards of Samarkand—"

"Hargoutai?" I broke in. "I remember you thought you'd seen him near Tuli when we passed last night."

"He was there," Bela nodded. "When I was dragged away from you, they took me before Tuli. At the sight of me, Hargoutai grew black with fury. He assumed you and I to be long dead. When he asked whether you were living, I wasn't in control of my temper. I said yes. He flew at me, wanting to know whether I had come onto the plain with you. At that juncture, the officer who brought me before Tuli's throne spoke up. He said that although he didn't recall a yellow-haired Frank—perhaps he didn't see you struggling by the roadside—he did remember a Circassian girl close to me."

"Go on," I said. My voice was low; an ominous sense of the workings of the hateful gods came over me.

"Hargoutai demanded that the girl be found and Tuli indulged him. It didn't take long. There were few girls of Lilith's type among the women forced to lie down and await death. She was hauled up before the golden throne fighting like a she-tiger. All at once a wary look came into her eyes. She recognized the scar on Hargoutai's neck—had you told her about it?"

Silent and grieving, I nodded.

"Hargoutai asked if she knew you. She was too frightened and angry to deny it. The Falcon went into another of his rages. Tore the clothes off her body. Started to whip her. Tuli laughed, but I couldn't stand it. I fell on them."

"And received the reward of eternal darkness?" I asked.

"Yes," replied Bela as he proceeded to finish the story.

He had been blinded with torches on Hargoutai's instructions. Lilith's valiant resistance ended when she crouched at the tar-khan's feet, whipped into misery.

"The Falcon must have had his blade in his hand—"

"Did he kill her?" I whispered.

"There were cries, confusion. I thought so at first. I heard her scream. Later they told me she'd seized the Falcon's sword and used it on herself to rob them of the satisfaction of executing her. I—I suppose her body is somewhere near here," he finished, hanging his head.

"But he didn't kill you."

"Oh, no! It was much more amusing for him to watch me stumble and stagger and try to stop the

blood flowing down my face. Finally I passed out.
I woke again to hear an alarm being raised, the
cry for retreat of the horde. I remember crawling
a little. No one came to disturb me until I heard
you approaching. If—if you wish to look for the
girl, I'll wait here while you do it. I'd be of little
help. Besides, she meant much to you. It would be
fitting for you to be alone with her."

I hesitated to leave him until he reassured me.
"Go. I'll be waiting here when you've done. The
black spell has passed. I'll do no harm to myself."

"That's true," I said. "Because you're still my
sworn brother. My hand will lead you in safe
paths the rest of your days. Together, we'll leave
this place—and make a mark before everything
ends." I was covered with cold sweat and trembling with anger as I gazed at the sky. "The Gobi
gods have punished me enough. I'll take no
more—ever."

The wind had picked up. It sang an eerie note.
The alien gods had heard my ultimate defiance. I
didn't care. There were other gods on my side
now.

"Rest now," I said, easing Bela to the ground. I
poured more water on the bandage hiding his
eyes, then gathered my gory robe about me and
commenced my search among the dead. I found
Lilith sprawled naked in the sand not far away.
Her fair hair spread down over her welt-streaked
back, catching the splendor of the sunlight in its
gilded threads.

My nerve almost failed me. For a moment I
was unable to turn her body over. But I did, gazing a long time at the deep wound that she'd in-
flicted on herself rather than bear the abuse and
the torture of Hargoutai.

Using my hands, I dug a shallow trench and

laid her in it. I kissed her face and crossed her hands on her breast in the mystic sign; she had spoken of seeing holy crosses in Nestorian churches in her homeland.

Covering her, I stood up and began to cry. I bent my head and wept a long time, without shame.

When I was in better control of myself, I said a wordless goodbye. In a way I had grown to love her. I loved her even more when she was gone, for only then did I understand how much she had meant to me. Finally I turned away from the poor grave and walked back to Bela, away from the dead to the one living thing on earth that was still mine to cherish and protect. The wind grew stronger, raising dust-devils among the rows of the dead and streaming the smoke of ruined Merv across the sky. I squatted down beside my brother, using my finger to trace patterns in the dirt between my feet. A strange, awesome power seemed to control me, guiding my hand, moving my tongue.

"Bela, we must go on."

"Where?"

"To find Hargoutai."

"James!" he cried. "After all he's done, you want to risk more—?"

"Risk?" I said in a somber voice. "I have nothing more to risk except my life. Losing that would be nothing. I've endured too much that's worse and so have you. Don't you wonder a little at why we were both spared again, brother?" I gazed at the sky. "I don't. Not any more. I have gods with me. Frankish gods whose names I don't know, but I know this. They've grown sick—as I have—of the workings of the Mongol gods. Sick of their heartlessness. Sick of their slaughtering.

244

I don't fear the gods of the Mongols any longer. My own gods are stronger."

Bela's mouth sagged. His voice grew husky. "James, you're mad."

"Aye, that I am. Mad from having seen too much death. Mad from letting myself be cowed by the spirits who rule the Gobi. I stood against them once and I feared them forever afterward, yet they never succeeded in striking me down. Oh, they tried. They tried in the Mangudai. They tried when Merv fell. Time and again they tried." My voice rose with the raw hatred of one who had been stupidly submissive. "I didn't know why they failed, but I know now. It's because my own gods protected me—and you, I think. And they've left us alive for one purpose. They hate the Gobi gods, and they hate the worst manifestations of those gods in human form. One is Hargoutai."

I could taste salty spittle on my own lips. Perhaps I spoke with the tongue of a trance-bound shaman. *Something* was moving within me, showing me almost all of the rest of what the Muhammadans would have called my kismet.

"I have to search for Hargoutai, Bela. Seek him out instead of waiting for his wrath to fall on me. I must kill him somehow, somewhere, even if I have to follow him to the world's end, and off its edge, and down to the nether places. I must kill him because my own gods *demand it!*"

"They—they must be powerful indeed, these new-found gods of yours," Bela breathed.

"They rule the whole earth and every man on it. Beside them—" Another defiant glance at the sky. "—the pretenders of the Gobi are infants. Cruel, willful infants." I drew a deep breath. "Can you stand up?"

"With your help."

"Good. I can't abide the stench of this place any longer. We'll head to the foothills yonder and try to find food, and some herbs to make a poultice for your eyes."

"My eyes don't hurt," he lied.

"Nevertheless, we'll dress them, then begin our journey. I don't know where it will take us—"

"Except to Hargoutai."

"Yes. Come."

I extended my hand. By the hour of darkness, we had climbed into the foothills and put the sorrows and shames of Merv behind us.

Chapter 7

The Wanderers

During the first three months after our flight from Merv, we dwelled in the hilly barrens to the northeast, unbothered, unsought, left to lick our wounds while the blowing sands of Khorassan gradually covered the stark remains of the city we had quitted. Bela recovered his strength and I recovered mine. But a part of me had died: When my beard grew long, its yellow was streaked with white.

One day we chanced upon an old Arab trader. He had but half a dozen mangy camels to bear his goods, and a single, louse-ridden youth to give him aid.

I traded a few words about the devastation of Merv for the first fresh meat we had tasted since setting forth.

It took perhaps an hour to gain the old Mussulman's confidence and convince him that we meant him no harm, that the wildness of our unshorn locks and the strange picture we presented, blind Mongol and gaunt Frank, boded him no ill.

At length he allowed us a second helping of food and more wine. Having tasted nothing but berries and the flesh of martens for some length of time, his poor fare seemed richer to us than the finest banquet in Merik's hall.

"Is the destruction of the pleasure city of Merv truly as great as you hinted?" the camel driver inquired.

"It is."

"Then what I have heard elsewhere must be true."

"What have you heard?"

"That all residents of the district are now forbidden to look upon the site of Merv. It is to remain abandoned until the end of time, covered by the sands and called Moubaligh—the City of Sorrows."

"I can understand why," I observed. "But I have a question on another subject."

He shook his head. "I want to hear all you know about Merv's fall."

"Then perhaps my question and your wish have a common ground." I told him, falling easily into the florid language of bargaining. "I note you have weapons among your goods. We have none. So if you would hear more from one who witnessed the destruction of Merv, let's come to an agreement. If you can see your way clear to spare us a single bow with arrows—or a blade, since you're armed with several—and if you will also give us tidings of the army of the fierce Khan, then I'll spin the whole tale of how we came down off the Gobi into Khorassan, fell into slavery, and were delivered. I'll also describe the wonders and spectacles of the wrath of the Khan at Merv. The story will take at least two nights to relate. But it's full of thrilling and frightening descriptions."

While Bela chuckled, I studied the old Arab. I feared I had been too bold, asked for too much. But I hadn't reckoned on the depth of his hunger for news and companionship. I suddenly wished I had promised a tale of *four* nights' duration. As long as we remained in his encampment, he must feed us and give us wine. And he was in no hurry to press on, commerce being poor because of the presence of the barbarian horde in Kharesmia.

I settled down comfortably and began narrating our adventures. All I omitted were references to my beloved Cathayan princess and Hargoutai the Falcon. My relationship with the latter was no business of anyone except the tar-khan, myself, Bela—and the gods who waited.

In return for my story, we received information about the progress of the Khan's war against the crumbling empire of the dead Shah.

In the north, the horde that had ravaged the country of the Kipchaks and Circassians had turned back at a river at the very gate of Frankistan. They had turned back in response to a summons the Khan issued to his far-flung tumans in the late summer months of the Christian year 1221.

The northern contingent was stopped while storming through the salt lands of the Bulgars. Together with other tumans, it turned back toward a central meeting place designated by the Khan. Although the great Genghis had thus far been victorious in Khorassan, all was not well throughout his empire.

As explained by our Muhammadan host, the main body of the Khan's horde had ridden up to the fertile Hindu Kush during the months just past. There, great indignities had been heaped upon the atabegs and other lords of Islam. They had been forced to labor as slaves while the Mongols lazed in silken pavilions, taking their pleasures from Islamic maids whose veils had been callously torn away. Turkoman and Persian emir alike were required to grovel before the conquerors.

I interrupted to ask whether the old man had heard anything about one of the Kahn's sons called Juchi the Guest, but he had not.

He continued his tale, describing how the conquered city of Heart had risen and overthrown the Khan's garrison. At the same time, Jelal ed-Din threatened the east with a new army. Now the trader's eyes glittered. His hands moved in broad gestures as he tried to outdo the extravagances of my account of Merv's fall.

Near the powerful Afghan city of Bamiyan in the ranges of Kho-i-baba, the Mongols had clashed with the revenge-hungry army of Jelal ed-Din. The outraged Mongols thereupon turned against Bamiyan itself. A grandson of the Khan—not Kublai but another whose name the trader could not call to mind—had perished at Bamiyan with an arrow in his heart. The Khan razed Bamiyan in the same fashion as Merv, creating yet one more place of desolation forever forbidden to members of the Muhammadan race.

The fickle Afghans promptly withdrew their support of the son of the Shah, who drew back past Ghazna into the valley of the Indus, hoping to cross the river and ally himself with the sultans of Delhi. But when the river proved too swift and deep, Jelal ed-Din defiantly destroyed his vessels and put his back to the Indus for a last desperate fight.

This time the Khan proved victorious, the trader reported woefully. With all his forces gone, Jelal ed-Din threw off his armor. Taking bow and sword, he leaped his pony down an embankment five times higher than a tall man, straight into the river. This courageous act earned the Khan's admiration, but not his mercy. Mongol tumans pursued Jelal ed-Din across the Indus but failed to catch him. Enraged, the Mongols sacked Mullan and Lahore and then withdrew, oppressed by the terrible Hindu heat.

"Meantime, an important governor of one of the Cathayan provinces died. Word of his passing was widely circulated." I guessed the dead governor to be the great Muhuli.

"Further," the old man went on, "beyond the white mountains whose slopes I have seen only once, there is restlessness so great, it has caused the accursed Khan to turn aside from storming the gates of Peshawar. He has withdrawn to Samarkand and is reported to be there now, preparing to move farther north to the River Syr. According to announcements circulated among the captive lords of Islam, he will hold a great council on the banks of the Syr in the spring. All will pay tribute."

He paused. "That, young master, is the full extent of my information. Allah be praised! The telling has truly brought me pleasure. You have stirred me with exciting stories, but a good listener is highly valued among my race."

Politely I replied, "And you have rewarded us by describing the Khan's plans for the spring. To my brother and I, this is more precious than gold,

251

because we must take ourselves into the Khan's terrible presence so that a debt can be repaid."

I turned and saw Bela nodding. His fists were tightly clenched. The tattered bandage hiding his eye's sockets fluttered in the evening wind.

I continued to our host: "I wish we could tarry here longer, but we cannot. At the first light of day, we must start for the Syr, thanking you for your hospitality during the past few days.

"May Allah illuminate the path on your journey," he responded. "May he also protect you—"

"From the Khan?"

Soberly he shook his head. "From yourself. You have bleak eyes, Man-with-nine-fingers. The sign of a terrible kismet, the wise men say."

Next day, we bade the old Arab good-bye and started north. We traveled mostly at night, avoiding villages as well as the roving bands of Mongols we sighted now and again.

As winter waned, we trudged on toward the site of the rendezvous by the River Syr. We looked like two pilgrims bound for a holy shrine. But the place of the Khan's forthcoming Kurultai was a dark Mecca indeed.

We drew ever closer to our destination. Spring turned the streams above the Amu to torrents. I had no formal plan to carry out when we arrived; I intended only to call upon my protector, Juchi the Guest, and seek his help in obtaining a hearing of my case by the Khan—a fair hearing, untainted by the lies and deceptions of Hargoutai the Falcon.

Thus it came about that we at last reached the fringe of a vast meadow sloping down to the Syr. I saw waterfowl winging from the marshy places and golden pheasants preening in the thick grass.

But the wildlife was colorless indeed compared to the splendor of the Khan's encampment.

It spilled down to the river, covering seven leagues or more. Silken-sheathed kibitkas dotted the land. The areas between swarmed with officers newly returned from the frozen wastes of the Tian-shan; with carts of gilt and lacquer; with strings of horned yaks waving their pure white tails; with camels adding the stench of their droppings to the mingled smells.

The camp was a stew of people: Mongols as well as the wide-headed Kirghiz; the lean captive Turkomen; emaciated Jews. The horse herds seemed to number ten thousand animals; the cook fires ten times that many.

Amidst the chaos and clatter of it all, I did not think Bela and I would be overly conspicuous. The sun had bleached my hair and beard and darkened my skin. We could have been just two more unspeakably filthy beggars among hundreds who followed the army. Certainly two ghastlier, dirtier specimens could never have trod the earth. Bela held a sword in one hand and rested his other on my shoulder. I carried a bow and quiver of arrows. Both of us were in rags, our bones full of aches, our flesh shrunk away to nothing.

Yet we found renewed energy as we descended the long meadow. Perhaps before the sun set, the game would be played out at last. The thought of it set my heart beating a little faster.

As we approached the camp, I politely hailed a Mongol officer. He stopped to converse outside a huge shed. Inside, I saw the accumulated riches from the Khan's pillaging: piles of rich garments sewn with threads of gilt and silver, numerous carved chests, and a gossamer mountain of veils decorated with pearls. The Mongol officer wore rich Turkoman chain mail which glared in the sun. His hand rested on a pommel of a scimitar with a Damascus blade.

Above the roar of a troop of blooded Arab racers thundering by, I said to him, "Sir, can you direct us to the yurts of Juchi the Guest? We seek an audience with him."

The officer laughed. He gazed curiously at Bela, then back at me. "What do beggars want with a noble lord?"

"I am no pleader for alms," I said, holding up my left hand.

It was as though I had worked magic. He turned pale and retreated a step. "Gods! It can't be you!"

"It is either me or my spirit. Both of us would like an answer, if you please."

"But—but your name has been written among those of the dead!"

Growing annoyed, I flexed my hand. "Come, does this look dead?"

He gaped at the four fingers. "No—*no*. I remember it well—as do most of the men of the horde. We gloried in the accounts of your bravery among the Mangudai."

"Then help me. Direct me to my protector, Juchi. I have important words to speak with him."

He shook his head dolefully. "If Juchi is your protector, you'd be better off returning to whatever god-forsaken land you came from."

Something in his eyes started my palms itching—the itch of fear. "Explain yourself," I said softly.

"There is none in greater disfavor with the noble Khan than Lord Juchi. He has been reviled as the next thing to a Tatar—and by his own

254

brother, Tuli! He has no yurts. He dwells apart, far up the meadow, scorned and without honor. It's true he sits daily in the Khan's pavilion, but he is not heard. He'll do you more harm than good."

Genuine dread touched me then. Bela's hand clasped my shoulder hard. He too was sickened to hear that our sole hope was futile.

"Tell me," I said. "How can Juchi have fallen so low? He's the Khan's eldest. Much loved!"

The officer gave a shrug. "He allowed Jelal ed-Din to escape at Urgench. When the Khan summoned him to Balkh and reproached him, Juchi denied wrong-doing, lost his temper, and called the Khan blasphemous names. Then he took his men and retreated in anger beyond the Sea of Aval. Next, the Khan demanded Juchi join him in the Hindu Kush. He pleaded illness and instead sent a gift of a thousand snowy ponies, but the Kipchak who delivered the ponies told the Khan that Juchi was not sick at all but hunting. Subotai Bahadur of the Raging Torrents had to ride beyond the Aral and fetch him here for the Kurultai. He came against his will, full of bitterness and despised by his father. So if you wish favor with our glorious emperor, don't seek the counsel or assistance of his son. If you do, I assure you your cause is lost."

Stricken, I asked, "What of the tar-khan Hargoutai? Is he present?"

"Indeed yes," answered my informant with a curious leer. "But he still bears many a scar from nighttime battles."

"Talk sense, curse you! What's this prattling about the nighttime?"

"Marks," said the officer, as if he were speaking to a clod. "Marks left by his favorite woman.

She despises him when he's rough with her, but I hear she submits peacefully if he's gentle. Unfortunately, Lord Hargoutai is not often gentle. That doesn't sit well with a Cathayan concubine."

"*A Cathayan*—?" I swear my heart nearly stopped at that moment.

"Aye," the officer said. "The princess? Surely you remember her—" He hesitated, suddenly nervous.

I imagine I must have looked like death itself as I whispered, "In my days at Karakorum, Lord Hargoutai had but one favorite Cathayan. She dwells among her ancestors. At Samarkand he told me he had sent her to them."

The officer grew more and more confused. "Why, if you mean Cho Soo, then a trick was played, and you have been cruelly served. You—*wait!* Now it comes back to me those days when you first came to The Black Sands. I seem to remember there was enmity between you and Hargoutai and its cause—" His eyes grew huge, just as the scales fell from mine and I saw at last treachery's true face. The officer's voice could barely be heard. "—its cause was this same princess of Cathay!"

"*You swear she's alive?*"

"I saw her only this morning!"

Bela heard and kneaded my shoulder in a fit of wrath that almost broke bone. Swiftly I drew from the stupefied officer a pledge of silence. To do it, I needed only to remind him I still carried the rank of gur-khan. I demanded directions to the pavilion of Genghis.

"Ghengis? Surely you would not presume . . . !" He was nearly speechless. "Not—not as you are—with no gifts? Filthy and mad-looking as a hermit of the wilderness?"

"Bela," I said, "hand me your sword."

The officer shuddered and gave me the directions. Then he shook his head. "Go on if you must. Should you and your blind companion die in the Khan's pavilion—"

"You think I will."

"I *know* you will. May a mighty bogodo come down from heaven and bear your soul to a warm place near the sun!"

He hurried away from us then, as though to avoid being contaminated. I rearranged my ragged robe, threw back my head, and laid my hand on Bela's, pulling him gently forward. He too shuddered.

"Madness and death are on you brother James! To go before the Khan in such a state invites divine wrath!"

"*I have put off this rendezvous for almost five years!*" A terror and a triumph sang in me now. "The gods of the Franks will wait no longer and neither will I!"

"I understand, brother," he sighed.

"I will leave you here, if you wish."

"No." Then louder, "No. My life is your life— short as they both may be. Lead on."

Chapter 8

The Justice of the Khan

We traveled up the slope of the meadow with quickening steps. A breeze from the Syr had sprung up, bending the long grass and rippling the manes of the several thousand Kipchak horses quartered to our left.

Gleaming like a sunlit cloud, the Khan's white pavilion waited at the top of the gentle rise. It resembled the pavilion at the emperor's dwelling place, except that it was much larger. It looked to me as if it might hold two thousand souls. Before its southern entrance, nine white yak tails on a staff stood out in the wind. My steps faltered no longer.

All at once a mortal terror filled me. Yet I could not stop. This moment had an inevitability whose power I felt like a great hand at my back. The moment had been part of my destiny—my kismet, if you prefer—from that long-ago hour when my Frankish father planted his seed within a woman I never knew. He—and the gods—had set me on a path leading straight to this place: the throne of the mightiest ruler in all the world.

I led Bela straight to the entrance where the silver table stood, noting that the simple fare of the table in Karakorum had been enriched by the addition of a dozen jars of Persian wine, joints of meat, and cups of golden mead. But hungry as I was, I wanted no food, only a final accounting.

I addressed the haughty captain at the table: "We seek audience with the great Khan and will not wait long for it."

Astounded, he raised his mailed arm to threaten me. "Be off, beggars! Join your companions at the dung heaps, where you belong."

I pushed his hand aside. "Wait one moment! You're speaking to a gur-khan of the horde, higher in rank than you. I order you to go inside at once. Tell the Wrath and Flail of Heaven that two of his loyal soldiers await his justice— namely, Bela of the horde and the Frankish man called James Nine-Fingers, whom you will recognize and remember by this sign."

I thrust my left hand in front of his eyes. Dirty and hideous looking though it was, the hand was familiar to him. A gasp of surprise whistled in his throat. Recognition lighted his slanting eyes.

"Go *now* soldier!" I said. With another fearful glance at us, as though we were tengri come to life, he turned and fled into the pavilion.

My heart beat hard until he returned. "If you are men and not ghosts," he said, "the Khan bids you enter."

At last, there was no turning back . . . .

No moments in my life, then or afterward, car- which we traversed the huge silken hall, followed ried a greater sense of peril than the moments in by the astonished eyes of a thousand tar-khans and lesser officers.

Halfway down its length, near the remains of a great dung-chipfire, Bela dropped his hand from my shoulder and walked unaided, gauging the path by the sound of my steps. Without looking around, I knew his shoulders would be stiff with pride.

Seated to my left and glimpsed from the corner of my eye, I saw Hargoutai the Falcon.

His powerful hands were knotted in the folds of his fur cape. The scar on his throat was livid. I had a fleeting impression of a face torn by confusion and hatred. I had never seen him show such an expression before. It heightened my certainty that we would come together at last and settle our accounts with one another for all time.

Near the dais sat the kindly Bourtai Fidjen, grayer than when I had seen her last. I saw the insolent Tuli, as well as the Khan's other sons, Ogotai and Chatagai, and a round-faced brat I assumed to be the little Kublai.

On another bench, occupying a position of honor but nevertheless clearly placed apart from the royal family, was my powerless protector, Juchi the Guest. He wore his prized sable cloak, and like most of the others gathered in the wind-billowed pavilion, he gaped at Bela and me with disbelief in his eyes.

Bela and I prostrated ourselves before the dais. Momentarily I heard the voice of the Khan bidding me rise.

Once more I stood up before the god-man, but this time the circumstances were far different from those of my first audience in Karakorum. Then, I had come before him almost as a supplicant. Now I would make demands.

260

Genghis Khan had changed somewhat. His face, still leather-tough, showed signs of age. And a certain weariness was visible in his eyes, boredom borne of too many victories, perhaps. But he still wore the black robe and golden girdle of his homeland in preference to the rich and no doubt stolen garments in which his courtiers were arrayed.

The Khan's seat was the magnificent golden throne of Muhammad Shah, fetched from Samarkand. In his lap lay the jeweled scepter and crown of that vanquished lord of Kharesmia. Beneath the chair, however, I spied a little square of dark felt, woven from the hairs of some Gobi beast. It was a curious touch, as though the conqueror of the world needed an ever-present reminder of the origins of his power.

The conqueror of the world now gazed down at two ragged, dirty creatures and registered quite human surprise.

"When the captain announced you, I thought he was drunk. The punishment for drinking on duty is loss of the head. But I see the captain is not in any danger—you are who he said you were. I see yellow in your white beard, Nine-Fingers. I am glad you are here."

Relieved, I watched him smile.

"Indeed, your sudden appearance brings a sort of miracle to this Kurultai. All in the horde knew you were captured in battle by the cursed Muhammadans at Samarkand. All presumed you dead—you and your comrade both."

"It is true we fell into their hands, Lord," I said slowly. "It is not true that it happened in battle. We were tied to trees in an orchard and left to be caught."

"Left? By whom?"

"By one who sits in this chamber. One whose life I demand as payment for his treachery— treachery not confined to the betrayal of two who fought loyally for the nine yak tails I might add. The treachery extends to the telling of a false tale of punishment. The tale concerned a certain Cathayan girl. The tale caused me to believe her to be dead though she still lived. I claim that such a falsehood sets aside the vow she made to the man whose life I claim in forfeit for his treachery."

My chest aching, I tried to gauge the expression in the eyes of the Kha Khan. I played the right chords to stir him. For an instant, it seemed I had.

"Tell me in a few words the evidence that is the basis for your accusations. I grant justice to those who have served me well, and in my sight, honor is priceless while treachery is unpardonable. Before you begin, however, tell me your betrayer's name."

From his penitent's place, Juchi the Guest flung me a glance of warning. I ignored it, turning to point. "There he sits, Lord Khan. Favored in your house and covered with honors. Hargoutai the Falcon."

With remarkable composure, my enemy drew his cape of marten closer around him and gazed at me without expression. My hands shook a little. I knew enough to fear him most when he showed wrath the least. He made no attempt whatever to deny my charges.

The Khan requested that I begin. This I did, giving him a brief recitation of my fate and Bela's since last we had stood before him with dispatches on the hill about Samarkand. Gasps came from those assembled from time to time. All

262

in the pavilion strained to hear each syllable. The brow of Bourtai Fidjen wrinkled with distaste. Tuli the Master of War frowned, too, though for a different reason, I suspected. I had upset a balance, accused one of his favorites.

And Juchi, my protector, kept darting those warning looks my way.

I tried to keep my voice moderate as I recounted the crimes of Hargoutai. At the end, I asked for his death. Still he did not move.

The Khan touched the tips of his fingers together, then turned and whispered something into the ear of Ye Liu Chutsai. The old scholar had come into the pavilion during my recitation and taken his place at the Khan's right hand.

Cold sweat trickled from my chin as I waited for the private discourse to reach an end. In the eyes of the Cathayan, I saw nothing but sympathy. Yet I knew his characteristic prudence would carry little weight in this matter. It would be decided by the Khan—on the basis of the Khan's law.

Straining forward, I caught a bit of the conversation, a few phrases from the old Cathayan. If I heard right, he was presenting his interpretation of the law: Should my account prove true, the vow of Cho Soo should be set aside. A man who demanded fidelity from some, while deceiving others, was in violation of the spirit of the Khan's law and not entitled to its protection.

"So," Genghis nodded at last. "My learned adviser concurs on at least one point. However, I must ask additional proofs. Do not be insulted, Nine-Fingers. The law requires it. You make no claim to being born of Mongol blood—"

"No, Lord."

"Therefore, while your story is acceptable

enough to me, to fulfill the law it must be validated by one whom the law says is beyond question." His gaze shifted to Bela. "Can you hear me well, soldier?"

"I can, Lord," Bela answered.

With a swift glance at Tuli, he continued, "I regret that because of the actions of my overly zealous son, a loyal warrior of the horde must spend the rest of his days in darkness. However, Tuli's actions are beyond the scope of this discussion. I will deal with him privately at a later time."

Tuli wriggled uncomfortably at that. But the Khan was no longer paying any attention to him.

"What matters at the moment, good Bela, is the truth or falsehood of all that Nine-Fingers has related. I ask you on your oath as a Mongol born: Is the accusation an honest one, honestly presented? Or has it been embellished to gain our sympathy?"

"There is not a word in it that is false, Lord," Bela replied, with such conviction that none but a fool would have disbelieved him.

"Then I call forth Hargoutai the Falcon, tar-khan of the horde," said Genghis Kha Khan.

In a moment my enemy took a place beside me. Then he moved one pace forward—a bold and deliberate affront. His features remained composed. Saying nothing, he faced his ruler and waited.

With a pucker of concern on his wide, flat brow the Khan spoke. "Once before in my presence— nearly five years ago, it was—we engaged in a discussion about a man's sacred oath and the importance of same. I declared that nothing is to be more highly prized than a man's own word. So speak, tar-khan Hargoutai. If what the Frankish man says is false, you have only to swear that, and under the law you bear no guilt."

Hargoutai the Falcon inclined his head slightly in my direction. I could not miss the cruel shine in his eyes. I grew lightheaded; failure loomed close. If he seized the opportunity the Khan had presented to him, I would be defeated and disgraced.

"Lord, I will deny nothing," Hargoutai said. "Every syllable is true."

He turned again, smiling just a little this time. I was too stunned to do anything but stare. A trap was being laid. But I did not know where.

"His story is true, and I would not call back a single act," he went on. "I treated this foreigner in a manner I thought fitting. I shall do so again—in combat. He demands my life? Very well. Let him see if he can take it!"

"Beware, brother," Bela whispered in my ear. "He wouldn't speak so or risk himself, unless there was a way for him to—"

I never heard the rest of Bela's speech; I was shouting: "Yes, Let's see! And let it be done before the sun falls today!"

While Juchi the Guest glared, trying in vain to convey something important that escaped me, the sly Tuli stepped forward.

"A reminder, if you please! Since we're dealing with a dispute involving law, the combat itself must be conducted in strict accordance with The Yassa, else it settles nothing."

Genghis Kha Khan gazed sharply at Tuli. His eyes widened as he realized something still hidden from me. I thought there was regret in his voice when he said, "My son has spoken correctly. I have gained mastery of the world by living according to The Yassa, and I have always urged my subjects to live the same way. The Yassa prescribes the rules for settling a feud. First, in contests of honor between Mongols, weapons of iron are forbidden. Although Nine-Fingers is not of our blood, in this instance, I consider the rule binding. So speaks the Khan; let it be done."

At last I began to see Hargoutai's game.

He stripped off the sleek marten-skin cape, holding it aloft. "This is not iron, noble Khan. Therefore I name it a weapon suitable to be employed in the fight. The Frankish upstart must likewise use his garments and windings, until one of us is muffled to death by the other."

Turning, Hargoutai cast a contemptuous glance at my tattered robes. I could almost hear the laughter inside his skull.

The Khan scrutinized me. He saw I had been trapped, yet he could not call a halt, having already set forth the conditions of the meeting.

As calmly as possible, I said, "The terms are agreeable to me. Even if I lacked these worthless rags on my back, even if I were naked, I would agree. And slay the tar-khan with my bare hands."

The words raised a murmur of approval among the assembled warriors. But I knew how empty the boast was. I was woefully unprepared for a duel on the terms mentioned. I had trapped myself.

Very well, then, I thought. Death is waiting. There are other things far worse. Cowardice, for one. I made no further comment about the position in which Hargoutai had placed me.

But Bela wasn't so tactful. "Lord Khan, my brother's rags can't match Hargoutai's cloak. Let me fight with him."

"Impossible."

"Then let me add my garments to his. If you do not, your law, your *justice* is a mockery!"

Tuli raised his fist to strike Bela for his insolence. All around the pavilion, I heard whispers of shock. But the Khan lifted his hand to still every voice except his own. "Do not rage at him, Tuli. A man who has endured the horrors which Nine-Fingers described cannot be expected to speak gently. His loyalty to his brother is to be commended."

Tuli flushed, pivoting away. More sternly, the Khan said, "Good Bela, the point is well if roughly taken. But you cannot fight beside your brother. The Yassa forbids it. You can, however, lend him whatever garment you—"

"I'll lend him an even better weapon!" a new voice thundered. Heads whipped around as Juchi the Guest stormed to the dais. "Though I am despised in the eyes of my father and of this company, I would be a pitiful creature indeed if I forgot an oath sworn in a boar's lair far across the high Tian-shan. I can offer Nine-Fingers no royal intercession. But I can place about his shoulders the one treasure dearer to me than all others on earth. And I will do so—gladly!"

With those words, Juchi undid the bone clasp at his throat. He whirled off his rich, heavy mantle of sable skin and threw it across my shoulders.

Angry glances darted between Tuli and his brother. The Khan, too, was affronted, but not so much that he forgot it was his son who spoke. Juchi was wise enough to fall on his knees before the dais, extending his hand and saying, "Lord Khan, do I have your permission to aid my sworn brother?"

Love shone in the Khan's eyes. He took Juchi's

hand and held it against his own forehead a moment.

"You do," he whispered.

Juchi arose. He averted his head so none could see how deeply he was moved, and slowly returned to his place.

But Jealous Tuli came snarling forward again. "One further clause of The Yassa I'd bring to mind!" His glance showed that his hatred of his brother had now been transferred to me. "It too cannot be set aside. Nor can it be softened by any intercession on Juchi's part. Since the days of Yesukai the Valiant, Khan of the Yakka Mongols, it has been forbidden to shed the blood of a Mongol of high station in a duel such as this. Hargoutai is a tar-khan. The—the foreigner is of lesser rank. Therefore, in the combat, Nine-Fingers may shed blood. But should he cause the Falcon to shed blood—aye, even so much as a speck—his life is forfeit. Let all who hear remember, so that the law may be carried out."

Thus the final trick was played. Well, I said to myself, at least there is satisfaction in a good death.

Tuli's insistence upon the condition did not sit well with the Kha Khan. Yet he clearly knew its rightness.

Hargoutai sneered openly at my sable cloak. The assembled noyons lamented my fate aloud. The hand of Genghis Kha Khan rose one last time. "Since all matters of protocol have now been settled, let there be no more delay. Make ready to begin the combat."

Chapter 9

The Last Combat

In a level area immediately to the north of the great white pavilion, a covered dais was hastily erected by Cathayan slaves. The yak-tail standard was planted at one corner. The Khan and his family took seats beneath the shade of its silken cover.

A great ring formed. During the time in which the Khan's throne was out of doors, hundreds of people had come swarming over the hillsides; word of the coming struggle between the tarkhan and a man returned from the dead had evidently swept along the bank of the Syr like a grass fire.

The sun burned my shoulders when I tore off most of my rags. I fashioned a clout for myself from pieces of the tattered garments, then took into my hands Juchi's precious sable cloak.

Hargoutai had a whole herd of sycophants assisting him, fitting him into light leggings and

269

lacquered breastplates. He wore nothing on his head or feet. The marten fur was wrapped loosely around one hand.

Tuli the Master of War joined Hargoutai's group to wish him good fortune. I had only Bela, muttering warnings in my ear.

I tried to reassure him that things would go well. He didn't believe it. Nor did I. In truth, I felt lonely and extremely small.

The crowd packing the slopes around the open space quieted suddenly. Hargoutai's followers left him, several taking places under large, colorful sun shades. All at once the silence was complete. The Falcon's painted breastplates glared in the sun. I gazed at him, then past him, my attention caught by the movement of two new arrivals—

The bearded Ye Liu Chutsai and a Cathayan girl.

My heart nearly stopped. It was Cho Soo, brought by the old counselor.

Across the intervening distance, her eyes sought mine, shining with a love I had thought lost to me forever. That long glance gave me courage as I walked out to meet my enemy.

Hargoutai the Falcon waited at the center of the ring. His face looked harder than rock. But it was sweaty, too. I hoped he was afraid.

Although I wanted to look at Cho Soo again, I did not. I crouched and sidestepped toward the man on whom I must focus all my attention if I meant to see another sunrise.

The main rules of the struggle having been established inside the pavilion, all other means of attack became fair. Hargoutai wasted no time. He leaped out, charging toward me before I was fully prepared.

The total strength of his hand and arm went

into a blow to my groin. Pain made me reel. A tremendous shout went up from Hargoutai's fawning followers as I fought to recover my balance before he struck again.

A dark cloud floated over my head and fell. With the battle only moments old, he had my head swathed in folds of marten skin. I gasped for air as he sought to wind it tighter and deprive me of breath. I could see nothing.

One of his hands groped at me through the fur. His palm found the outline of my face and clamped on tight. I snapped my sable cape behind his legs, working by feel and blind instinct. On the second try, I caught the loose end and tugged hard.

I upset him. He let go of my head. Instantly, I tore away the marten skin and flung it in the dust.

Hargoutai was staggering backward. He almost fell, but a savage forward jerk of his torso restored his balance. I rushed to him, twisting Juchi's cloak into a sort of rope which I proceeded to loop behind his head, cross at the ends and pull, throttling him.

Distant voices reached me: Bela's, and Juchi's, too, calling encouragement. I paid little attention, having enough to do to keep the sable rope tight and avoid the kicks and clouts Hargoutai aimed at me.

I dodged his hands and feet as best I could. But he was fast—and desperate. His nails caught my ribs and tore my skin.

Groaning, I held on to the ends of the sable rope. His other hand slashed at my other side and held fast, the clawlike nails digging almost to the bone. Inevitably, my grip on the cloak weakened.

Some of the purple drained from his cheeks. He

twisted his head over and sank his teeth into my wrist, smearing his mouth with my blood.

I tried a knee to his genitals, but he dodged away. While I was perched uncertainly on one foot, he kicked it. As I fell, he freed himself from the cloak wound around his neck.

He retrieved his own marten skin as I tumbled in the dust, losing Juchi's cloak. Then he leaped high, coming down on my belly with both his feet.

I tried to rise, but the wind was knocked out of me and I couldn't. He flung himself full length upon me, his cloak between us, strangling me.

My head rang and buzzed. I was too weak from the long journey; unable to heave him off. He prisoned my legs with his own hard thighs, bunching and knotting the marten skin over my face. I tried biting through the cloak, but that too failed.

He pressed the fur harder, until I could get no air through my nose or mouth. But doing it kept his hands occupied, and left mine free.

I flailed about, trying to lay hold of the sable skin I had dropped. Blind as I was, I couldn't do it. Then I thought of the tulughma—the sweeping tactic. As I gagged beneath the fur, I raised my arms and reached for Hargoutai's ears.

He bit a finger on my right hand nearly to the bone. I screamed and jerked my hand away, feeling the flesh tear. But I caught his other ear, and eventually the first, too.

It may have presented a ludicrous sight, that ear-pulling, but I heard no laughter. Any trick was fair when only one man would leave the field alive.

Hargoutai didn't try to bite me again. His strategy was to choke me to death before I tore his ears from his head—which he knew I would not do; I dared not make him bleed.

Fearful of this, I let go and fastened my hands on his unseen throat.

He used one hand to try to pry my fingers loose. When he let go with that hand, I gained a little freedom and air space under the cloak. So he was forced to employ both hands to press the cloak down again. Thus I could keep choking him, while I gathered my strength for a push that might be my last.

Screeching, he once more attacked the hands on his windpipe. He dug and scratched—and at that instant, I wrenched my shoulders to the right. Little rocks raked my back. But the hurt pierced the daze in my mind. I gained precious seconds as his one hand grappled with my two. I twisted my head out from under the hem of cloak and drew in a lifesaving draught of air.

I had a brief glimpse of the dust-clouded field on which we struggled. I saw Juchi's sable, almost within reach. I extended my arm but could not quite touch it. Like a madman, I fought to push myself a little closer, the rocks gashing my back again.

But I caught the cloak and jerked it toward me, just as Hargoutai wadded the marten fur and slammed it down toward my face.

I bunched my fist in the sable and struck at him. The blow landed on the side of his head. He rolled away from me, snarling, and I staggered upright while he floundered.

Taking part of the sable hem in each hand, I closed on him spreading the ebon shroud for him to see, then wrapping it swiftly around his head and pushing him down. Once more I folded the cloak around him and again feeble cries sounded through the fur.

I knelt on his throat and chest, holding the cloak fast with one hand while I pinned his thrashing arm with the other.

Gradually, the thrashing of his arm became weaker. At last it flopped out, limp. Only the fingers worked, closing, opening, then closing again. A shudder rippled through his chest, his belly and hips, then set his heels to drumming in the dust.

At last he lay still. I had strangled the life out of the incarnation of the evil gods.

Rising, I almost couldn't believe I had won. I tottered toward the rim of the crowd where I saw Bela towering, the rags about his eyes flapping in the wind, his arms raised in jubilation as he listened to those shouting my name.

The cries became a roar. I staggered on through this chaos of sound, seeking among the bobbing faces the one most dear to me.

All at once, the shouting stopped.

"The life of the Frank is forfeited," I heard Tuli cry. "There's blood on Hargoutai's cheek."

"The blood of Nine-Fingers," someone shouted. "Look, he's covered with it."

And so I was.

But Tuli shook his head. "No, I watched closely. Nine-Fingers never touched the Falcon's cheek where it's bleeding. Look!"

Heartsick, I reeled back to where sly Tuli had drawn aside Juchi's sable cape. I bent down and saw that he told the truth. A place below the Falcon's glazed left eye oozed red—rubbed raw on the ground as we struggled perhaps. But under the law, I had spilled his blood.

Directing his words to the dais where the Kha Khan watched the proceedings with dismay, Tuli shouted, "Send forth the imperial sword-bearer! Let him cut down the Frankish dog where he stands. The sacred Yassa has been violated, and no man flaunts the law of our father the Khan."

Then Tuli gazed at me, wrath and laughter in his eyes. I had killed the tar-khan he had championed. I had disgraced him and would pay a price. "Sword-bearer!" he screamed. "Come here this instant!"

Chapter 10

...And a God Wept

"Lord Khan! Wait but a moment! Hear the plea of a soldier!"

Astonished, I turned to see the man who had uttered the shout a moment after Tuli's. It was Bela, prostrate before the imperial dais.

The Khan gave him leave to rise and speak. In a clumsy way, groping for words but weighing each with a burden of love such as I have seldom known, Bela said, "Lord, one night years ago, when my life was endangered by a cruel Tatar in the horde, James the Frank fought the Tatar in my behalf. He offered his life in place of mine. My own existence has become sour and worthless since the sights of the world were taken from me. I have grown weary of stumbling when others walk upright with ease. Therefore, I call into force that provision of The Yassa in which this is written—the tengri will accept another man in the place of one condemned."

"Bela, *stop!*" I cried, stumbling forward. "I'll take the punishment! I would not have..."

As though I didn't exist, he continued his entreaty: "Oh Khan, you know the warrior James has many good reasons for clinging to life. The love of the princess of Cathay is now his by right. And he wishes to ride westward to the land of his own kind, Frankistan. Since I have none to love me save this same blond Frank—and I prize his life above my own—I beg you to grant him safe passage throughout your whole empire, letting him take with him the princess Cho Soo while I remain and accept the sword-bearer's cut."

"I am touched by your pleading," the Khan said, stroking his mustache in a thoughtful way. "And you are entitled to make such a request, since the law is exactly as you say it is. There is not only generosity but a certain wisdom in your request. Jame Nine-Fingers is still a young man, and healthy, while your worth is diminished by your sightlessness."

I knew the Khan did not say that out of cruelty; it was the truth. Bela understood. Still, it pained me to hear my good comrade so quickly dismissed. I ran through the crowd, flinging people right and left until I reached the dais.

"Lord Khan, don't listen, I beg you! I won't send him to death in my stead. . . ."

"Silence!" was the Khan's reply. Once more he gazed down upon my blind companion of so many dark and dangerous paths. "You revere this Frankish man so greatly that you would freely sacrifice yourself for him?"

Bela tried to answer but could not. Tears in his eyes, he nodded.

A radiant pride lit the Khan's face, hateful to me then but wondrous to remember.

"Do any dare deny the courage of the Mongol race?" he whispered. "Through such loyalty have I gained mastery of the earth! Still a life must be claimed. I accept yours. When Nine-Fingers and the Cathayan princess are gone from us, it shall be taken. It shall be taken before the sun falls. Scribe! Come forward and write out what I shall dictate. A scroll giving Nine-Fingers and his woman safe passage from here to the borders of Frankistan. . . ."

I fell into a screaming rage, born of exhaustion and torment. I remember ranting and fighting those who tried to calm me. I remember crying Bela's name time and again, until a blow struck my head, and then another, and my protests were stilled by the darkness that claimed my mind and grieving heart.

"Beloved?"

I felt the touch of a cool cloth, dripping with water from a brook running through a poplar grove.

For the first time in many hours, I wakened to full consciousness, wakened to the rosy dying of the sun and the gentle nicker of a pony unhitched from a lacquered Cathayan cart standing nearby.

Wakened to the radiance of the face of Cho Soo as she knelt beside me.

She pressed the cloth to my brow, then kissed my mouth. Her lips were incredibly soft. There was a balm in their touch—

But not enough.

"I was afraid fever had claimed you, beloved. You were not awake, yet you raved and cried out when the Mongols locked us in the cart and brought us this far from the river."

I struggled to sit up. "Cho Soo, listen to me!

The sun's not down yet. We can't have come far. I'll ride back. I *must* ride back, before the sentence is carried—"

I stopped. The ball of light in the west sank out of sight behind a bank of clouds just over the horizon. Little golden chimes on the cart tinkled sadly. I stared at the sky, knowing the truth:

It was too late.

"The pain will pass," Cho Soo whispered when I put my head on the softness of the embroidered silk covering her breasts.

"Never," I said.

"Yes, beloved, it will. I have felt the same kind of pain. Many times while you were gone from me. I thought of slaying myself, so sorrowful had life become. Yet I remembered the vow, the one you made in the hay bower so long ago. I knew that the pain I felt on the tar-khan's couch would one day be gone. And I knew the pain was better than death, which destroys all hope, all joy, and the promise of joy forever."

"You're right, I suppose. It isn't easy to bear. He was a good friend."

She stroked my face. "I know, my darling. I know."

Gradually I accustomed myself to the bitter loss. After a time I kissed her again, and to my astonishment felt the stirrings of a passion of which I thought myself incapable.

In silence, I said a last good-bye to the memory of sweet and generous Lilith of the Circassians; then a longer one to Bela. Finally I closed my arms around the body of my lovely Cathayan girl and bore her backward on a bed of fragrant grass, stilling my pain with a sweeter pain of a union beautiful beyond my power to describe.

At the end, with the sky pitch dark and starry

above us and the night-birds of Kharesmia crying in the distance, we lay together under a robe, our bodies bare and our souls, too. The hurt of losing Bela was almost gone.

Almost . . .

But the gods who had given me triumph over Hargoutai were not finished with me yet.

Cho Soo and I were sleeping in the open, unafraid for the first time since we had met. Yet that night, too, there was pulse-thumping fear as I woke abruptly to see torches glimmering beyond the poplars.

The pony whickered. Hoofs thudded. Dust clouded over the stars.

I thought I had gone mad.

When the dust cleared and the moon gilded the cart and the trees and the pony, a figure stalked toward me, a huge, hulking figure with a clean white silk wrapped around the forehead. Beyond the poplars, a shadowy escort of mounted officers watched while I leaped to my feet, wrapped a cloth around me and hid Cho Soo's nakedness with the robe.

A few steps away, the man halted, fists on his hips.

I hardly dared to say the word:

"*Bela?*"

"Aye, who else?"

I ran forward, clutching his arm. I laughed and cried at the same time, telling him I couldn't understand the miracle.

"No miracle," he shrugged, then added, "Well, yes, perhaps—though not entirely a happy one. Before the sun went down last night, I heard a god weep like a man."

"Why did the Khan spare you, brother?"

"Because there was one more substitution of a life for a life—as permitted under the law. Juchi the Guest refused to let me die for you. He wanted me safe—to thwart Tuli, I think—and took a great risk to bring it about. He demanded to take my place."

"To be *killed?*"

"Yes, James. He bowed his head and bared his neck, but the sword-bearer fainted away at the thought of slaying the Khan's son. Then Tuli took the blade—all too eager—but he couldn't do it either. There is much evil in Tuli, but not so much that he could murder his own brother.

"Finally, the Khan stormed down from the dais and snatched the sword into his hands. He raised the sword over Juchi's neck and—" Disbelieving, Bela whispered the rest. "And after a moment, he trembled like a leaf in a storm. He dropped the sword in the dust. He wept, James. *Wept.* Genghis Kha Khan, who made the law, could not carry out the law. Not against his own flesh and blood."

"You could not have seen all that, Bela."

"I saw it in my mind's eye. Ye Liu Chutsai was at my side every moment, describing it." He shook his head. "Do you realize what has happened?"

"Yes! You're alive!"

"I mean something of much vaster importance in the universal scheme. The Yassa is broken, destroyed—perhaps forever. The Khan himself did the deed. I thought him a bogodo—a god made flesh—but I learned otherwise. The god-spirit may move within him, but he's a man just like us."

"In his sixtieth year, if I remember," I murmured. "Growing old—"

"It must have been tragic to see. I was glad I had no eyes then. But the old Cathayan scholar served. He told me everything: How the Khan stood there in the last red light, reduced from godhood and weeping tears in the dust until Juchi embraced him. Even then, the Kha Khan kept sobbing. He knew he had failed himself, and his law, and his people."

"Who helped you come here?"

"Ye Liu Chutsai. He arranged for the protection of those riders yonder."

"I could ask for no greater blessing."

"Be thankful you were sent forth when you were, brother." Bela's head lifted toward the moon. "Be thankful you didn't hear the sound of Genghis Khan in tears."

Shortly, the Mongol officers rode back eastward. When the morning sun crept up from the horizon, we turned our backs to it, setting out in our small cart, my great comrade, my best-beloved princess of all the earth, and I—the three of us.

We went out from the land where a mighty god had lived for a brief time. Together we took the first steps on a road of a thousand leagues, to find new lives—and perhaps an answer to the riddle of my origins—somewhere along the distant shores of Frankistan.

We went with great joy. But there was a certain sadness, too. A god was dead. Only a man born Temujin remained. I doubted we, or the world, would ever see his like again.

About the Author

With publication in January, 1976, of the fourth volume of The American Bicentennial Series, John Jakes became the first author in history to have three novels on national best-seller lists within a single year . . . climaxing a twenty-five-year professional writing career which began with sale of a science fiction short story (for $25) to *The Magazine of Fantasy and Science Fiction* in 1951. A native of Chicago and still a Midwestern resident, Jakes sold his first story while in his second year of college, and his first book—an historical Western for young people—twelve months later. Since then he has published more than fifty books and two hundred short pieces ranging from science fiction to suspense, and fiction and nonfiction for young people, including a biography of the Mohawk chief, Joseph Brant, and a history of the TIROS weather satellite program. Most of this work was produced while Jakes held creative posts with advertising agencies, working on behalf of some of America's largest companies; he left advertising in 1970 to write full time. He remains an avid community theater actor and playwright (eleven of his plays and musicals have been published), as well as a lifelong history buff. His interest in history led to half a dozen historical novels—originally written under his "Jay Scotland" pseudonym—which Pinnacle Books is now publishing in completely revised, uniform editions.

Two rich blooded, romantic historical novels by "America's favorite storyteller*"

*(*The New York Times)*

____**I, BARBARIAN** The days of Genghis Khan, the fiercest and most terrifying days of man since the birth of civilization. Against this forceful and dramatic scene weaves a love story as bold and as powerful as the mighty Khan himself. It is a tale of a brave young warrior from Frankistan and his love for a beautiful Oriental princess, a concubine of the Mongol king. A spellbinding novel of romance, intrigue, and adventure, storytelling at its very best.   P971 $1.50

____**VEILS OF SALOME** The story of Salome, the beautiful Judean princess, duty-bound to the service of her father, Herod Antipas, and victimized by her mother's selfish ambitions. It is also the timeless and moving love story of the princess's lost and hopeless love for one man, Marcus Catullus, physician of Rome's Fifth Imperial Legion. Set in a time of the greatest decadence, at the same time the world's single most influential period, it is a magnificent saga of human love and inhuman agony—a woman who had to lay her pride aside to win the man whose love she desperately wanted.   P972 $1.50

Both by **JOHN JAKES,** author of the American Bicentennial Series, the only writer ever to have three books on the national paperback best-seller lists at the same time!

ARE YOU A LATE MOVIE FAN . . .
OR A DYED-IN-THE-WOOL
HOLLYWOOD BUFF? If so, here
are some stories of the stars
that will keep you up even later!

DO YOU KNOW HOW TO . . . ?

(Pinnacle Books can help you)

DO YOU KNOW HOW TO?
(Pinnacle does and can help you!)

Save gas!
_____THE GAS SAVER'S GUIDE,
Callender & Woods   P437   1.50

Defend yourself! (and stay trim with exercise)
_____THE BEGINNER'S GUIDE TO KUNG-FU,
Dennis & Simmons   P701   2.50

Look younger and feel *younger?*
_____THE PURSUIT OF YOUTH, Rae Lindsay   P833   1.75

Read faster, think clearer, and express yourself better?
_____SPEED-THINK, Hans Holzer   P919   1.50

Perform feats of magic?
_____HOUDINI'S BOOK OF MAGIC TRICKS,
PUZZLES & STUNTS, Harry Houdini   P970   1.50

Get rid of aches and pains?
_____SHIATZU: Japanese Pressure Point Massage,
Anika Bergson & Vladimir Tuchak   P916   1.50

Play bridge? (learn while you laugh!)
_____BRIDGE IN THE FOURTH DIMENSION,
Victor Mollo   P700   1.25

Win at backgammon?
_____WINNING BACKGAMMON, Lawrence   P262   1.50

Make up a TV commercial?
_____DOWN THE TUBE, Galanoy   P091   1.25

Become clairvoyant?
_____HOW TO DEVELOP YOUR ESP, Smith   P246   1.25

Outwit today's stock market?
_____PANICS & CRASHES, Schultz   P516   1.50

YOU CAN ORDER ANY OF THESE BOOKS RIGHT HERE:
Please add 25¢ per book for postage and handling up to $1.00—
free thereafter

Pinnacle Books
275 Madison Avenue
New York, N.Y. 10016

_____Check here if you wish our free catalog

The Thin Book

By A Formerly Fat Psychiatrist

Theodore Isaac Rubin, M.D.

The famous bestselling guide to healthful weight control: medically authoritative, scientifically accurate, psychologically sound.